UNDER THE SUN

Hanne Marie Svendsen

HANNE MARIE SVENDSEN is best known for the intriguing blend of realism and fantasy in her novels and short stories, notably the award-winning novel *Guldkuglen* (1985, published in English translation as *The Gold Ball* in 1989) and the recent success *Unn fra Stjernestene* (2003, Unn from Starry Stones), about life in medieval Greenland. Since her debut novel *Mathildes drømmebog* (1977, Mathilde's Dream Book), Svendsen has published nine novels, two plays, three collections of short stories, three children's books and two radio plays.

Born in 1933, Svendsen began her professional career at Denmark's Radio, where she became deputy head of the theatre and literature department. She also taught at the University of Copenhagen, and published several critical books before devoting herself to writing fiction full-time. Inspired by her many journeys abroad as well as by storytellers from her native Skagen, the northernmost town in Denmark, she has become a consummate storyteller herself, experimenting with narrative techniques and exploring the transformative power of art, dreams and imagination.

MARINA ALLEMANO holds a Ph.D. in Comparative Literature and teaches Scandinavian Studies at the University of Alberta, Canada. She has previously translated Suzanne Brøgger's *A Fighting Pig's Too Tough to Eat and Other Prose Texts* (1997) and also published a monograph in Danish on the same writer, *Suzanne Brøgger. En introduktion* (2004). Presently she is working on a monograph on Hanne Marie Svendsen.

Some other books from Norvik Press

UNDER THE SUN

A Novel

by

Hanne Marie Svendsen

Translated from the Danish by

Marina Allemano

That which is, is far off,
and deep, very deep;
who can find it out?
What has a man
from all the toil and strain
with which he toils
under the sun?

Ecclesiastes

Originally published in Danish by Gyldendal under the title
Under solen (1991)
© Hanne Marie Svendsen.

This translation © Marina Allemano 2006.

*A catalogue record for this book is available from the British
Library.*
ISBN 1-870041-62-3
First published in 2006 by Norvik Press, University of East Anglia,
Norwich NR4 7TJ.

Norvik Press gratefully acknowledges the financial assistance given
by the Danish Literature Centre towards the translation of this book.

Norvik Press was established in 1984 with financial support from the
University of East Anglia, the Danish Ministry for Cultural Affairs, the
Norwegian Cultural Department and the Swedish Institute.
e-mail address: norvik.press@uea.ac.uk

Managing editors: Janet Garton, Michael Robinson, C. Claire Thomson.

Cover design: Richard Johnson

Printed in the UK by Page Bros. (Norwich) Ltd, Norwich, UK

THE DREAM

And what happens when we wake?
What happens is that,
as we are accustomed to a sequential life,
we give a narrative structure to our dream,
though our dream has been multiple
and simultaneous.*

Jorge Luis Borges

* Jorge Luis Borges. *Seven Nights*. Tr. Eliot Weinberger. New York: New Directions, 1984, p.28.

1

Margrethe Thiede Holm dreamt that she was dead. She stood on a big hill and looked down on the town. The wind shook her, wanted her to lift off, but she leaned back, sank her feet into the sand among the prickly stubs of straw. Her body still had enough mass to stay put.

Far below in her bed, the name Margrethe Thiede Holm was written in black letters above her white face, a large square face with deep furrows around a receding mouth. But up here the letters had detached from each other, drifted away like colourful kites and clouds at sunset, ivory-coloured E's, a pink A with its contours partially dissolved, the I a bluish violet, T's and R's floating in different directions, copper-hued and orange-red. The pale Holm had already disappeared in the horizon, far away over the sea. It didn't really belong to her name although she had carried it with her for many years during her life. The wind soon wafted her own letters away, and she turned into nothing, a little condensation in the cloud cover, merged with the greyish blue sky behind the clouds in the sunset. But still her body carried some weight.

She braced herself, making herself heavier yet. The nightgown lifted and spread out like a sail above her legs with their prominent blue veins. Far out on the lead-coloured sea a wreck appeared, its masts and girders forming the letters WRECK against the horizon. Now it keeled over, slid further down into the waves. K, C, E, R disappeared, and only a toppled-over W was left of the ship.

Far down in the other direction, the town slept under the street lamps and the orange-coloured lights from the harbour. She could see roads and houses on both sides, greyish yellow walls touching the street or buildings hidden further back in gardens with white-painted picket fences. The apartment building where Lily Lund had lived as a child was there. She thought she could detect the cabbage smell from the stairwell. But hadn't that house been torn down? No, it was still there, floating above a deserted parking lot, a light showing in the window where Lily Lund was sitting, dangling her long, skinny legs. Her face was hidden behind the curly reddish-golden hair. Lily, watch out. You'll fall. But it is Harald who falls, falls onto the grey surface of the courtyard.

She lowered her face to protect it from the wind and blinked away the small wind-tears that had formed in the corner of her eyes. Here was the spruce plantation where Carl went for his solitary walks on the paths that were covered in loamy carpets of brown pine needles. Walked and walked. What was he thinking about? And close against her ear, she heard Niels Buus' voice saying: If I don't have any red on my palette, I'll use green.

Faces appeared and disappeared again. She turned and could suddenly see all the way down to the main street and the big buildings, the post office, the hotel. Her gaze penetrated the red wall, and she was now in the taproom with the brown-stained tables. Eyes lit up like flames in the light from the hanging lamps. The room vibrated, disappeared in the tobacco fog, emerged once again, was transformed into glass and chromed steel, mirrors and fluorescent lights were everywhere, figures moved around, back and forth, without looking at each other. And behind the counter stood Egon.

The wind took hold of her. She tumbled backwards a bit and turned around again. Far away, the lighthouse twinkled, and behind it, partially hidden, was the lighthouse keeper's house with its rows of tall small-paned windows under the grey-tiled roof. The lighthouse keeper's house is our dwelling. Why do you say dwelling? It sounds so silly. But that's what it is. You dwell there, and then you become a corpse.

Harald fell and became a corpse. And Carl and Lily Lund and the other one with the white furry hands. I have killed a human being.

Margrethe Thiede shook her head lightly as she stood there in the dream on top of the hill. She looked further, far and wide, right through the lighthouse keeper's house towards the cottage with the three little old men. The light swept over the cottage in calm circles, and the three little old men stood outside by the hollyhocks and called her over to where they were standing.

Were there any hollyhocks? Yes, the sun was shining above them. She could see their sticky brown eyes among the pink petals. Bees were buzzing, and she slowly slid her finger down a hairy stem. She thought that she might visit the three old men far down there, back in time. To chat with them just like she did then, even though she didn't always understand what they were saying.

But the wind blew them away. Kites hovered in front of her eyes. She could barely make out their colours when they moved sidewards or upwards in sudden jumps, whipped by the wind gusts. Some of them collided. Pink, orange, ivory. A, T, E. No, now the T blew away. The reddish yellow kite flew out over the water, and she was just AE, a murmur, a mumble, then nothing.

UNDER THE SUN

2

Once upon a time.

From chaos and fear comes the fairy tale. The beautifully dressed fairy tale steps out of the shadow plays of life, of its confusions and tangles, but it only carries along whatever fits into the pattern. Once upon a time. And they lived happily ever after.

Once upon a time there were three little men who lived in a house in the forest.

These are the men that Margrethe Thiede will meet. She is lying in her bed dreaming that she is dead, standing on the windy hill looking down on her life. She is an old woman; her vision is blurred although sometimes she can see very far. But she is also a little girl who believes in fairy tales and who visits the three little men that lived in a house in the forest.

There they were, way back in the past. They were really there, in the real world, or in what we call the real world. They didn't live in a house, however, but in a black-tarred cottage. And it wasn't in the forest but on the edge of the spruce plantation south west of the lighthouse.

They had lived there for as long as anyone could remember. The townspeople called them Sem, Kam and Jafet after Noah's three sons who got stranded on a mountain and became the first men on the new earth. They themselves didn't use any other names, but Jafet became Jaffe because it rolled more easily off the tongue. Moreover, they were as like as three peas in a pod – if you didn't look too closely – small and sinewy with dark complexions and lively yellow-brown eyes under wiry, grizzled hair. They made their living fishing from the beach and by fixing things for folk that could afford to have their things fixed. People thought they were skilled but complained that they couldn't always understand what they were saying. They were different and didn't fit in with the community. They didn't fit in anywhere else, for that matter; they kept to themselves and didn't mingle much with others.

– And how can they live in that mess, Margrethe Thiede's mother said. She was by no means a tidy person herself. She was a Carrot Fairy who dashed back and forth between the house and the fenced-in kitchen garden where she would pick lettuce and parsley and pull edible roots from the soil. She reigned over soup pots and preserves, she stuck flowers in water, brought in windblown laundry from the enclosure behind the lighthouse and took hold of reality as if her chores had a hidden meaning and she always knew what she was doing. But in the evening, when Margrethe Thiede's silent father came in after a day's work, and she had attended to her husband's supper and gone to rest in her chair, her hands that usually had a firm grip on things suddenly became restless and unsure of themselves. It was as if she, after all, didn't believe in the reality that she had mastered during the day.

Later on she would climb upstairs to the small bedroom and tell fairy tales to Margrethe and little Harald, Margrethe's younger brother with the golden curls. She knew all the fairy tales in the world and talked about Snow White and Rose Red, the Princess in the Glass Mountain, Cinderella, Snow White and Sleeping Beauty as if they were close friends and relatives of hers. Dangerous creatures lay in wait everywhere: witches, trolls, elves, bad fairies, giant serpents and three-headed dragons. But the girls, who appeared somewhat wavering and spineless and were satisfied with things that they shouldn't have accepted in the first place, were always saved, not by their own hand, but because the king's son or the poor lad who had gone to the end of the world, and even further than that, had struck out with his magic sword, awoken the sleepers and uttered the word that would make the troll explode into a thousand pieces. And a prince always happened to pass by and ask the girl if she would like to come with him to the castle and be his beloved queen.

Margrethe would rather be the king's son or the poor lad who went out into the wide world.

– I don't think so, the mother said. – But there are some girls that can do things for themselves, too. Rose Red and Snow White weren't afraid of the evil dwarf. And think of the princess who chopped off her pinky so she could get into the glass mountain and save the seven brothers.

– I would chop my pinky off too if it could save Harald, Margrethe said. But she wasn't sure if she were telling the truth.

Harald was too small, he didn't understand anything and babbled quietly in his crib till he fell asleep. Margrethe wanted to hear more.

– Tell me about the woman who walked into the sea.

– That's not a fairy tale and not a story for children either.

– You've told it before. I want to hear it again.

Once there was a woman who lived in a lonely place somewhere near the sea. One day her soul turned grey, and she couldn't imagine any greater happiness than meeting death. But she had a husband and children, and she couldn't shed her responsibility. So, she took in her youngest sister

17

and taught her to mend and cook. After some time she noticed that her sister was kind to the children and that she and the husband had begun to look lovingly at each other. She then put on her best dress and walked into the sea. And so the story ends. It's short but not sad, for she did what she had to do.

– I hate that story, Margrethe said and sat up in her bed.

– Why, then, do you always want to hear it? her mother asked and tucked the blanket around her.

– Because I hate it. Why didn't she just go somewhere else. And if she cared so much for her sister, why didn't she give her her best dress too. Now it just got spoiled.

– It's only fair that she kept a little for herself, Margrethe's mother sighed. – And where could she go, the poor thing.

– Just somewhere out in the world where she could experience other things. She could have gone to see the three old men who would give her precious gifts. Or found a prince who would take her to the king's castle.

– East of the sun and west of the moon. That's where you will end up, late or never, said the mother. Then she leaned back in the chair, rocked her head back and forth and gazed far off into the distance.

But in the morning when Harald and Margrethe woke up, she was once again the Carrot Fairy, fresh as dew and full of confidence, ready to conquer new territory and gain new subjects for her kingdom of kindness and care. She was the one who could made the sun rise and the rain fall on the dry earth. She wasn't permitted to doubt things, and she couldn't let anyone down.

– Bring the old men some soup, she said. – They don't have anyone to look after them.

They had someone – once. The three little old men had

been children too at one time and had had a mother who looked after them. The oldest folk in town could remember having seen her, a small bent-over woman who never spoke to anyone. From their grandfathers and grandmothers they had heard that she, one day, had arrived on foot from the south with a child at each hand and one in her belly. She hadn't looked too bad, then. People said that she had been put ashore somewhere on the coast, been rowed in from a big ship where they no longer could be bothered with her, a whore or a refugee, no one knew the details. She could only make herself understood with gestures, but people did figure out, though, that she was hungry and didn't have a place to stay. So they gave her the cottage in the spruce plantation where no one else wanted to live anyway. And she had made a living by doing this and that – opinions differed on this subject – until the boys were big enough to support her. She never learned to speak the language, but her sons could make themselves understood although their speech was odd. In those days there wasn't much education to be had.

That's how the stories about the old men and their origin were told in town. Margrethe, who was curious by nature, asked questions and didn't always understand the answers she got. She was very preoccupied with the three little old men. To her they belonged in the fairytale world with its clear borders, although reality and its many details, of course, have a tendency to dissolve fairy tales and erase their contours. Also later, when their language use became the basis for her shortlived fame, in Margrethe Thiede's mind the three men were part of the fairytale universe. But we will get to that later.

– Please, take them a little soup now, said Margrethe's mother, the Carrot Fairy, who is also the daytime ruler of reality. – Since their mother died, and that's a long time ago, they haven't been eating very well.

Rain clouds drift against the sky. The sun has disappeared. Margrethe Thiede runs down round the hill with a pot of soup to visit Sem, Kam and Jaffe whose speech pattern later became the foundation for her brief fame in linguistic circles. But they wouldn't have known that. They stand outside the cottage by the hollyhocks. Were there any hollyhocks? Oh sure, the thin petals droop a little, weighed down and whipped by the rain. And the three old men are there, calling her over to where they are standing. They are babbling and laughing.

Fish tied together two at a time, their tails swishing against each other, hang to dry on the drying frame. Inside the cottage, it is dark. In the back room quilts and blankets are piled up on top of boxes and old bedsteads. This is the old men's bedroom. From the outside, you step directly into the sitting room which is lined with tools and implements, mud-covered spades, a sharp-toothed saw, a fishnet, an axe with its handle pointing up, the edge of its head visible under a dirty bandage.

Jaffe lifts the rings off the cast iron stove with a stick so Margrethe can put down the pot. The red fire leaps up against their faces for a moment. When she turns around she notices that on his hand, Sem – who is sitting on one of the four rickety chairs around the wooden table – is wearing a bandage as well.

– Have you hurt yourself? she asks, having first brushed crumbs and dust off the chair she wants to sit on.

– Sem took the axe, chops wood, the axe slips, Jaffe explains as if it was just another joke or an everyday incident worth noting. Jaffe was the nicest of the three and the best storyteller. But these three old men always laughed when Margrethe Thiede visited, laughed till the deep lines in their grimy faces nearly cracked. And she felt unsure of herself. Were they laughing at her or at her mother and the soup pot?

– Cuts have to be cleaned, she says adult-like. – Otherwise animals will get into them.

– But Sem points at the axe and then at his bandaged hand. – The blood here and the blood there, he says. – They help each other. The axe gets better, and the hand gets better.

– And so the axe must be bandaged because Sem cut himself on it? Margrethe Thiede shook her head and felt as if she were the only adult among three old playful children. They knew all the words, but used them differently. She felt like an onlooker who couldn't penetrate their world.

– Yesterday the sun was shining, she said in a conversational tone.

– Yesterday the sun shines, Sem repeated. The soup was bubbling on the stove, and he signalled to Jaffe to set out the plates. At least they had plates although they were old and chipped.

– Was shining. The sun was shining yesterday.

– Yes, Sem nodded. – Yesterday the sun shines.

– Tomorrow it might shine again, she continued tentatively. She wanted to be their teacher and help them speak correctly.

– Tomorrow the sun shines, Sem beamed. Sometimes she thought that the pupils in his yellow-brown eyes weren't round but narrow horizontal black lines, like goats' eyes or the devil's eyes. Jaffe had two pupils in his left eye. That's how you could tell him apart, but he was also the youngest, the kid brother that the other two teased, ordered around and treated with a certain amount of indulgence. Still, sometimes Kam was aggressive towards him. Kam was the most choleric of the three.

The dog ran inside and rubbed against Margrethe's legs. It was greyish-white with black spots, short-legged and big-bellied. The dog expected to be helped up on one of the chairs and have its food served while Jaffe had to slurp his soup standing. Margrethe didn't approve of this. It was a sign of poor upbringing and bad table manners.

– A dog is an animal, she said. – A mammal. And she thought about the wall pictures in her classroom at school. None of the animals on the pictures looked like this mutt.

– That dog is mammal, Kam repeated and lifted the bowl to his mouth so he could drink the soup. Small beads of grease ran down his cheeks.

– No, a mammal. The dog is a mammal. Inside her head, Margrethe Thiede pointed with a cane at colourful pictures of cats and dogs, tigers and lions.

– You are mammal, Sem laughed and stretched his bandaged hand across the table to reach her. She pulled back a little and glanced down at her blouse where small bumps had lately begun to show. Jaffe shoved the dog aside to sit on the chair himself. He did it to be polite to Margrethe and because he could see that Sem had embarrassed her. Not that he agreed with her.

She didn't understand them. They used the same words as she did but differently. They didn't think in terms of the past, the present or the future. To them a thing happened only once, or it happened again and again. And it was irrelevant to them when it happened or had happened or was going to happen. From under their stringy grey hair, they looked at the world through their yellowish eyes, but it was another world they saw.

– They are very primitive. They are hardly human, Margrethe Thiede's mother said while on her knees in the garden, pulling big greyish-yellow carrots from the soil. – But they are grateful. Today another bucket of lobster was left outside our door. They must have bartered for them in town. We will eat them tonight with pepper and vinegar.

– I want to know more about them, Margrethe said and kicked with her foot in the dirt. – Why isn't there anyone who can tell me something. They themselves can't even figure out who they are. They get everything mixed up.

– Try asking auntie, the mother said and straightened up while brushing the dirt off her apron. – I have a tin of cookies that you can take along.

This aunt, a younger sister of Margrethe's maternal grandmother who had died years ago, lived in an apartment surrounded by knick-knacks – porcelain figurines, bowls with gilded edges, candlestick holders of metal, French clocks, decanters with painted flower motifs, delft lamps on small flimsy tables between heavy upholstered furniture. She lived among doilies, lace curtains and velvet portieres in rooms that were like a hothouse because the radiators were always turned up at full tilt, even in the summer. Here she received or expected to receive regular visits from people who would bring their gifts – flowers, pastries, chocolates – and in return be offered cherry wine served in a crystal glass. She was the town's information centre, sat in her easy chair, small and hunched over – at times dressed very scantily with a hairdressing cape or a dressing gown covering her slight shoulders – nodding her bird-beaked head that was crowned with a tuft of greyish white hair. She had become independently wealthy after a very short-lived marriage. They said that the husband had simply lain down to die in order to get away from her.

Auntie, for that's what everyone called her although only Margrethe's mother had the right to call her this, was very near-sighted and for that very reason completely shameless. Because she herself saw the world around her through a fog as blurred shapes with vague contours, it never occurred to her that others might take exception to her shrivelled calves with their scars and knots, her shrunken thighs that were covered in blue spots, her shoulders and upper arms whose bones rattled under a thin layer of speckled skin. She displayed herself with an air of assurance that was unfamiliar to the townspeople and cackled happily while poking her bird-beaked nose into a world that she could barely make out. People took notice of this, but they also accepted it. Auntie was auntie and the whole town's eager gossip.

When a visitor came she would try to get out of her chair in fits and starts in order to get the cherry wine that the domestic help had left on a tray in the kitchen. Margrethe didn't like auntie getting up from her chair. She was afraid that her fragile body would collapse and fall onto the carpet and lie like a sack of bones with her bird-beaked face carrying on with its cackling and rattling at the top of the heap.

If the truth be told, Margrethe found her visits to auntie both exciting and creepy. It was easy to imagine her as a witch. That she one day might change into a good fairy, dressed in a tailor-made suit and lace-collared blouse, her hands full of priceless gifts, did not enter Margrethe's mind. She didn't think that far while she ran up the flight of stairs with her mother's cookies and her own thirst for knowledge about the three little old men, rang the doorbell and opened the door that was always left unlocked during the day.

– My, you have grown tall, auntie clucked. – And fat too, methinks. Her skinny arms flapped up and down against the armrests of the chair. – Shall I get the cherry wine? No, you'll manage on your own. And if you'd rather have fruit juice, there is some of that out there as well. Sit down over here on the footstool. No, move closer this way.

She smelled sweetly of old age and perfume. Margrethe wasn't keen on sitting too close.

– The cookies are good, auntie said munching slowly. – Your mother knows how to bake, I'll give her that. Is she doing all right otherwise?

Margrethe nodded.

– She and your father weren't really meant for each other, you know, auntie said and bent forward a little, making the tuft of her hair jump. – But she was betrayed. Her sweetheart took off, and she went after him. And my sister, the poor thing, who had never been away from town, had to go and bring her back home again. He walked with a limp, but apart from that he was a nice specimen of a man. You have probably never heard this story before?

Margrethe shook her head.

– So then it happened that your father wanted her, auntie continued and straightened herself in the chair again. – The Thiedes weren't pleased. They always thought of themselves as being special. But it's not a good thing being too proud. Has your grandmother told you about her brother-in-law, the captain?

– No, Margrethe said and moved further back on the stool.

– We always heard stories about him. Now he is long gone, of course, but in those days he sailed abroad on large freighters. He was a man of importance. At least that was the impression one got. Every time I met your grandmother on the street, she always managed to mention that now the brother-in-law had been home again with shawls and gold jewelry and silverware and I don't know what else. They were completely wrapped up in this man.

Margrethe nodded. She had seen silverware at grandmother Thiede's but never gold jewelry. They were probably locked away in a chest.

– But then, you see, one time he went sailing with a large cargo of spices. He has also fifty barrels of whale oil on board that were stored above the spices. And during a storm the barrels came loose because they hadn't been tied down thoroughly. They knocked against each other and broke and oil seeped down into the hold and destroyed all the spices. Do you know the smell of whale oil?

Yes, Margrethe knew the smell.

– Phew, auntie said and pecked at the air with her bird beak while puckering her small mouth. – But he had to stand for an inquiry and was quarantined. It was all in the paper. And after that we didn't hear so much about him.

– That's a shame, Margrethe said. – He wasn't the one who had tied the barrels down, after all.

– He was responsible. He who carries the responsibility has to pay for the consequences. That's how it is.

Responsibility. It was such a heavy and unyielding word. It smelled a bit like whale oil.

– Stuck-up. That's what they have always been. But still, your father got the girl he wanted, even if the Thiedes didn't want her and she herself had preferred someone else. But they have all been well served by his choice, the aunt continued and leaned back in her chair triumphantly, as if she were the one who had arranged it all. – I could have wished her someone more light-hearted. But he is a reliable person, even if he is a bit stiff. And she is good to him. She probably thinks that it is the only decent thing to do. I guess that you didn't know anything about all this.

Margrethe knew nothing and felt uncomfortable listening to all this confidential talk. It was intriguing but also wrong. Auntie said things that no one else in town would ever mention with a single word. Words seeped out of her as if she herself were a barrel of whale oil that had come loose of its bearings and now rolled around on the deck. The barrel wasn't responsible, and neither was the sailor who should have secured it in place. But the captain was. And a mother was a mother and a father a father. They simply existed and oughtn't to have a past. Yet, she wouldn't mind hearing more about the mother of the old men.

– Hm, the aunt cackled letting her thoughts fly off in new directions. – That was before my time. They said she was a whore. The fishermen visited her at night. I wonder what she did to avoid having more children. Do you know what a whore is?

– Yes, Margrethe nodded.

– You can tell by just looking at them. It is in their eyes. That girlfriend of yours that you spend so much time with, the one from down the tenement house, she will become a whore too. Just you wait and see.

– Lily Lund, Margrethe volunteered.

– That family has always been in poor shape. They have never been able to keep their lives together. I assume that her mother cleans houses?

Margrethe nodded but kept silent. She was not going to be tempted into betraying Lily Lund, and evidently auntie didn't know any stories about the three little old men. They didn't interest her.

– Don't lock the door, the voice shouted from the sitting room when Margrethe was on her way out. – There will probably be other visitors.

And Margrethe walks through the town, pulling her bicycle along, passing the new apartment building. She walks through the long main street and on to the winding streets where the old houses are low, nestled in their gardens. It rains lightly. There's hardly a breeze, the sky is grey and heavy. She hunches her shoulders, bends her head. Raindrops run down the back of her neck, and suddenly she feels as grey and heavy as the sky.

It is boring in this town. Everyone here is boring, and if not boring then bad. They say things that are inappropriate, offensive and smell like whale oil. Margrethe Thiede doesn't want to have any responsibilities, and she doesn't want to stay in this town. She wants to go out in the wide world and seek her fortune, and preferably right now. But how do you do that, and where do you go?

For the time being she would walk down to grandmother Thiede's where she would have to stand on newspapers in the hallway until the rain had run off her clothes, after which she was permitted to enter the sitting room.

Grandmother Thiede had things under control and didn't say or do anything inappropriate or offensive. She never told stories, and everything she said related to the real world; it could be measured, weighed and controlled. But you didn't have to worry about this, for what grandmother Thiede said was contained within clear boundaries, it was truthful, solid and trustworthy, just like the silverware that she kept in her wall cabinet: spoons and forks, pastry forks and teaspoons in long rows on trays lined in blue velvet.

There were also serving spoons whose ornamental handles had designs of twining flowers and clusters of fruit, and a large heavy soup ladle in a delicate leafy pattern. That one was an heirloom and couldn't have been one of the sea captain's gifts.

All this silverware was laid out along with gild-edged coffee cups and fourteen different kinds of baking when grandmother Thiede occasionally had ladies over for an afternoon gathering. Otherwise it was kept hidden away in the dark cabinet and only taken out to be polished once a month. Sometimes the Carrot Fairy and Margrethe were summoned to help out, but it was hard for them to please grandmother Thiede. Things could only be done in one particular way, which was the correct one. Grandmother Thiede had fixed rules for the folding of the starched white tablecloths, for doing the dishes in the proper order, for using the right tea towels for glasses or cutlery. The Carrot Fairy often bungled it, sinned against the rule book and was punished with a look from grandmother Thiede's grey eyes: That's what I thought. It's exactly what I expected. That's how they are in that family. Why couldn't my son have stayed away from this girl. It was all written in her eyes. Margrethe was now able to read most of it and thought, too, that her mother was a bit clumsy now and then. But only in grandmother Thiede's house.

Twice a week grandmother Thiede had a visit from her son, Margrethe's father, who followed his mother around the house and in the garden to be instructed about things that had to be adjusted and repaired. He dogged her footsteps, nodded and made sure that everything was done the way she wanted it. In this manner he made amends for the fact that he had married into an unstable and dissipated family for whom moderation was an unknown concept, a family that told fairytales, was slovenly and easily tempted by prospects that had no foundation in reality. Otherwise he was nice enough to the Carrot Fairy and let her reign in her own way. But his mother he never contradicted.

Margrethe was bored at grandmother Thiede's, especially on Sundays when the whole family gathered for dinner. Nevertheless, she went there regularly once a week on the day the weekly magazine fell through the letter slot, with pictures of royal families and stories about life out in the big world where much had to be endured but where you would usually find happiness in the end. Grandmother Thiede knew all about the royal families. She was as familiar with their kinship relations as she was with the townspeople's families and who was related to whom. Apart from that, the big world didn't interest her. Her own world was enough.

And now that the water has run off her clothes, Margrethe is given permission to sit at the table with the magazine in front of her. Today she finds that boring too. The real kings and queens look like all other people, and the fortunes that people in the magazine stories find for themselves don't seem very appealing after all.

Grandmother Thiede didn't know anything about the three old men's ancestry. She thought that perhaps their mother had been a gypsy. – And we know what they are like.

A few years later, when Margrethe Thiede had completed the first and longest part of her education, she borrowed a tape recorder from the teachers' staff room. It was a big, heavy monstrosity, but she herself had also grown big and heavy and had no trouble carrying it.

She dragged it around the hill and into the cottage where she put it down on the table. Sem had died the previous winter. Nobody had really heard anything about his passing, but in any case he was gone, and Kam and Jaffe had weakened due to old age. They cheered up when they saw her, sat down by the tape recorder, poked at it and tried to figure out how it worked.

During the summer she paid them many visits and eventually made them feel comfortable with the machine. They babbled and laughed as they used to do, and afterwards she rewound the tape and let them hear what they had said.

– Kam speaks now, and Kam speaks before, Jaffe said. – Time is inside the box.

– And Kam will speak tomorrow if we play the tape when I come again, Margrethe answered. She felt that she understood what they meant, to some extent. But not completely.

– Why won't you move into the old-age home? she asked. – The council office can arrange it for you. You'll get food there every day and you can listen to the radio.

But they shook their heads and didn't want to think about moving away from the cottage.

The tapes were put in the closet in her room. They stayed there, hidden and forgotten, until she returned to town after Harald's death.

3

Evening and winter darkness. The light from the lighthouse sweeps over the sea, glitters on the water surface, pulls away again, turns around itself, is projected onto the hills where small patches of snow have settled on top of dead creeping willows.

Margrethe Thiede's father has climbed to his office in the lighthouse. He attends to his work. That's what fathers do.

Down below couched behind the towering structure is the house. Light is visible behind the many small window panes. Suddenly two of the windows become dark and stare blindly into the night. Then the light pops on in two windows upstairs. A sleepy glow spreads over the deserted courtyard. Soon Margrethe's father will come out of the door in the corner, a little out of breath after the climb up and down the many steps. He will cross the courtyard, pause for a moment and listen to the wind that whispers quietly in the darkness and then slowly walk up the cement steps and into his home.

Margrethe lies upstairs in her nightgown, curled up under the heavy feather quilt. At the opposite wall in the room, her mother fusses at the crib where little Harald is on the verge of falling asleep. His eyes are closed, the long yellow-brown eyelashes touch his cheeks. He makes sucking noises in his half-sleep and smiles inwardly to himself. Harald always smiles that way as if he was hiding a secret. People will pat him on his angel hair, tickle him under the chin, and he will pull away, not in an unfriendly

way but with a clear signal that you may look but not touch.
– How lovely he is, the ladies say when they come out to the
lighthouse for coffee. And he smiles to them and withdraws,
guarding his secret. He is different. He is not of their kind.

Margrethe easily gets irritated with him. He is so
helpless although he is no longer a toddler. He reckons that
others have to do things for him. When they go to
grandmother Thiede's for dinner, Margrethe has to pinch his
arm to make him sit properly. No one scolds Harald, they
don't have the heart to do it. Margrethe doesn't know if she
likes her younger brother. But she does love him. Which is
a different matter.

– Mama, tell a story.

– Shush. Harald is sleeping. You can read something to
yourself. It's about time we had that attic room done up. You
need to have your own room.

– Just a short one. The one about the three little men
who had a visit from the bishop.

– You can tell me the story while I finish here.

Margrethe knows it by heart and doesn't have to look
for the book. Once upon a time there were three little men
who lived alone on a small island. It was way back in the
olden days when most people were heathens. One day a
pious bishop came to the island to educate the three old men
and tell them about the faith. He stayed with them for a
whole day, and they listened to him and admitted that they
had been ignorant about many things. In the evening when
the bishop was rowed back to the mainland, he suddenly
saw the three men skip along on top of the waves in pursuit
of the boat. They motioned to him and begged him to
explain once more something in the articles of faith that
they hadn't quite understood. Then they thanked him for his
patience and fine teachings and walked back on top of the

waves with light steps. But the bishop sat in his boat in deep thought.

– Didn't you leave something out? Do you really understand the story?

– Yes, I do, Margrethe says. – Our old men in the spruce plantation are also heathen. They wrap a bandage around the axe when they cut themselves on it.

– They are just superstitious.

– It would be better to say simple-stitious, Margrethe suggests. Super sounds more important than simple. And grandmother Thiede thinks you are a heathen too, even though you go to church with dad every Sunday.

– That grandmother Thiede. She is so stubborn, her mother sighs. She smooths out the quilt, puts the clothes away. In a little while she will go downstairs to make his coffee.

– Let him do it himself, Margrethe suggests. She thinks that her mother makes too much of the men in the house. – Won't you come over here now. Sit down on the bed here and tell me a story. Something scary that's not for Harald.

The mother's busy hands stop moving about and rest now calmly in her lap. She closes her eyes and breathes deeply. Then she gets up again. – No, not tonight. Tonight you'll have to do your own reading. The fairytale book is on the night table.

And Margrethe picks up the book and leafs through it. She is sleepy, and the mother's voice reaches her like an echo from within the darkness.

Once upon a time.

Once upon a time there were three little old men who lived in a house in the woods.

No, that's not how it begins.

There was once a poor widow who lived in a small cottage. In front of the cottage she had a garden, and in the garden were two rose bushes, one with white roses, the other with red. She had two daughters. They looked like the two rose bushes, one was called Snow White and the other Rose Red. They were as good and pious and hard-working as two children could be in this world, and in the evening their mother sang by their bedside.

What did she sing?

She sang: Fortune's roses of delight, In thorny gardens shine so bright, The thorns are all for me, A rose I keep for thee, Fortune's roses of delight.

Why are all mothers bad in fairy tales?

But that's not so, Margrethe, only stepmothers are.

And Snow White and Rose Red ran about in the woods and picked sweet red berries. The animals never hurt them in any way but approached them trustingly. The hare nibbled cabbage leaves out of their hands, the roe grazed right beside them, the stag ran happily past them, and the birds stayed put on their branch and sang for them in full chorus.

We'll never part from one another.

Never, for as long as we live.

Nothing evil could harm them, and if they played in the forest till it turned dark, they just lay down to sleep on the soft moss until daybreak. Their mother never worried about them, and when they sat down at the edge of the cliff, a child in white clothing stood nearby and watched out for them.

That's not a story. It's an old glossy picture in an old book. Now it slams shut, no, the book falls open up again. There are so many pages, so many pictures that flutter past each other.

We'll never part from one another.

Never, for as long as we live.

There is the younger brother who is transformed into a deer. He has drunk from the spring that transforms people. Snow White holds him on a leash made from grass and her own brown hair. But he tears himself loose, runs swiftly through the forest pursued by the hunters and the baying dogs. He is a shadow, a brief shudder in the grass, gone.

And Snow White walks through the forest wearing a small dress fancied out of paper. Her mother made it for her and sent her out in the forest in the storm and the cold to pick fresh wild strawberries. She sees nothing but the snow. Nary a green blade of grass is visible on the white ground, the trees are spun in a web of diamonds, and hard snowflakes beat against her arms and legs while the sun sets and the wind rips the paper dress to shreds.

Then she arrives at a little house. Hollyhocks grow along the wall. No, there are no hollyhocks. All the flowers are hidden under the snow that has piled up against the windowpanes.

Come in, say the three little men, standing in the light from the open door. Come and warm yourself by the fire, and perhaps you'll share your soup with us.

The snowstorm rushes past her eyes. The wind tears at the paper dress. The door is shut, the house is gone. Far away she glimpses a light from a window.

The snow pelts against her arms and legs. She runs through the snow and reaches the door. She stretches out her hand to knock, but there is only the empty air and the snow that whips against her from every direction.

There is the house, buried deep in the snow blanket. She runs through the howling wind, stretches out her hand.

Why did your mother send you out in the cold and the storm?

I have to pick wild strawberries. Where do I find them?

Come inside, say the three little men, standing in the light from the door. Come and warm yourself by the fire, and perhaps you'll share your soup with us.

And they give her a broom so she can sweep in front of the door. There, under the snow, grow the most delicious deep-red strawberries.

But Rose Red is locked up in a tower in the forest that has neither door nor stairs. Every evening she leans out the window. Rapunzel, Rapunzel, let down your hair. She leans out the small window, and the prince climbs up to her.

Poor child, says the old woman. You don't know that the bridegroom who is waiting for you is death himself.

The robbers arrive with a young maiden, give her three glasses of wine to drink, one red, one white, one yellow. Then her heart bursts, and they tear off her clothes, place her on the table, cut her into pieces and sprinkle them with salt.

But Snow White walks through the forest and reaches the sea. Earth ahead of her, water behind her. And dry land appears in front of her, but only where she stands. The deep sea is on both sides, and the fog is so thick that you can barely see your hand in front of you.

But Snow White continues. She is looking for her seven brothers who, because of her, have been changed into ravens.

You'll have to go to the end of the world, then, and further yet.

She makes her way to the sun. It is so very, very hot, so hot that it will eat up all the people in the world. She continues and runs to the moon. But the moon is so very cold and angry, and when it sees her, it says: I smell human flesh. Finally she arrives at the stars. They are friendly and gentle, and each one of them is sitting on a little stool. Only the morning star has risen, it gives her a bone and says: With this you can open the glass mountain. Your brothers are there.

And she runs to the end of the world and far beyond. There, suspended in the air hangs the glass mountain. It sways back and forth, it's not so easy to find the key, and the key doesn't fit. She twists and turns the key, then coaxes it but all to no avail.

She then cuts off her pinky and uses it for a key. It slides easily into the lock. There is the troll with the three heads, the troll with the six heads, the troll with the nine heads. Forward, go. She must carry on. Light ahead of her, darkness behind her. And the trolls crack in the sun, turn to dust and ashes while the seven brothers flutter above her head, each one minding his own business.

But where is Rose Red, where is the mother in the cottage, where is the roe that disappeared into the forest.

The Bogeyman took them. Who is the Bogeyman? She has to guess the name of the troll. How does she find the word that will close and seal all the cracks.

She walks down the country road. She wants very much to have some company. People approach her, stop and greet her, join her for a while, sometimes for a longer while, turn off at a side road, vanish, and she is alone once again.

At this point she encounters a tall man wrapped in a cloak. She can't see his face, only shadows, hollows and jutting angles where his face should have been.

You're all alone on the road, he says. Would you like me to join you?

And who are you, then?

I'm death, says the man without facial features.

You're just and fair. All people are equal to you, and you don't discriminate between rich and poor. Yes, I would like you to join me.

And she continues down the long road. He is by her side, like a shadow. He is always near her, there is no getting away from him.

And they live happily ever after.

4

It's morning once again. Margrethe Thiede is awake in her bed and stretches her body. Her dreams are forgotten, and she is now on her bicycle riding down the grey country road from the lighthouse towards town. Heather-covered hills roll down to the sea on both sides of the road, only interrupted by the small spruce plantation where the three old men live.

This is where Margrethe Thiede rode her bicycle every morning, both as a child when she attended the local primary school whose tall red buildings framed the two playgrounds, and also later when the town had expanded to include a naval base and a secondary school.

If she turned her head to the left she would see the white sea spray from the surf on the beach and the sun braking through the low golden clouds far out above the water.

But she rarely looked to her left or her right for that matter, not at all during the winter darkness but not much in the summer either. She pushed hard on the pedals and lowered her head against the wind that forced tears to trickle from the corners of her eyes.

Colourful stripes and whirling wheels appeared behind her eyes, and a face or part of a face would emerge: Harald's chubby baby cheeks under his angel hair, her mother's eyes which in the daytime made things in the real world fall into their proper places but in the evening became unfocused and restless, her father's mouth that clamped down on words that were never spoken. Why didn't he spit them out instead of letting them slosh around in the hollow of his mouth until he finally swallowed them.

She also saw the teachers' faces. The insane Miss Iversen whose head jerked back and forth in yellow and black swirls when she shook Lily Lund who had worked forever on the same knitted sock until it was so tight that it couldn't even be stretched to fit a very small child. And Mr Andersen's lack-lustre but friendly eyes: You are clever, Margrethe. You have an ear for language. We'll have to do something about that. She felt slightly uneasy at the sound of 'we': that would mean Margrethe as well as Mr Andersen.

And she was too heavy, too hot-tempered, awkward in all ways. Nobody loved her, nobody understood her. And why did she have dull, brown, straight hair plaited in a single braid. And why did she have greyish blue eyes and not violet blue ones like Lily Lund, or real sky-blue eyes like Harald. Everybody was stupid, stupid, stupid. That's what Margrethe Thiede thought while pushing the pedals. And to top it off, today was cold and really humid. All she wanted to do was to lie on her bed with a book and curl up around the bit of warmth that was still left in her from her sleep.

But when she rode into the morning darkness or the half-light of dawn, she pushed all her emotions into the pedals, up and down, up and down, through the sleepy town where the smell from the bakery hit her so that the faces behind her eyes changed into pastries and dancing buns. At home at the lighthouse she had eaten porridge and coarse homemade bread for breakfast, but she was still hungry.

Lily Lund was waiting at the school gate, her curly reddish golden hair smelling faintly of cabbage from the stairwell in the tenement building. Lily Lund had a mother-of-pearl face. Blue veins pulsated under the skin in her

41

forehead. She could eat as much as she wanted without getting fat. But she didn't have much of an appetite. Margrethe was her protector and took her into the school yard that was full of flailing arms and skipping legs. Lily Lund was afraid of all the noise and the insistent display of physical activities. Nevertheless, Margrethe, the dependable protector, could sense a touch of pride in her, just like in Harald.

The gangly Carl Holm stood by himself as usual and watched them with his muddy eyes that couldn't decide whether they should turn grey or brown. His head looked fragile, the skin was stretched tightly over the bones, the ears were longish but delicate. He wore short pants well into the autumn season although he was among the older kids and several classes ahead of Margrethe and Lily Lund. You ought to feel sorry for him because his mother always wore a beret and stayed up all night cleaning house and singing hymns. During the day she stayed in bed and suffered from nerves. Margrethe would have liked to befriend Carl Holm and hear more about this mother who let her son wear short pants although you could tell from his legs that he was cold. But it was a bit embarrassing to be a friend of Carl Holm. It didn't give you any prestige in the school yard. That's how it is. Many of the things we do are unkind and wrong, and yet we pursue them to protect our own reputation. To be fair, Margrethe Thiede and Lily Lund would occasionally talk to Carl Holm, but only when no one saw them.

But Egon had prestige, wherever he got it from. He now approaches Lily Lund and Margrethe who are sitting in a quiet corner of the schoolyard with their bags in front of them. Lily Lund is leaning forward and scratching her knee.

– There's Egon, says Margrethe. – I wonder what he wants.

– He's crazy, says Lily Lund. But there is admiration in her voice. And something else too. A kind of tenderness.

Egon stands in front of them with his legs wide apart. He moves his ears back flat against his skull. No one but Egon can do that. A gob of spittle flies from his small mouth and lands on Margrethe's shoe.

– Stop that, you pig, she yells. – We don't like you.

– Lily does, Egon says and steps closer. – And you're just a hothead.

You never know at whom Egon is looking. His eyes don't move together. One eye looks straight ahead, cold and warlike. The other turns a little inward and smiles slyly. His cheeks are fat and white but powerful.

– Come here, he says and tugs at Lily Lund's thick hair. – I want to show you something.

She gets up and signals to Margrethe to come along.

By the wooden fence that joins one of the walls of the school building, Egon has thrown a bag that has been tied shut with a string. Something inside is twisting and turning. The bag bulges out, hangs limply, bulges out again. What can it be, inside that bag.

– Watch, Egon says, loosens the string with his short fat fingers and opens the bag. It is full of squirming grass snakes, brownish grey, glistening with flat heads that poke up and recede back into the pit of the bag.

– Yuck, it's disgusting, Lily Lund says and steps closer.

Egon ties the bag shut again and hangs it up on the fence pole.

– So you think it's disgusting, he says and pushes Lily Lund aside. – Move back a bit and watch this.

And he pulls a couple of arrowheads out of his pocket, positions himself in front of the fence with his arm lifted and begins to throw. The first arrow nails the bag to the fence at the top, the next one goes right through the paper where it bulges out the most. Suddenly the whole bag hangs limp.

– I'm going to throw up, Margrethe Thiede yells. – Come on Lily. The bell's ringing.

– They can hang there now, Egon says. – And nobody will know where they came from.

– They'll find out. They'll know it's you who did it, Margrethe shouted back over her shoulder while dragging Lily Lund along.

After school – Margrethe had brought a packed lunch to school and was able to satisfy her needs somewhat if not completely, and at home a reheated dinner was waiting for her – Margrethe Thiede and Lily Lund drifted about in the streets. They didn't stay long at Lily Lund's where her father was lying on the chesterfield with a newspaper over his face. There was a sour smell of defeat and laziness about him. They sat on the doorstep and exchanged glossy pictures and beads. They drew hopscotch grids on the sidewalk outside the tenement building in the sun, skipped on one leg pushing blue and emerald-green glass stones in front of them with their foot. And they dawdled along the streets down to the harbour to see if there was anything going on there. They are Snow White and Rose Red on an adventure seeking their fortune. We'll never part from one another. No, never, for as long as we live. And they meet trolls, withered old dwarves whose beards they cut off with a small pair of scissors, witches who threaten them with a cane. Princes are nowhere in sight. They'll probably show up one fine day. When will one fine day arrive?

– There's nothing special about boys, Margrethe said. –

Why is it always the boys that go away and fight trolls in real fairy tales.

But Lily Lund thought that it was a pretty good arrangement. She was a little lazy by nature, Lily Lund was.

– You can't catch me, you can't catch me, Margrethe Thiede and Lily Lund sang when they ran through the streets, hiding behind fences and street corners and poking their heads out, making fun of people that passed by, making grimaces, giggling away, flailing their arms around, ducking and darting off, their arms wrapped around each other's waist.

For they knew that the town was full of witches and trolls and old withered dwarves. In any case, it was full of peculiar creatures that could have popped right out of a fairy tale. Perhaps they were crazy.

Miss Iversen, who with her yellow hands curled tightly around the scissors couldn't cut the patterns straight and who shook the girls' arms or pinched them with pins when they whispered to each other during class. Crazy. The irate teacher Myhl, his bald head red as blood, spending his life among foetuses in alcohol, stuffed birds and wall pictures of lions and tigers. Crazy. Anders Stiff-Belly who paced back and forth down by the harbour and offered passers-by the opportunity to drum on his distended stomach. Crazy. The Grasshopper, who instantly jumped out of the way when meeting someone on the street. Crazy. And Miss Anthonsen who suffered from lupus and blew her house up with dynamite to get rid of the rats. Crazy.

Yes, the town was a cave full of trolls where Snow White and Rose Red were held captive until the princes would come and free them.

– – –

Auntie's tuft of hair appeared in the window with the lace curtains, and she asked them to come up to her hothouse apartment where she proceeded to inquire about Lily Lund's parents, whether her father was still unemployed and if her mother stayed out in the evenings much.

Afterwards she began in her cackling and spluttering way to tell her own horror stories about girls who were raped by their fathers, about Emanuel who slept with his mother in a double bed till he was forty, about Eline who drowned herself because her sweetheart had betrayed her, about the lady in the clothing store who was an illegitimate child and had to call her mother auntie because no one was to know. And of course we all knew. But that was all before your time.

And it was all before their time. It had happened in their town many years ago and had since turned into stories with a beginning and an end. Some of the stories seemed old-fashioned, but they were frightening nevertheless. And there were probably still things that happened secretly which came to the attention of Margrethe's mother's aunt when she poked out her bird-beaked face and interrogated her numerous informants. One day these would become stories as well. Who knows, perhaps Lily Lund and Margrethe would appear in some of them?

– How is your mother doing, Margrethe. I haven't seen her for a long time, it seems to me. Did she get a new winter coat? Yes, when it comes to her needs, he is not quite so frugal. But generally speaking, they like to hold on to their money, the Thiedes. Except for the time your grandfather was conned by the missionary who preached in the mission hall and afterwards held a prayer meeting with the men and talked them into investing money in his coffin ships. Those are dead ships. You know that, don't you. And the sailors that get a berth on board, they'll also die. But that's the way we'll all go, after all.

And auntie gathered her hairdressing cape closer around her neck, drew a sigh, began coughing, sipped some cherry wine that was handed to her, and then continued her cackling. Now it was all about the school teacher who was dismissed because he led his students astray, the boys, that is. And one can only guess what he did to them. It's not a pretty thought. One of them had his anus torn. Well, you're big enough to hear about these things. Yes, those poor people.

Lily Lund was listening, her head bent over a glass of juice while Margrethe tried to stop auntie. She was ashamed. Even though Lily Lund was somewhat timid, she was by and large indifferent to the small town. Margrethe wasn't. Between these abysmal horrors and abnormalities was the grey country road of normality that she was expected to travel, just like her mother who had chosen to become a Thiede and therefore was bound by the name.

In the same way that grandmother Thiede found royal families interesting, auntie took a great interest in abysmal lives, all very innocently and without it changing anything in her daily routine. And in spite of saying things that ought to be left unspoken, she abided by the rules and norms of the town. She had money of her own and reigned supreme in her hothouse empire just like grandmother Thiede reigned in her small house with the family silver.

But Margrethe was drawn towards the abyss and knew that it was dangerous to peer over the edge.

– We won't talk about that, the father said when she tried to bring up some of auntie's stories at the dinner table. He always just wanted to talk about things that had practical

47

applications in everyday life, and everything that was freaky, and wrong because it was different, was up to the professionals to look after, if necessary. But the wrecks, those that had fallen into the pit and now lay there squirming, they were not to disturb life on the grey country road, the very road that Margrethe was destined to travel. It was her obligation, but to whom, though, was she obliged?

Without being able to put it into precise words, she sometimes thought to herself that perhaps the problems lay hidden in the language. If she could just disentangle herself from the web in which the town's language had caught her, she would be able to see more clearly and find her own way out without fearing the abyss. But for the time being she would lean over the edge, shudder and pull back.

And it wasn't just a coincidence – this she learned from auntie – that nearly all the mad women were unmarried. For although some people evidently didn't need the institution of marriage, the majority found it a safeguard and stronghold for all that was considered right.

The maddest of them all – she had a document to prove it, they say – was Miss Arthur who had worked at the municipal office for many years until, one fine day, she annnounced that she would retire in order to prepare for her wedding to a count and admiral who in a short while was expected to anchor at the roadstead and bring home his faithful bride. On this occasion she was going to be presented at court and had acquired books on conduct and etiquette and had a silk dress made in pale yellow with a pearl-embroidered bodice and a train. Because the postman at this time had delivered a letter with a monogram on the back to Miss Arthur, townspeople were made to believe that there was some truth to her story about the count. But when Miss Arthur began showing up at the harbour dressed in her gown and train with an old rust-red coat draped over her shoulders, standing at the end of the pier curtsying and acting up, they quickly grasped that she must have misunderstood something or other.

Now many years later she still wandered about town with the train tied around her middle, just below her belly. She didn't hurt anyone, and nobody bothered her. But when Margrethe and Lily Lund sneaked up behind her on the street, she turned around and threatened them with her cane.

Crazy. Possibly Egon was crazy too, but in a different and more deliberate manner. He knew exactly what he was doing and could hypnotise Lily Lund to the point of her standing petrified in front of him, her eyes bulging and her mouth open, ready to let out a scream that never came.

Margrethe sensed now and again that the two of them shared a secret bond. They didn't fit into the category of the 'right people', but neither were they wrecks. They were indifferent and outside the norm, each in his or her own way.

And take Egon now, what kind of strange creature was he strutting about like that as if he owned the whole world. He was never short of money, which he stole from his parents who were in the restaurant business and had irregular work hours and who led an irregular lifestyle. He bought soda pop and chocolates – or perhaps he stole those as well – and hid his cache among the fish crates from where he would call Margrethe and Lily Lund when he wanted an audience for his experiments. He caught insects, trapped them in a glass where they buzzed around helplessly while trying to perform their normal routines within the confined space until they dropped to the bottom, their legs twitching – and died. He caught rats with his hands, pried their jaws open and gave them their own tails to chew on.

– Yuck, said Margrethe Thiede and Lily Lund. But Egon was tireless and invulnerable. Even when he later came under the care of the Child Welfare Office and was monitored every week. With his hands deep in his pant pockets, he would stare at the woman who was sent to check on him and give him counsel, his one eye looking sternly at her, the other turning inward in a little secretive smile. – Everything's going just bloody fine, he said. – Nobody has complained about me since the last time. That Egon.

One day Margrethe saw him sitting on a fish crate with a newborn kitten on his lap. A thin line of saliva ran from the corner of his mouth. He held the squirming and whimpering animal tightly with one hand, and with the other he drove a knitting needle into its belly and out through the fur on the other side. And now another knitting needle in through the neck and out somewhere under the tail. The kitten collapsed and lay limp. And Egon stroked it, almost lovingly.

Lily Lund had run ahead and stood in front of him, swaying, her fingers tightening and then relaxing just like claws. She whimpered quietly, her head rocking back and forth.

– It was going to be drowned anyway, Egon says and glances up at Margrethe.

– Stupid jerk, she yells and slaps him across his face. – I'll never talk to you again.

Then she grabs Lily Lund by her shoulder and pulls her along.

5

Margrethe Thiede's father went about his work quietly and without a fuss. He wasn't about to make inroads on the language. When he said something, he had already formed an opinion that no one could possibly change.

One evening at supper time, when Margrethe, as usual, had eaten leftovers warmed up from the meal that the rest of the family had consumed at noon, he nodded in the direction of his daughter. – Mother says that she is gallivanting about town. Why can't she come home right after school and help out in the house and with Harald.

– She does her homework with Lily Lund. And besides, I don't have that much work to do, Margrethe's mother said. She looked at her husband, who normally didn't comment on the running of the household but who took it for granted that his meals were served, his shirts pressed and that the sun rose and set at appropriate times. It was the responsibility of women.

– If that girlfriend of hers is so important, why can't she bring her out here. Perhaps it would be good for her to see a proper home, the father said and retreated back to his usual silence.

And that's how it happened. In the afternoons Lily Lund bicycled out to the lighthouse with Margrethe, had the loose buttons on her blouse sewn back on, drank tea and ate homemade bread and poundcake. Lily Lund seemed strangely unfamiliar to Margrethe when she saw her in the Thiedes' house. She was very polite but always with this little arrogant smile at the corner of her mouth as if she saw through it all and wasn't impressed. She made the Carrot Fairy nervous with the result that Margrethe was scolded. Sit properly, Margrethe. Don't shovel your food, Margrethe. Don't be a glutton.

Why couldn't she be a glutton? When there were other people present, the Carrot Fairy put on a mask and knew precisely what was right and what was wrong, what the townspeople would approve of and what they wouldn't accept. Why did she deem it necessary to wear a mask for Lily Lund who, when all was said and done, didn't belong to the town at all. Was the Carrot Fairy afraid of Lily Lund who sat there with her teacup like a well-mannered girl – though no one had ever taught her any manners – obeying all the proper rituals, but in a somewhat exaggerated way, Margrethe thought, making a little too much of it, subtly pointing out that these rituals were too exotic for her and truly ridiculous. Was that it? Was that what the Carrot Fairy sensed, and was it her own doubt that she feared? She wished for Margrethe to travel straight down the grey country road without looking to either side and without demanding more than what was feasible. That's what security was all about. But it wasn't security that Margrethe wanted. Under no circumstances. And yet, her attempts at rebellion lacked conviction, were too intense, too clumsy. She had no allies, for Lily Lund was a traitor who would watch her and the Carrot Fairy with a little shadowy smile, her head tilted back in an arrogant pose. Margrethe was at a loss. She had to defend the Carrot Fairy and show that her mother was not what she appeared to be. And at the same time she had to prove to Lily Lund that she also despised everything that the Carrot Fairy insisted on pretending that she was.

– Mom, tell me a story. – Tell me about the woman who came back from the dead.

– Oh, that's just a silly story about a wife that died, and then her husband shut all the doors and windows in the house and caught her soul. And in that way she came back to life again.

– The three old men also know a story about a soul that was trapped in a box, Margrethe said. She was disappointed that Lily Lund never wanted to come along when she went to see Sem, Kam and Jaffe.

– What is a soul? What does it look like? Lily Lund asked, pursing her lips.

– I don't know, said the Carrot Fairy. – In the olden days people believed that it looked like a butterfly.

– I thought it was only heathens who believed that, said Margrethe's father who had just walked through the door. Lily Lund got along really well with him. He didn't show any cracks. She also took a fancy to Harald and enjoyed drawing pictures for him. Lily Lund was good at drawing.

Margrethe watched the two heads bent over the dining table and felt let down. She sensed that the people she had chosen to protect were conspiring against her, letting her know that they shared something she was not part of. She collected the cups and helped the Carrot Fairy carry them out to the kitchen. Nobody expected Lily Lund to help out. She was a guest, and besides, she was playing with Harald.

– Her teeth are somewhat neglected, but she is turning into a good-looking girl, the Carrot Fairy said and looked critically at her own daughter. – So would you if you ate a little less. At least your teeth are fine. And your hair.

– You should try and curl the ends and let it hang loose. Or grow a fringe, Lily Lund said and hooked her arm under Margrethe's. A fringe would suit you. You could colour it

53

too. More brown or perhaps a tint of red.

– Are you crazy, Margrethe said. – My father would never allow it.

– What business is that of his? Lily Lund said and held her head high, tossing her shock of reddish golden hair that framed her nacreous face with its light sprinkle of freckles over the nose. The boys at the school gate had begun to whistle after her. Margrethe trotted along beside her, condemned to be the guardian and observer of those boundaries that define the good and the proper. That's what she was brought up to do. But she didn't feel at home anywhere, either at the lighthouse or in town, either in Lily Lund's world or in the Carrot Fairy's tales.

During the years when Lily Lund and Margrethe Thiede attended primary school and grew taller and developed both here and there and in all ways, the town also experienced a bout of growth and enterprise. Perhaps it was due to the initiative of a new mayor, or perhaps the town had just dwelled in its sleepy self-suffiency for so long that it was bound to wake up and stretch its limbs or else stagnate completely.

The harbour was expanded, and it was decided that a naval base should be built. A new big shipyard was constructed in addition to several fish-meal factories where the workers contracted respiratory diseases due to the dust and the handling of formaldehyde products, with the result that the hospital system also had to be expanded. And so it goes. One man's loss is another man's gain.

In the north-east end a new residential area with rowhouses and apartment buildings sprouted up. It was known as cabbagetown, and not because people appreciated this rather useful vegetable. But the houses had modern kitchens and bathrooms of a kind that were not seen in the older part of town. However, the brickwork quickly began to crumble away, and rain leaked through the roofs, all of which led to complaints to the town council and protest letters to the contractor in charge of the buildings. Nothing came of this, of course, since no one would take on the responsibility. Tenants in cabbagetown got used to having to put buckets out under the leaky spots every time it looked like rain, and eventually they forgot that it was possible to live in houses where all this wasn't necessary.

Finally a secondary school was built. In the beginning it was housed in the old school for skippers, but later it was moved into its own grey buildings with an assembly hall decorated by an artist from out of town, and with real washrooms that could be locked from the inside.

Margrethe Thiede was recommended to the secondary school by her teacher Mr Andersen who came out to the lighthouse on a visit and was served coffee and poundcake. He spoke eagerly to the parents about her academic abilities. Margrethe sat in a corner, sulking. She didn't think that she needed Mr Andersen to speak for her.

Lily Lund, whose father had died on his very own chesterfield and whose mother cleaned houses during the day and brought boyfriends home at night, took a summer job as a waitress at the hotel. After the summer vacation, she was going to attend the secondary school too. Her grades were not the best, but the new school needed students, and most of the teachers thought she had abilities although she seemed reluctant to make use of them. The regular visits to the lighthouse had ceased, and in the afternoons she and Margrethe wandered around town or at the harbour as before and told each other everything that was on their minds.

Carl Holm had left town after his mother had been institutionalized. And we don't need to mention the rest of the people, except for Egon.

Egon had started as an apprentice in a butcher shop as arranged by the Child Welfare Office. He cut up bloody chunks of meat with painstaking precision and wore a white coat with rust-brown stains across the front, surrounded by meat cleavers and knives, his one eye turning inward in a little smile. The butcher didn't think that he had ever had a more skilful apprentice than Egon, but he also mentioned in a confidential tone that he sometimes felt uneasy when he watched the way Egon stroked the carcasses lovingly before the blade fell, exposing the flesh that was covered in grey membrane, and splitting the white bones. Lily Lund saw him from time to time on the street or in the hotel's pub where he ordered beer, even though he was under age. He wasn't interested in staying in town for much longer.

Strictly speaking, Lily Lund wasn't really allowed to serve alcohol either, but in the pub with its low-hanging lamps suspended above the tables, no one paid much attention. She moved back and forth between the counter and the tables, carrying mugs filled with amber-golden beer, avoiding all the hands that stretched out to pat her on her arm, hair or other more intimate places. She seldom smiled, but earned money, much in the summer, less in the winter where she only helped out on Fridays and Saturdays. Now she could buy watercolours and good paper.

On Sundays when decent people went to church or for a bicycle ride – as did the lighthouse family with a squeaky-clean Harald and a reluctant Margrethe who was still living the family idyll although she didn't quite believe in it any longer – Lily Lund was painting, her hair streaming behind her in the wind. She painted pictures that didn't look like anything recognizable and showed them to Margrethe, who couldn't judge their merit. Later on she showed them to an artist from out of town who frequented the pub and drank with the locals. He was excited – by the watercolours, and by Lily Lund too.

She seldom expressed any enthusiasm herself. But during her breaks she would sit with the painter at his table and put up with his wandering hand that would sneak in under her hair and caress her neck. She had nothing against people taking care of her as long as she could choose for herself. If the painter showed interest in her pictures, she would welcome him. He already had a name for himself, had been commissioned to do the large frieze for the school's assembly hall; he was a man of the moment, so much was understood although he was probably boasting somewhat. Lily Lund was tired of school. She was on her way out, and perhaps the artist could be her passport to the world that she wanted to explore.

Margrethe met him one evening in the pub. She had attended a concert with a string quartet in the hotel's big hall, and Aksel and Anders, who called her Buxom and who shared her cultural interests, had accompanied her and suggested that they look in on Lily Lund after the concert. Margrethe wasn't so sure that Lily Lund wanted to be observed in her evening role, but she trotted along as she always trotted along when the boys gave the sign. She was at this time unhappily in love, not with Anders or Aksel, but with a language teacher who had bespectacled, brown velvety eyes and an unruly lock of hair that he constantly had to brush away from his forehead. As a consolation she compensated by reading big novels on the bed in the attic room where she could sob in peace, unless Harald came up and teased her. After one of those bouts of weeping she felt weak, relaxed and a little sheepish. Reality was waiting for her and shouldn't be neglected. So she took her bicycle and rode out from the lighthouse to meet Anders and Aksel who called her Buxom and who had spots on their chins.

Incidentally, she wasn't musical like Harald who could make strange melodies trickle out of the piano in the sitting room at the lighthouse. But she had prepared herself for much work ahead if she were to be a cultured person.

This evening the painter sat under the hanging lamp with a couple of the permanent residents, the glass blower and Mats Mathies. Artists or semi-artists; in any case, they could make things. Whether it was art or not was up to the individual to judge.

The glass blower's pitchers and vases could be seen in many places around town and out of town as well. He sold quite a bit to tourists and was a nice-looking man, dressed in a normal way according to the town's customs.

Mats Mathies was different. He had long black hair that was a little stiff and greasy as if it had been pulled out of an oil barrel. His eyes were greenish, and he had black stubble on his cheeks. In one of his ears he wore a small golden earring which was something that many in town found peculiar for a man to wear. His family had for many generations been dealers in charlatanism and racketeering. He himself had admitted that much, and it was most likely the truth. Moreover, he had been at art college and had served as a military man abroad, but he didn't talk much about that. Now in the summertime he pulled his cart around the neighbourhood and sold necklaces, wooden carvings and his own paintings of ships in stormy seas to the tourists, always tipping his broad-brimmed hat as he went along. Business wasn't bad.

– I admit that I have thrown myself into the arms of

commercial market forces, Mats Mathies said and winked to Margrethe. – Not everyone is as honest as that. She was fond of him, but he drank too much.

The artist put his arm around Lily Lund's waist, and she leaned against his shoulder and stared straight ahead with a vacant look. It was difficult to know what she was thinking, but she seemed to wake up for just a moment, and with a nod to Margrethe and her companions invited them to sit at the table.

The glass blower and Mats Mathies talked about what kind of war ships were going to be stationed at the harbour. If the idea was to keep their whereabouts a secret, it was very odd that the ships were exposed so that everyone and his brother could see them. There was also a submarine in the deep water off the coast to the north west. The periscope had been sighted from a fishing boat, and later on the same day the vessel, a big grey monstrosity, had moored by the quay. No one in the harbour knew of any details, but it was rumoured that it was on a trial run and that the folks in the Navy Department were well aware of it and ought to have issued warnings so that the fishing boats could look out for their trawling nets. This evening the submarine had taken off again, and the whole thing seemed to cause a great amount of disturbance at the fishing grounds. But they probably didn't care about that up there in the offices where armchair generals made the decisions without consulting the people.

The artist butted in and held forth on the arms industry, on big capital and the corridors where the centralized powers with their secret agreements ignored ordinary people's needs. He thought of his paintings as being political manifestoes against insidious oppression and the abuse of power. – And you're most welcome to draw inspiration from them while you're pondering all your acquired wisdom, he added.

Aksel and Anders poked each other in the side and guffawed. They were interested in culture and found politics contemptible. But Margrethe Thiede listened carefully to all these words that were never uttered at the lighthouse. They lit something in her. Only, she had a hard time understanding how the artist's frieze with its abstract pattern of shapes and colours could be a political manifesto. On her, it had a sleepy effect.

– It's closing time now, Lily Lund said and cleaned off the bottles and glasses with impatient hands. She hustled them out the door and whispered 'See you' to Margrethe before closing the door and turning to her artist, who stayed behind.

Margrethe bicycled to the lighthouse in the windy night. Towards the north west the desolate heather-covered hills hid the view of the sea. Out there a submarine was lying in wait.

Now it is a sunny day in late autumn. The sea is greenish blue and dotted with little white foamy crests, even out there on the high seas where waves normally roll in calm and broad movements. The water shimmers, is agitated, doesn't know what it wants, can't get a grip on itself because the wind keeps nudging it, now from one direction, now from another, capriciously as if teasing it. The sea tries to build up a couple of tall waves and send them off towards the pier, but before they get that far, the waves lose their strength, flatten out and splash foolishly against the big rocks where slimy green seaweed moves in twists and turns.

Lily Lund and Margrethe Thiede sat on the pier's heavy

guardrail with their legs dangling, Lily Lund's thoroughbred legs with their slender ankles – wherever she had those from – and Margrethe's solid legs that had begun to shape up. In the bright afternoon light Lily Lund appeared greenish, a little seasick. When she was a child, her hair had smelled of cabbage, and she had always been afraid.

– Egon has quit his job as an apprentice, Lily Lund said. – I'm leaving pretty soon too.

Margrethe gave her a sidelong glance. She said it in such a straightforward manner as if it were the most natural thing to say: I'm leaving.

– My mom doesn't care, Lily Lund continued. – And I'll just tell them at school that I have to withdraw because I have to go and look after my dad's sister.

– But isn't that what you're going to do? Margrethe asked.

– My dad doesn't have a sister, Lily Lund answered and smiled to Margrethe who had never felt fear and yet had no courage.

Lily Lund was calm, cold and strong. She wanted to join her artist. Margrethe knew that all too well. She wasn't in love but just waiting for something to happen. She wanted to be an artist herself.

What did Margrethe want? She who was plopping around in a quagmire of feelings, all confused, unhappily in love with teachers, film stars, characters in books that she devoured with a great appetite? – I'm interested in literature and politics, Margrethe said and drew a circle around her, signalling that she too was different. But she herself didn't really know what she meant by that. In her mind politics was still a vast and completely foggy concept. She had a vague sense of it as a place where you would be able to tell good from bad, only it was based on some other criteria than those used at the lighthouse and in town. Wasn't that what it was supposed to do, separate good from bad. Or perhaps she had misunderstood something?

Lily Lund didn't care. You couldn't talk to her about things like that.

– Give my regards to the artist, Margrethe said to Lily Lund's profile behind which reflections from the sun were bobbing up and down on the flowing waves. With him she was also unhappily in love.

Lily Lund promised to write but left no forwarding address behind.

6

So now Lily Lund had left, and who knows where she had gone. Just leaving the town behind her, believing that people like her can look out for themselves.

Margrethe Thiede missed her and didn't make any new girlfriends during her last years in secondary school. On the other hand, she devoted quite a bit of time to her younger brother Harald. He had been by himself a lot during his early childhood at the lighthouse when he was his mother and father's pride and joy – an angelic child with blond curls framing his chubby face. Now that he had grown taller and leaner, he would move so lightly as if his feet didn't have to touch the ground when taking a step. He still didn't have many playmates. He was something out of the ordinary and was aware of it, but he didn't disclose his secrets easily, at least not to Margrethe. For the most part he lay on his bed and listened to music, strange drawn-out notes that reached all the way to the attic room where Margrethe sat with her homework. Now and again he came to her room, seated himself in a chair, whistled, stood up again and walked around restlessly until she closed her book and asked what he wanted.

Nothing. He didn't want anything. He looked at her with his light blue eyes that hid this little arrogant smile of his. Was just a little bored. Would leave again, now. And he smiled to her and then became the foundling, the child descended from a moonbeam, a traveller from an unknown planet.

Once Margrethe had stood in the shadow of the lighthouse and listened to Harald entertaining some unfamiliar children in the middle of the yard about life on the planet where his real home was. Up there they spread a dark blue blanket over the sea in the evening so you could walk on it. The blanket moved up and down with the waves, it was like walking on a trampoline, quite amusing, but still it was more fun walking on the clouds. Everyone on his planet could do that, and it was also necessary because the dragon king, who looked like a giant lizard with a green head covered in armour, lived in a deep gorge at the southern rim. He ran back and forth along the edge of the gorge, snorted and spewed fire from his nostrils, and the best way to tease him was to skip from one cloud to another, right above his head, and spit into the tongues of fire, and then when the dragon king tried to stand on his hind legs, you would jump way up into the sky.

– Try walking on the clouds, said the children who were visiting with their parents.

No, Harald didn't think he wanted to do that. Down here the air was far too heavy, and it would make you heavy too. Sometimes he even felt that it was too much trouble to breathe. The colours up there were also much nicer. They had colours that had never been seen on earth. If he had to describe them, he would have to use ordinary earth words. But they wouldn't do. The colours were completely different.

– You're lying, said the children and moved closer to him. – Try walking on the clouds. You're afraid.

Before they had a chance to push him, Margrethe rushed in and suggested they play games and have some juice to drink in the dining room. But afterwards she had shaken Harald by the arm. – Why do you tell such rubbish.

Don't you see that they laugh at us.

– But it is all true. And it is very boring to talk with people who only know earth words.

Harald was fair, radiant and self-assured, but shy at the same time. He had often irritated her. Yet she loved him helplessly and understood that he could not adjust to this monotonous life at the lighthouse and in the school with classmates who weren't able to approach him because he would never allow anybody to be near him. Not even Margrethe, although he would appeal to her feelings sometimes. He was bright but lacked concentration. He was bored and didn't behave like other boys. Something was wrong with him, but she couldn't figure out what it was, for he never let down his guard. She was worried about him but didn't know why herself.

When she tried to hint at some of these things to her mother, the lighthouse keeper's wife stared at her with a blank look on her face, grabbed the top of a carrot plant, picked a couple of nasturtiums, hurried inside to find a vase, reached out for a duster on the way, shook the cushions and turned her back on the girl. She didn't want to hear anything bad about Harald who might not perform all that well in school, but he was a boy after all and had other things to occupy him. Harald had always been something out of the ordinary ever since he was an infant.

Harald, Harald, my heart and soul.

– When I grow up, you and I will travel together, Margrethe said – By then I will be ...

– A bank clerk, Harald interrupted and turned the corner of his mouth down. The father had talked about getting her a position as a trainee in the bank.

– Definitely not, Margrethe said. – Do you think I will stay in this town all my life.

As the exams were approaching, she was studying hard and keeping mostly to her books. One day when she wanted to visit Kam and Jaffe, they had disappeared. The cottage was closed down.

– They must have left, her mother said. – Perhaps they had relatives after all.

– Perhaps they are dead, Margrethe said.

No one saw them again. The cottage was forced open, it was empty except for the kitchen table with the four rickety chairs and the tools leaning against the wall. Margrethe imagined that one night they had taken each other by the hand and walked on the sea in the middle of a moonbeam.

But she didn't have time to think any longer, either of Harald or of the old men. She was reading. And after that came the exams and all the parties where Anders and Aksel would carry her shoulder-high and pretend to groan under their burden while she would float above faces that were shimmering in the light and in the darkness.

And Margrethe is dancing in a blue dress inside a mirror while a voice close to her ear is singing about red roses for a blue lady. She is tall but no longer fat, just chubby, her face all soft hollows, eyebrows heavy below her fringe, skin like cream and peaches. She feels good inside that skin. She smiles to herself, pulls her lower lip up to cover her teeth that are a little too big and bulky in her wide mouth. She purses her lips. A mouth to bite with, a mouth to kiss with. She smiles to her mirror image again. Her dimples are showing.

Her dance partner had retired into the cigarette smoke while she had been rocking on her feet in front of the mirror. Red roses to a blue lady. She bent her head to the side so her brown hair would touch her shoulder. At the bottom of the mirror she could see a pair of long trousers. They moved back and forth in front of an easy chair where a girl in a white skirt sat with her legs pulled up under her. Now the girl got up, and the two of them danced together.

Margrethe Thiede felt warm, a little sleepy, indifferent. Anders came over and put his arm around her waist. How did people find each other, two by two. A shudder running down your back, a tickle in your stomach. You are the one I want, now, always, for just a moment. Margrethe Thiede was swaying and couldn't quite recognize the girl in the mirror.

A few days later, auntie with the bird-beaked face and the hairdressing cape came on a visit to the lighthouse. She wasn't actually wearing her hairdressing cape but a suit, a lace blouse and a hat. She had arrived by taxi and had been more or less carried up the stairs by Anton Cap who retired to a corner of the room after having placed her in the sofa.

Auntie had big plans, wanted to get out of her hothouse and travel abroad before she died. Margrethe was to accompany her as a nurse and companion.

– That's not possible, said the Carrot Fairy. – You are obviously not well.

– Tougher than you think, auntie cackled and struck her head forward above the coffee table that had been set in a hurry with a hemstitched table cloth and the cups with the floral design. – My money is not going to rot. I want to spend it on myself, and no doubt there will be a handful left for Margrethe so that she can go and study. Her appearance has improved over the years. But she is too big. That type doesn't get married.

She is crazy, the father said. – She will squander it all. In his opinion the money should be left in the bank and draw interest. But the Carrot Fairy agreed with auntie, and for once she was not going to make sure that things remained the same as always. Harald said nothing. After all, he wasn't invited to come along.

And if there is a fairytale anywhere, this is the one, and auntie is the good fairy although in a rather special role. She sits in her seat by the window with a cane between her knees, surrounded by suitcases and handbags containing the entire household pharmacy while the train lets off steam, moves away from the platform, and the faces of father, mother and Harald slowly disappear. She doesn't hesitate to demand that the window be closed at once for the draught. Ordinarily you don't do such things in town. You sit patiently and wait and let the cold penetrate you until a kind soul of his own accord thinks of asking whether it isn't too windy. You don't ask other people to do you favours just like that. And auntie doesn't even ask. She orders people as if it were her right to do so. Evidently it is possible to behave like that. And the young man sitting in the corner with drops of perspiration on his forehead has already taken his jacket off but jumps up nevertheless and shuts the window while Margrethe desperately rummages around in the hand luggage looking for the turtle that auntie has purchased for the occasion and keeps on a chain of small silvery beads, which doesn't prevent it from disappearing among the bags and blankets.

Because the trip was a journey of cultural education for everyone involved, the destination was the south. The turtle was crawling on the floor of the train compartment and made acquaintances. Margrethe felt a little embarrassed about her traveling party now and again, but she carried out her responsibilities in a good-natured manner, took care of the luggage, got taxi cabs to the hotels and negotiated with porters and waiters. Auntie didn't care much for ruins, and she quickly tired of the art galleries. She didn't see very well either. When Margrethe disappeared into the large cool rooms, auntie would often sit on a bench in the sun. And when Margrethe came out again, auntie would be surrounded by admirers, men and women but especially children. They were allowed to touch the turtle that would blink and look confused and retract its head into its shell.

– You must go and look at this painting, Margrethe said and held out some postcards. – There are plenty of mothers with infants here on the square, auntie answered and strutted in the company of her new friends. – You better show me some real men. These pipsqueaks won't do. And she let herself be manoeuvred inside to gaze at a cardinal with a fleshy face and cruel features. She walked right up to the painting. – He looks a bit like your old school friend, now what was his name? Oh yes, Egon. But this one here is not cross-eyed, auntie said.

She took to wearing blouses that exposed her bird-like chest, flirted with the young waiters and grabbed them by their sleeves with her thin blue-veined hand. She wanted attention and got it. But she wasn't petty and made sure to show Margrethe off too. – Lovely girl, she said and leered. – Lovely girl.

No, really, it was not easy traveling with auntie who had cut herself off from the town and was now drifting here and there, following the impulses that emerged from her confused brain. You would have thought that the turtle would be a stabilizing factor. But not so. The turtle began to look more and more like auntie herself and was completely unpredictable. Margrethe discarded her lists of all the things they ought to see. The whole thing was anarchy and chaos, amusing, but also exhausting.

They were sitting on a patio drinking wine under a roof of green interlacing branches. A long-haired violinist was carrying on in the background. Then he came closer, leaned over auntie and played close to her cheek.

– They should see us now, auntie said and winked at Margrethe. – But we won't say anything.

When Margrethe came home, she remembered the journey as a kaleidoscopic jumble of colours. It wasn't so much the paintings, the statues or the ruins that stayed in her memory. It was a wall covered in green ivy, red wine poured from a pitcher decorated with a floral motif, a shaded entrance gate against an open courtyard with a fountain in the glaring sunshine, a dark-haired head that for a brief moment had leaned over her own. But most of all she remembered the little brown turtle that in spite of its slow movements constantly disappeared into every nook and cranny and was later recovered, its head retracted into its shell.

Two weeks after their return, Margrethe left again to commence her studies.

7

And the big city was a fairy castle, burning with excitement. People fluttered in and out of gates and doors, lit up for a second and disappeared again, then others appeared right behind or further ahead. Margrethe Thiede had a strong sense that these creatures hardly weighed anything, were like moving lights. They never touched the ground but took off from stairs or the grey pavement and floated upwards like balloons that were filled with talk. They were always talking, without breaks as if the act of producing sounds in itself was worth something, and often it made no sense at all what was being said. They buzzed and fluttered around her. The world they created with their language was different from the one she knew, lighter, without substance and responsibility. They were strange and amusing, the fairy people.

In the beginning she got lost in the streets and had to ask for directions before reaching the boarding house for women that her father had found for her. It had to be a place where you could leave your daughter with some reassurance of safety, a place with house rules and regular, ample meals. Here, every morning and evening Margrethe passed through a gate that had the inscription: 'May the Lord watch over your coming and going', which you could only hope was the case, for the area was rather shady with ladies standing in the doorways, holding shiny handbags and surveying the street. One night, late, when she walked home at a slow pace and stopped for a moment in front of a shop window, one of them whispered to her: – You can't stay here, little sister. This is my district. It was quite possible that in the dark entranceways behind the girls with the shiny handbags there were also sadness and tragedies, poverty and poor living quarters. Margrethe Thiede knew this deep down, but the reality of it didn't surface to her conscious mind. This city was a fairy castle where tiny creatures flew in and out without anyone taking anything very seriously.

She didn't see Lily Lund anywhere. Lily Lund had never written to her.

Anyway, she, Margrethe Thiede, is busy with her own things. She is successful in her new life as a student. At first she sat quietly in the lecture hall, consumed with the mistrust that her upbringing had taught her about city intellectuals. She was amazed by this odd, meaningless verbal outpouring where people talked way too much compared to what they were actually saying. Later she begins to participate herself. Her professor likes to provoke her; she is hot-tempered after all and not afraid to take part in heated discussions if it should come to that. She also learns that you can play on words and tell jokes that play on different meanings. She hadn't known this before, and she is aware that her attempted jokes fall flat sometimes. But now she is not scared of speaking out in public, she thinks carefully first, knows what to say and doesn't just let words automatically follow one upon another. She was brought up to follow rules for good behaviour, but apparently they don't apply here. But she sticks to her own practice anyway which is probably the most sensible thing to do.

– Pardon me, but perhaps I haven't quite understood

what you were saying, she interrupted her professor during one of the first lectures. She really didn't understand it. He is confusing and funny, or perhaps he acts confused in order to be funny. He pokes fun of everything and says the opposite of what he means.

– It might be because I don't express myself clearly about topics that I haven't thought out completely yet, the professor answered, scratching his forehead under the strands of hair that have fallen out of place. – But the most obvious explanation is that your frame of reference is too narrow.

The autumn sun cuts through the windows in the big room. All around her the other students are scribbling in their notebooks. She is just as clever as they are. Of that she is certain.

– And what, then, does frame of reference mean? she asks.

– Background knowledge, the professor answers curtly and looks at her closely for a moment. – Notice your formulation: Perhaps haven't quite ... What was that supposed to imply?

– Politeness, Margrethe answers. – I didn't understand a word.

– Exactly, the professor says. – Politeness and courtesy. Cortesie, derived from the word meaning court. As is befitting at court. But you are not at court, young lady. Among other things, courtesy means that people have acquired a set of rules that makes it possible for them to interact and express their opinions without causing offence. Do you know the expression 'diabolic courtesy'? Well, I see, but you'll get to that one day. Courtesy is a set of ritualized social conventions and useful in many ways. I myself have had to acquire several principles of good manners over the years that were not considered important in my proletarian childhood. But as the rituals differ from group to group and become increasingly opaque, politeness can give rise to many misunderstandings. I'll try to repeat what I have just said.

He is irresistable, that professor. He looks like Jaffe although in a slightly bigger and much younger version. His body vibrates under his jacket. He has the same restless movements, the same toss of his head that makes his hair fall over his forehead, the same yellowish brown eyes. She has always been a little in love with Jaffe.

And now Margrethe Thiede is on her way upstairs to a big hall where she has never been before. Later in life, she will enter the hall again but then as the main performer wearing a silk dress, black with a green leafy pattern. However, she doesn't know this yet although she dreams about all her future exploits.

You reach the lecture hall from a wide staircase flanked by busts resting on pedestals that are recessed on the landings. They represent men who all look very important. Who could they be? We'll have to find out somehow.

Inside the room, chairs have been set out in rows facing a podium. The walls are lined with dark wainscoting and above the panels hang paintings illuminated by small lights – these paintings are also for the most part of distinguished-looking men. Presently there are mostly women in attendance in addition to the students. The men are probably too busy being important to go to lectures.

There are, however, quite a few people there. The lecture of the evening has been arranged by the Language Society, which provided the hall, and by the students, who have persuaded the professor to speak without an honorarium. Margrethe is going to do the introduction. She is proud of having been chosen and has spent a lot of time preparing herself although she only has to thank the professor and the Language Society on behalf of the students.

The professor's manuscript is lying on the podium. He gets up from his seat and walks quickly to the back of the podium, climbs the two steps to the platform, adjusts the lamp on the lectern but gets his hand stuck in the wire, and when pulling his hand back with a sudden movement, he accidentally sweeps the sheets of paper over the edge of the lectern. Margrethe jumps up, bends down, gathers the sheets and passes them up to the professor.

– There is jam on this one, he says, holding a sheet up to the light, inspecting it carefully. – Strange, he mumbles and waves the paper in front of him. – Personally I seldom eat jam. My wife prefers marmalade.

– You are not supposed to talk about jam, Margrethe hisses. It is part of her responsibility to make sure everything goes smoothly. – People are waiting.

The professor then begins his lecture. He talks about the great leap in the evolution of mankind when humans not only were able to see objects and to project images of them in their brain but also were able to turn these images into concepts independent from their specific circumstances. When a bear was not just some bear that stood right outside the cave, or the bear that mauled my wife last year, but a bear in general, so that people could make strategies as to how to defend themselves against this particular animal species. It would of course have been possible to categorize the animals in very different ways. According to colour for instance. But that would have been impractical and without any purpose. The linguistic contract that we enter into with each other is first and foremost governed by practical goals.

It was all very clever and interesting, but Margrethe felt that he popularized it somewhat. She thought about dogs. There were so many kinds, big ones and small ones, some that were short-legged or long-legged, others that were of uniform colour or a greyish white with black spots just like the cur that belonged to the three little men – I wonder what happened to that one, she thought – and yet they were all dogs.

– Look at the ladies, the girl next to her whispered. – They soak it all up. He is popular with the women. They fall for him one after the other. It is odd for he is really an ugly little man.

Margrethe didn't think he was ugly. He looked like Jaffe.

Now people applauded, the lecture was over, and the questions from the audience began.

– Why is modern poetry so incomprehensible, and why do young people use such awful language, an older woman asked. She was a member of the board of the Language Society, and Margrethe had dealt a bit with her in connection with the arrangement. She was also one of those people who talked incessantly.

For a moment it looked as if the professor was going to lose his composure. Then he leaned over the lectern and smiled amiably to the woman. – 'Poetry is not jam but fruit that grows.' Do you recognize that quote? No, hardly. On the face of it I don't believe that your two questions relate to my lecture, but you can probably answer them yourself by examining how many sterile and tired clichés you use in the course of a single day. Language innovators are the ones who will rediscover the world for us, and I don't just mean the artists who might be of varying quality.

And the professor leaned back in the chair pleased with himself while the students applauded madly. The girl next to Margrethe was certain that he had alluded to them. However, that turned out to be a misunderstanding, Margrethe discovered, when she joined the professor and some of the others for a beer at the pub.

The professor brought various tapes to the linguistic classes with language samples that he asked the students to analyse in terms of pronunciation, vocabulary and grammar. On one of them you could hear a high-pitched, somewhat child-like female voice with very open vowels. From the monologue addressed to a nearly silent male, it appeared that the speaker preferred marmalade to jam, yes, that she actually considered jam something rather vulgar.

– Conversation at the breakfast table, the professor said. – It is my wife. You will be able to study her in real life at my home. Her speech belongs to a linguistic substratum formed by girls' private schools and by landed property. You seldom find it as purely cultivated as in this case, which is not uninteresting in itself. By the way, marmalade originally meant jam made from quince.

The wife was quite nice, tall, a little bony and extremely polite. However, Margrethe couldn't help noticing that she didn't enjoy having so many unexpected guests. In this respect, and in some other ways as well, she reminded Margrethe of grandmother Thiede.

The professor was showing off his wife. He was proud of her, yet ridiculed her at the same time. And with her stiff little smile she put up with it while she conversed in her little-girl voice with the open vowels.

77

The professor mocked everyone, including Margrethe, who sat and listened in his classes with pursed lips. She wanted to catch him being inconsistent; sometimes he got away with it too easily and brushed it off with a joke, she thought. In spite of all his grandiose words about language, he was a peacock himself and was cut from the same light cloth as the big-city types. That was what Margrethe thought.

– So, our lady from the provinces, he said, without ever asking her if it was alright to address her in this familiar way. – Tell us what is on your mind, you, the queen of understatement.

– I'm expanding my frame of reference, she said and looked up at him and smiled.

And she was in love with the professor, who now and then would pat her on her arm or other places absent-mindedly when he passed her, but otherwise he didn't make any advances to her, which disappointed her a bit. She was in love with the professor but also in a medical student with whom she was closer. He seemed very experienced and yet childish. With him she argued because she needed to argue very badly, but it was never very serious. First and foremost she was in love with herself during this period. – Ahh, she said when standing in the shower at the boarding house, her face turned up against the jets of water that tickled her soft skin. Imagine, getting so much enjoyment from your skin. This was a new experience.

She went out a lot and made use of the big city's offerings. – You can't stroll in this area, little sister, said the ladies with the shiny handbags when she walked home late in the evenings to the boarding house where the Lord watched over her coming and going. Once she thought she saw Egon standing in the doorway of a restaurant. Then he was gone, and she felt no urge to look for him. She had never cared for him, and besides, he belonged to a very different world. This city was aflame and got her excited. Everyone fluttered back and forth, and she herself was beginning to lose her substance.

During the holidays she visited the lighthouse but seldom stayed on for a longer period. Everything was going well in the usual quiet way, apart from auntie, to whom she had wanted to deliver long detailed descriptions of her conquests and exploits, but who had fallen down the stairs and without any protest had succumbed to death. After that the Carrot Fairy had to clean up all her junk, which had grown to include several additional ceramic figurines and vases since the trip abroad.

Even the turtle got cleaned up and was brought back to the lighthouse. Whenever Margrethe looked at it, she missed auntie who had turned out to be the good fairy and, in her own way, a bright spot in Margrethe's life. She didn't see much of Harald when she came home. He went his own way, spent time with friends or lay on his bed in his room and listened to music.

8

But what about Lily Lund, what had happened to her? Once in a while she popped up in Margrethe's thoughts just for a split second. Where in the world would Lily Lund be?

Where are you, Lily? Margrethe asks, drinking her tea in the dark dining room at the boarding house. The tea pot under the tea cosy is on the sideboard, but on the table that is covered in oilcloth for breakfast and later in white linen for dinner are bread, cheese, marmalade, butter and eggs, and Margrethe is hungry. She is hungry and dissatisfied with her relationship with men. The medical student irritates her because all the words in his universe must be very precise, which makes his universe rather limited. And the professor, who usually gives her praise, has made fun of her latest assignment.

Where are you, Lily. I wish I could talk to you.

Here, answers Lily sleepily from a place not far away. She lies in a sun-filled bedroom and stretches herself next to a young man. He is stocky, not very tall, and his entire body is covered in golden down. Lily Lund presses her nose against his shoulder, and in his sleep he stretches his arm out and pulls her closer towards him. But he is very warm, and she draws back a little. She thinks she likes him but doesn't quite know why she is here, in this bedroom, in this apartment, with this young man.

Here I am, Margrethe.

Who, then, is that fellow lying beside you. The one who is so warm?

But you know that. It's Berre. You always wanted to discuss politics with Berre.

And it is indeed Berre. The prince that looked up at Lily Lund in the window in the tall tower and begged her to let down her lovely hair so he could climb up and rescue her. Perhaps she hadn't counted on getting rescued, but now she has to resign herself to the situation. Berre is the one who built wind turbines and water treatment plants.

All that is later, Lily. We will get to that eventually.

Margrethe walks over to the sideboard and pours herself another cup of tea. Lily Lund rolls over towards the edge of the bed and lowers her feet to the floor. All that is happening right now, at this very moment. And what kind of a moment is that? In her assignment Margrethe has written about foreign cultures where each individual lives in his or her own time and where people don't believe that you can draw a line across time as such and identify the moments where things happen simultaneously. There are also languages where time doesn't move forward in a straight line but slide around itself. And what about time out there in the universe where it is very different from what we perceive here. She was very proud of that part of her analysis, but the professor had crossed it out with red ink and written that she should stop philosophizing and be more concrete instead.

There is still some cheese left on the small plate. Margrethe has forgotten to turn the toaster off. She might as well toast another slice of white bread.

I really wish I could talk with you, Lily. Then we can tell each other all the things that have happened lately, just like in the old days.

In the old days Margrethe Thiede and Lily Lund strolled around town, talking about school, boys and what to do with themselves. Right now, in this very moment, Margrethe flips her piece of toast, and Lily Lund gets out of bed, carefully. Later, some time in the distant future, Margrethe discusses politics with Berre and goes for a walk with Lily Lund along the harbour front. And Lily Lund goes back in time, to the time just before the present moment and tells Margrethe what happened when she moved away to find her artist.

Up there in a tall old building Lily Lund is sitting on a mattress with her legs crossed. It is in the artist's work space, cheap rent with cold water in the kitchen and a toilet downstairs in the inner court yard which the artist and his friends never feel like using. Outside the city he has a farmhouse and a wife who looks after the house as well as the artist, and who cooks meals and sprinkles wild flowers on the table cloth for decoration.

The artist knows that you have to be brutal in order to do your utmost. He suffers from anxiety attacks and depressions when he is unable to work. He is a good painter, and he owes it to his talent to organize himself prudently. He needs a wife that is a wife.

Lily Lund is his muse. She is allowed to draw a little herself if she sits quietly and doesn't talk about her own plans and if she refrains from pacing the floor restlessly and turning the paintings that lean against the wall with their backs facing the room. The artist is a vessel that must be filled with admiration daily. Lily Lund doesn't admire him any longer.

She now stands by the door with her knapsack and the portfolio with her drawings. The artist is painting. – Are you going out, he nods absently. – Get some bread and a couple of beers when you come back up.

She shuts the door and and goes down the stairs. The streets stretch ahead of her between tall dark buildings. Slush. Evening. The moon, the old lump of stone, shines high above her among restless clouds, but she doesn't see it. She walks through sleet and drizzle, is caught for a moment in the lights from a passing car that make the drops sparkle in her thick hair. She presses the drawings against her chest, lowers her head and disappears down the stone steps to a pub in the basement, appears again a little later and continues her evening walk.

Somewhere outside a cheap hotel with posters showing women with hard-pumped breasts and buttocks, Egon eyed her. Was it her? Yes, wasn't it? He stretched out, looked in her direction, took a couple of steps and turned around again. He was the doorkeeper, the bouncer, a trusted employee. He couldn't desert his post.

That's how Lily Lund spent her time, walking the streets. Once in a while she would sell a drawing or a watercolour in a pub, sweep up the money angrily and refuse to sit with the patrons and listen to their drunken nonsense. – Don't sulk, woman. Come over here and be nice. But why should she be nice? She walked out of the room, away from the faces with their shiny eyes and moist lips, away from hands that reached out for her and tried to pull her down on some lap or black-stained chair. For a moment she might have been tempted by the warmth. But she didn't want to end in the gutter and fall into oblivion. She wanted to paint.

– Let me suffer all the pain I can bear, she said, turning her face towards something or other up in the sky, perhaps the moon. – Let me suffer all the pain I can bear if only I can paint ten paintings that are worth something. But it was not a tenable agreement. She knew that.

She slept in attic rooms and bed-sitters, stayed with casual acquaintences, young people who, like herself, drifted through the streets but had a hide-out and an extra mattress to share. A couple of them believed that they were in love with her. That was okay with with her as long as they didn't expect any emotional involvement on her part in return. They could take care of her, look after her basic needs, lie with her on a mattress or a creaking chesterfield, but she didn't allow them to thaw her heart with their warmth. That she couldn't afford. She was meant to paint and to have ice for a heart. And tomorrow or perhaps another day she would look up a professor of painting whose address she had been given. One day, when she had a sufficient number of works to show him. She dreamt about a giant canvas with colours and figures swirling around in perfect harmony with each other. But only if you looked at it from a great distance. And she stood quite close to the canvas with her brush and couldn't step back far enough to see if her strokes had the desired effect. If she stepped so far back so that she could see the whole image, she would never be able to reach it again. Perhaps she would ruin the whole thing, and why was there no one to help her?

She started to feel tired. The days trickled away. It was overwhelming. She herself trickled through the streets, kept to the doorways at dusk and merged with the shadows. The knapsack that lay by her feet had an identity. It was a knapsack. But was Lily Lund really nothing, just a pool of pale grey light and darkness, mostly darkness here in the doorway where she was hiding out.

That was how she stood when a man came out from the house across the street. She could see him approaching her, feet in pointed black shoes, legs in jeans, a black box equipped with a glass lense dangling on the background of a patterned sweater. She couldn't see the rest of him, but she felt his eyes on her.

– Look up, he said. – No, not at me. Look sideways towards the street. Lean against the wall. Feel the wall. Yes, good.

Click, it said, click, click. – And now tilt your head a bit to the side. Drop your head. No, straighten up again. Don't give in entirely, there must be a sense of resistance. Tight, dark resistance. Inside you. Your hair is fine. Look at me. Hate me. Do you hate me? Good.

The camera clicked. She did what he told her to do, hated him. He stood in front of her wearing black shoes and jeans. The tips of the collar on his dirty white shirt stuck out over the patterned sweater. The muscles on his neck were moving. His Adam's apple moved up and down while his jaws spat out the words and then closed again. His nostrils were two large black holes, and she couldn't quite make out his deep-set eyes under the heavy brows. When he put the camera away she noticed that one eye was a little bigger than the other.

Later she came to realize that he was handsome. She could tell from his self-portraits, from the early one where his curly hair covered his ears and where he had applied make-up to make his eyes sparkle, like electricity, above his cheekbones. And the later ones where his hair is cut short and his chin thrust forward above an unbuttoned leather jacket and arms in chains. But back then in the doorway she saw his face as separate features and wasn't able to put the pieces together.

He came closer, grabbed hold of her blouse and pulled it open. – That's it, I want to see your collarbone. No breasts. No, that's good. And now look at me. He stepped back again, lifted the camera to his eye and began to click.

85

She was hypnotized. She looked into the camera's snake eye, swayed and turned following his instructions, leaned her head back, rubbed her body against the brickwork, looked like a protrusion on the wall.

– Good, good, he said. – No, don't disappear from me. Cross your arms. Stick out your chin. Hate me. Good.

– What is your name, he asked and finally slung the camera over his shoulder.

– Lily Lund, she said. He had dragged everything out of her. Now he was taking her name as well.

– I'll make you famous, Lily Lund, he said, turned around and walked towards the house.

– What about me? she shouted and ran a few steps after him. He stopped, hesitated, turned his head a little.

– Come along upstairs.

And Lily Lund grabbed her knapsack and the portfolio. She didn't even know his name.

It was a big house with many storeys, the linoleum on the stairs was worn, the greyish green paint on the walls was peeling. The windows were full of cobwebs, and the narrow banister had been polished by the touch of many hands. Not exactly an elegant staircase, even Lily Lund could see that, although she was not very familiar with elegant residences of the well-to-do. She climbed slowly behind the man who hurried up the stairs with light steps. On one of the landings his black shoes disappeared. Far above her she heard the sounds of pounding on wood and the jingling of keys. Then she followed the curvature of the banister and finally stood in front of an open door.

She stepped into the dark hallway where a number of chains of various sizes hung from the rack among the coats and furs. She didn't pause to look at them but followed her host through several dimly lit rooms, some with curtains instead of doors, until they reached a big room where the drapes by the windows were drawn. Two figures, a white and a dark, were lying close together on a sofa in the corner.

– Get up, you two. We're going to work. I feel inspired to work.

Two naked men got up slowly and jumped back and forth, probably to get the muscles working. Both had their heads clean-shaven, their faces were sleepy and empty.

– The black one is Ben and the white one is Dan, the host said looking quickly over his shoulder. – I'm Roy Vige. Find a place for your knapsack and get the heavy chain from the hallway.

He began to switch on lamps and set up cameras. He unfolded white umbrellas and placed them in stands. He took the chain Lily had brought and tied it around the waists of Ben and Dan so they stood like two Siamese twins, chests touching, a white leg crossing over a black one, white shoulders to one side, black to the other. – And now the profile. Ben, close your eyes. Dan, look straight ahead.

And Dan stretches his neck and bends his white, shaven head backwards. A skin-fold at the back of his neck appears. Lift your head a little, Roy Vige says. A white Adam's apple rests halfway on a black shoulder. Dan and Ben in white and black profile.

Here as in all the other rooms pictures hung on the walls. Dan and Ben viewed from the front and the back, chains around their waist and down between their buttocks. Their muscles shining as if rubbed down with oil. There is one with Ben curled up inside an oval frame. He pushes his shoulders up against it but is forever unable to prize it open. And here Dan is sitting astride a chair, his hands resting on its back. He is wearing a leather vest with a star but nothing on his lower parts, his member dangling in front of him between the bars of the chair's back. It is so troublesome, this sex. It creates delight as well as despair. But not in Roy Vige's pictures where the show of sexuality is heightened by glistening muscles in leather and chains. It is all effect and macabre aesthetics. Although Lily Lund could recognize the beauty of the pictures, she didn't really care for them.

All the faces were without emotion, empty of pain and joy, apart from Roy Vige's self-portrait from his youth where his intoxicated eyes glowed from narcotics. When Lily Lund's picture later was hung on the wall, her face too was empty. She posed with her thin arms folded across her chest, looking dismissively and defiantly at the world. There was no painting in that face. But it was beautiful and porcelain-like, mysterious-looking and very small under her heavy hair. Below the picture the caption read: Lily Lund. Platinum Print. – I'll make you famous, Lily Lund. Was that the way she was going to be famous? As raw material for the photographer's aesthetic that only sought to capture the state of loneliness and the beauty of emptiness.

All people and all things came to look alike when reflected in his camera. They all conveyed the same message: existence as a vacuum with tiny shadowy strokes of senseless pain. A peeled cucumber squirmed under his lense. A bluish black eggplant swelled menacingly in bright light and deep shadow. Even the flowers that were tied in exquisite bouquets and purchased from special florists or the bunches that he bought from street vendors became separate entities that looked hostile without contact with each other. Beauty. Emptiness. Loneliness.

That's how reality was depicted in Roy Vige's pictures,

but it obviously wasn't the same everyday reality that Lily Lund experienced in his big old apartment where there was room for her too. She stayed mostly in the kitchen where she would sit on the table and draw by the window that overlooked the grey roofs and the green-tinted copper roofs of the towers. The pigeons were cooing on the ledge. Way down in the courtyard you could see laundry hanging on the clothes lines. She didn't have to go anywhere else. She was safe as long as she wasn't in the way.

Ben lugged the groceries upstairs in big bags and would later be in the kitchen, bare chested, an apron tied around his middle, marinating meat and chopping up vegetables. His knife flashed in and out of heads of lettuce, sprigs of parsley, blood-red tomatoes and brown mushrooms from the field. He hummed and buzzed while working and once in a while he would sweep Lily Lund off the kitchen table to make work room for himself. But never in an unkind way.

Sometimes he argued with Dan who sat in their shared bedroom by a clacking typewriter for hours on end in the long afternoons and let himself be waited on. Exactly what he was writing he didn't disclose to Lily Lund. He only dropped the hint that it was a big and significant novel.

But Dan, too, was Roy Vige's slave. The white slave, the black slave, both would come when the master called. They would bow their clean-shaven heads, twist and turn their bodies, kneel with their muscular asses turned up, pose with chains and gunbelts, hands curved around their cock. Close your eyes, Ben. For there was too much joy in Ben's gaze. He enjoyed exposing himself. Dan was more hesitant, he was older, his muscles already sagging a little, the skin on his ass dimply. He looked straight ahead, saw old age and the body's deterioration down the road. Ben rubbed his forehead against Dan's shoulder and passed his hands over his rib cage. Their relationship was one of familiarity, tenderness alternating with irritation. But in Roy Vige's world of beauty under the bright lights, all emotions from daily life were erased. Only the shape of their bodies and the expession of painful loneliness in their faces were left. Silver Print. Platinum Print.

Dan and Ben were Roy Vige's slaves. Not Lily Lund, with whom he seldom interacted. – You have a nice little talent, he said and looked down at her drawing pad. – And what do you intend to do with it? You are completely lacking in technique. There isn't much to go on.

But how did you acquire technique, Lily Lund thought. And was it really necessary. In here it was warm and safe, and there was never any lack of food. No one mentioned that she should move. She could stay in this warm cave and eat and grow big and fat, her icy heart turning to slush. Once in a while it occurred to her that she ought to move on. But she was too lazy. She felt that she belonged here.

Sometimes it happened that Roy Vige had a fit of rage. Dan had been at the beach and came home with sunburned shoulders and was only white where he had worn his swim suit. – You people are taking advantage of me, you're fleecing me, Roy Vige bellowed. – Get out of my apartment. When I come home tonight, you're out of here.

Dan sat down and began to write on the typewriter, his blue veins pulsing in his forehead. Ben daubed lotion on his shoulders. He didn't care, and so Lily Lund didn't care either. And when Roy Vige came home in the evening, he would start working and explore how he could use Dan's blistering back against the backdrop of a dark velvety blanket that was hung on the wall.

– It quickly passes, Ben said. – Once he threw the carving knife at a gallery owner who was going to censor his pictures. We were up here in the apartment in the middle of a meal, eating a leg of lamb. Whoosh. And the knife came flying right past his ear. No, he was hit in the ear, I remember it now. He was bleeding onto the potatoes.

– And then what? Lily Lund asked.

– Then we drank another couple of bottles of wine, Ben said amicably. – It was such a nice little gentleman dressed in a suit. He took fifty percent for himself.

Now and then there were visitors, young men that Roy Vige had picked up at some bar, new models, female admirers. On these occasions Lily Lund withdrew with Dan and Ben, but not so far away that they couldn't be summoned and see to the serving of refreshments and to make sure that nothing went wrong or was derailed altogether.

– Get out, go to bed and leave me in peace, Roy Vige said and entered the room where Dan was reading a magazine and Ben and Lily were playing cards. But usually he called for them to have the guests thrown out. He quickly tired of the new young men, and the female admirers bored him.

– And Lily Lund drew less, ate more and became heavier, teased Dan and played cards with Ben. The place felt safe and cozy, like a lazy afternoon. She wanted to stay in the trolls' cave forever.

But one day, and it wasn't one of those fine days but a very ordinary cloudy day, just like the day when Lily Lund was sitting in the kitchen, gazing through the window and half-dreaming with the drawing pad in her lap – one such day the chains in the entrance way were jangling and a strange creature steps in, wanders through the rooms, parts the curtains until he finds Roy Vige and nails him with his gaze.

'The Killer Angel' was the title Roy Vige gave to his first portrait of the young writer Uwe T who wore tight black pants and a black leather jacket, and whose narrow face was the colour of red bricks. There was also a tinge of red in his light blond hair that stood straight up, swaying and hovering from the top of his head as if it had been sprayed or was being held up by a built-in wind machine. He was black and red but looked nevertheless like a slim root vegetable that had just been pulled out of the ground. Perhaps it was because of his eyes, which, despite their small size, dominated his face. They were not round or oval like eyes usually are, but square or rather rectangular, two small pale blue rectangles standing on their end, making his face seem even longer and narrower.

The gaze came from far away. From where? Perhaps from Uwe T's interesting interior that was hiding behind the black pants, the black leather jacket, the long brick-red face under the bizarre hair tuft.

Dan and Ben had found him at a get-together at one of their acquaintances' places, where he had stood in the corner with his back turned towards the other guests. When Ben approached him – no one else in the room had thought of doing this – he turned around and looked at the gathering with his rectangular eyes.

– We will give him to Roy, Ben said and put his arm around Uwe T's narrow shoulders and dragged him away from the party, followed by a reluctant Dan who later admitted that he had found this gesture too spontaneous and rash.

At first Uwe T had stiffened up and offered resistance but had come along to Roy Vige's apartment after all as if it didn't matter to him where in the world he stayed. He had recently, it turned out – and Dan knew this already – published a remarkable novel, very long, very difficult and evidently very promising. Uwe T insisted that none of the critics knew what to make of it. Most likely they hadn't finished reading it either.

Dan had read it and found it overrated. Ben never read anything but comics. But many years later when Margrethe Thiede and Lily Lund once again went for walks along the harbour front and exchanged stories about their lives, it came out that Margrethe had spelled her way through it. She still remembered the descriptions of insects, cockroaches in the big city, wasps on a dilapitated summer porch, mosquitoes around the bog, mayflies that stuck to the clothes in black blotches.

Ben fell in love with Uwe T, hopelessly and unhappily, for the young writer was never friendly and seldom forthcoming. Lily Lund observed how the relationship developed and how Dan for each day that went by became increasingly whiter from anger and jealousy. He and Ben argued every day, and Ben broke down in the kitchen, put his arms on the table and sobbed into the salad. – I want to die, he wept. – The only thing I wish for is death. And his hand squeezed around the carving knife, but then relaxed again.

Roy Vige wanted to photograph Uwe T's rectangular eyes and catch their pale blue light. He wanted to photograph like he ususally did at hours that suited him. But Uwe T was no slave. – I don't have time right now, he said and disappeared through the doorway. Maybe in an hour's time. Maybe tomorrow.

– Now, Roy Vige shouted. – Right now. But Uwe T turned his back on him and slammed the door behind his shiny leather jacket.

Roy Vige became irritable and took to wearing sunglasses. Dan hammered away on his typewriter till the walls began to shake, and he too refused to sit for Roy. When he wasn't writing he lay on the sofa staring at the ceiling with his hands folded under his clean-shaven head. Ben lumbered back and forth like a big sloshy lump. You could stir him with a wooden spoon, but he himself couldn't be bothered to get any food or wine. Roy Vige flew through the apartment and flung the door open to the room that Uwe T occupied and where he, pencil in hand, was observing a spider. All around him there was shouting, weeping and breakdowns. But he didn't care, he was only interested in his own affairs and was no slave.

One day when Lily Lund had been out shopping – for someone had to buy the groceries, and Roy Vige still remembered to leave money on the shelf in the kitchen – she saw a large moving van by the front door. Roy Vige was standing at the top of the stairs and gave directions to the movers who carried his things downstairs. – I'm going abroad, he said and looked as if he just remembered Lily Lund's existence this very moment. – Uwe is coming along, for the time being. You can stay in the apartment till the end of the month.

Dan moved to his sister's place. Had he really had a sister? Ben wandered around in the apartment in his sloshy manner for a while, patted Lily Lund absentmindedly on the head and talked about a commune where he had an old friend. Then he disappeared too. Lily Lund walked around alone in the empty apartment, looked at the bright outlines on the walls where the pictures had been hanging. Lily Lund. Platinum Print. Dan and Ben. Silver Print. The Killer Angel. She didn't really know what to do with herself.

Somewhere out there in the darkness Egon was waiting. Perhaps Lily Lund sensed this, but she wasn't conscious of it.

One afternoon when she stood by the open window facing the street, a young man passed by. He looked up and waved to her. She leaned out, her hair shimmering in the sun. From down below it looked as if her face was floating in the air, surrounded by this mop of reddish golden hair. The young man wanted to climb up to her but chose instead to enter the front door and climb up the many stairs. She let him in and took him through empty rooms to her own where there were still a few pieces of furniture left. He didn't know what to say, had no real reason for being there except that he wanted to see her close up. He made her nervous. He was so full of life and couldn't sit still out of sheer vitality.

Gradually she realized that he hadn't come to take over the apartment. She relaxed a little, permitted herself a smile. He was boasting, had wild ideas, there wasn't a thing that he hadn't done or wasn't going to do in the future. He was actually a car mechanic, but the work had bored him and therefore he and a friend had started a business selling wind turbines and fibreglass blades. Beautiful towers whose propellers turned and created new energy from the air. It hadn't been all that successful, though. Due to a fault in construction, one of the blades had crashed to the ground and broken at its base. When it fell, the rhythm of the tower's vibrations went haywire, a bulge formed on the tower and the whole thing collapsed. The factory would cover the damage, so the buyer wouldn't suffer a loss. Still, they had to close the business, and now he was working as a mechanic again. But he had many other ideas. Renewable energy, that's where the future lies.

He related all this hurriedly, almost in one breath. Everything happened so quickly with that turbine that stood so tall and straight, beaming against the blue sky and then suddenly collapsed. Lily Lund didn't understand everything he said, but he laughed a lot, and the late afternoon sun lit up the empty grey walls with the lighter squares where the pictures had hung. A little later he suggested that she could move in with him since she didn't have a place to live. And Lily Lund, who wanted to paint, just not right now, not now but later when she felt the urge and necessity once again, Lily Lund, who didn't quite know what to do with herself, accepted his offer.

A couple of months later she married him. Click: Lily Lund in front of the town hall. Click: Lily Lund with an infant. Click: Lily Lund with yet another infant and a toddler by the hand. Things are happening fast for this man who wants to sell energy and create new sources of energy himself. Here he stands, wearing swim trunks, his chest puffed out, his eyes squinting in the bright sun that shines through his light curly hair.

These are not Roy Vige's pictures. They are amateur snapshots that capture the moment lovingly: Lily Lund is smiling. Lily Lund is holding the children close to her. Lily Lund tries to be what is expected of her, a good mother, a good wife to a husband who is full of energy and who wants to conquer the world. She gets up, wakes up the children, tiptoes into the kitchen to make breakfast. She has arrived at the clear light called reality. Some people cannot cope with that, however.

And meanwhile Margrethe is drinking her morning tea at the boarding house. They cook good food at that boarding house, but still she wants to move away soon. She has been promised a room at the student residence. The professor will surely be satisfied with her next assignment. She has too much to do to think about Lily Lund and their childhood together. She has almost forgotten life at the lighthouse, the father, the Carrot Fairy and her younger brother Harald.

9

Sheets of light upon sheets of light. Along the horizon the sky is a pale blue, but above it is a broad band of black edged in gold. Sheets of light upon sheets of light. Golden mountains rise from red gorges. And still higher up wispy rose-coloured clouds glide past and dissolve in straight and feathery lines against the greyish sky.

At the top of the lighthouse amidst the drifting colours stands Harald. He can see the entire horizon. The entire world is spread out in front of his feet. His hair flaps against his chubby young cheeks. No, his hair is short, his cheeks thin. His eyes shine deep inside his skull.

Walk on the clouds, voices are whispering close to his ear. Up here the air is lighter. Here you become lighter yourself.

Walk on the clouds. You don't dare, the voices shout from down below, down there where everything is heavy and solid, where the colours cannot escape from the constricting darkness, where words fall with a thud like stones in a shaft, earth words, earth language, everything lumped together in suffocating solidity.

But the sky is one big painting of hues. The colours are singing to him and drown out the voices from below. Now comes the alto solo with the orchestra in the background:

I slept
From deep dreams I awoke
The world is deep

Deeper than the day would be
Deep is its pain
Deep is desire
Deeper than the woes of the heart
Pain will pass
But all our desire seeks eternity
Deep deep eternity.

And Harald climbs up on the railing and from his high jump
walks out onto the clouds.

It was a nightmare, and it was real. Margrethe Thiede was
called home in the middle of the semester. Her books
remained open on her desk. Later she would return, pack
them up and cancel her room. She would of course come
back again, and then she could stay at the student residence.
Right now she was needed at home.

She had to look after everything, arrange the funeral,
choose the coffin, select the hymns. Her mother had taken
to her bed, the kitchen garden had gone to weeds. – I lack
the strength to do anything.

In the living room the ticking of the grandfather clock
sounded sad against the dusty surfaces. The father drew a
line through the dust on the table with his finger when he
came in to eat his meals. And now it was Margrethe who
had to take care of him.

– What was it with Harald? she asked. – Surely you
must have noticed that something was wrong. Why do you
always have to pretend that everything is all right.

She hated her little brother because she had failed him.
Now he had taken revenge. Life wasn't good enough for
him. It was good enough for everybody else, but not for him.

– I didn't see too much of him, the father said. – He kept mostly to himself. He stayed upstairs in his room and listened to music. And then he did his school work, I guess.

– He played truant, you know he did. Why didn't you say something to him. Why were you afraid to say anything?

In her brother's room, the attic room that had once been hers, a pile of clean clothes was sitting on the chair. On the table were books, poems copied on note paper, a school book with words scribbled in the margins, no diary, no personal notes. On a shelf in the bookcase was a radio next to a row of cassette audiotapes, recent rock groups, classical music.

There was a tape in the machine. She pressed the button, and long deep notes rolled towards her. Then an alto voice cut through, spoke to the orchestra, enticingly with authority, full of seductive pain:

But all our desire seeks eternity
Deep deep eternity

She turned the machine off, ejected the tape and looked at the label. A symphony of sorts, she didn't know which one. It was the last thing Harald had listened to.

– Did he take drugs? she asked the doctor who had come to give the mother an injection. Margrethe was standing in the hallway helping the doctor on with his coat. Outside the rain was beating against the windows.

– Not as far as I could tell, said the doctor and pulled his cap down over his ears. – At least not when he died. About a year ago there was that dirty business. They stole the emergency supplies from the fishing boats and cut up the rubber dinghies to get at the morphine. What a mess!

– And was Harald involved in that?

– Harald, that nice boy. I wouldn't think so. He kept mostly to himself. Some said that Egon had organized it. That he was the ringleader and sold off the goods. But the case was never solved. Now we have changed the system so the skipper himself is in charge of the medicine and it stays with him. But there have been break-ins at my house too.

– Egon, Margrethe said. – I went to school with him. Has he come back to town?

– He is on his way to becoming the rich man of the town, the doctor said and opened the door a little. The rain was gushing in. – No one really knows where he gets his money from, but there are rumours of course.

He shut the door again and put his bag down. – Egon was employed in some dubious business where ladies were made available. Yes, young men too if the preferences went in that direction. They say that this establishment was often frequented by a member of the town council. I won't mention any names, but he has a big executive postion in the bank as well. Egon managed to get wind of his sexual habits, and naturally he wasn't keen to have that publicized.

– Do you mean that Egon blackmailed him?

– You can perhaps say that. In any case, all of a sudden he was back in town with a large bank loan and made investments in the hotel. They say that you can get anything you want down at Egon's as long as you bring money with you.

– I don't believe that, Margrethe said and opened the door for the doctor. – Not here in this town.

The doctor shrugged his shoulders and disappeared in

the rain. – Look after your mother, he shouted back through the wind gusts. – She is very ill.

Margrethe Thiede went for an evening walk. She walked along the beach towards town. The wind had tapered off, it had stopped raining, and the moon hung like a sad yellow lump above the dark sea. Margrethe Thiede's feet in black moccasins moved across the sand. She was thinking. She had many things to think about. The Carrot Fairy was ill and had lost her vitality. She was in bed, and when Margrethe came to offer her some food, she turned her head towards the wall. – My good little girl, she said and patted Margrethe's hand. But coldness oozed from her fingers, and she didn't mean any of the things she was saying. They were all echoes of old formulations, old phrases that contained a life of sorts until fear suddenly broke the shell. – Take good care of yourself. You have too much to do. Did your father have something to eat? It didn't mean anything. In reality she didn't care. She was exhausted and had set aside her responsibilities. It was all the same to her whether the sun rose and set at appropriate hours. She, herself, preferred to remain in the dark with Harald, of whom she never spoke again.

And then there was the father who waited helplessly for the meals to be served. He took no initiatives. He figured that things would continue as they always had, and that Margrethe would look after him just like her mother had. What should she do with them, and with herself? She would have to find a housekeeper. She couldn't just leave them like that. For the time being, she would have to stay.

By the breakwater sat a lonely figure. The moon reflected in the water below the figure and gleamed in one of his eyes when he turned around. It was Egon. He looked as if he had been sitting there waiting for her. He pointed at a big stone beside him, gesturing for her to sit down. But she remained standing in the moonlight.

He leaned back a little and spread his lumpy furry paws out so they each rested on a stone. Around him you could hear the lapping of the waves. – Hello, Margrethe, he said. – It has been a long time.

He was heavier now. The jacket was tight across his shoulders, and his facial features almost disappeared in puffed-up greyish-white flesh. He looked unhealthy. But one of his eyes winked slyly at her. – So, how is it going with you, Margrethe, he said.

– You have gotten fatter.

– And richer. Much, much richer. He patted his breast pocket. – Soon I'll own the entire hotel. And more is to come.

– Did you know Harald? she asked and kicked some pebbles with her foot.

– Harald, your younger brother? Yes, why did he do such a thing. He was a strange lad.

– Did you know him? she asked again. – Did you see much of him?

– I see, so that's what you want to know, he said, folding his hands behind his head and spreading his legs far apart in the sand. His belly bulged out over the top of his waistband.

– Yes, I would like to know, she said and looked at him.

– Knowing him is too strong a word. He never said very much. But he came down to the hotel once in a while and got himself a sodapop. There isn't much to do in terms of entertainment in a town like this. He was a pretty boy, Egon said with a roguish smile in his eye. A pretty boy and no coward at that. You couldn't suggest to him that there were things he didn't dare. He was game for anything. But he was stuck-up.

– And then what? What happened to him?

– He said that I had dirt in my head. No, not exactly like that. He said I was an Earth Climp, wherever he got that expression from. Anyway, I wasn't offended, it is better to stand firmly on the earth.

– You lured him into doing something, Margrethe shouted and clenched her fists. – You're going to pay for that.

– Now, don't get carried away. Egon got up with difficulty. He had also grown much taller. – You think too much. Thinking isn't of much use. I don't care for people who think too much or for those who are stuck-up.

– For you want to keep everything down in the dirt, don't you? That's what you want.

– Let's talk about something else, Egon said good-naturedly and began to walk along the inside of the breakwater. – Whatever happened to Lily Lund. Do you know anything about her?

Lily Lund is dead. You know that very well, Egon. You are the one who knows that Lily Lund is dead.

No, that is later, much later. Margrethe is down by the harbour, standing beside Egon who is looking even fatter and more unwieldy in his wheelchair. But right now she is at the beach, digging her shoes into the wet sand.

– Lily Lund is married and has children, Margrethe said. – I met her a couple of months ago. She has turned into a real housewife.

– Not Lily Lund, surely. She is not the type. Egon stopped and scratched his cheek.

And suddenly Margrethe saw Lily Lund and Harald reflected in each other's faces, the same fragile arrogance, the same contempt. They were surrounded by the roar of life, but they only heard it as an echo, lost as they were within themselves. She wanted to shake Harald. Wake up, real life is looking at you. But Harald had disappeared into the clouds, no, he had fallen down onto the grey cement in the courtyard where his body lay bloodied and broken, down into the coffin, down into the ground. She had not been able to protect him.

– Goodbye, Egon, Margrethe Thiede said and walked back towards the lighthouse. The moon, the sad yellow lump, sailed past her high up in the sky.

Margrethe Thiede stayed in town. This was not how she had planned it. She had figured that she could return to her studies, her friends and her new life when the practical problems and the initial grieving had been dealt with. But she couldn't make herself leave.

The mother didn't get better and now refused to get out of bed. Why get up at all, bring order to the chaos, look after things and make the vegetables grow? Perhaps she had long had her doubts about the necessity and meaningfulness of all this restless activity. She had disciplined herself, observed the rules, done what was right in order to live a life. And in a small way she had also enjoyed it when the boundaries of the structured world had embraced her, making her feel snug and safe so that she would forget about the dreadful emptiness outside. Now she had lost her clear day vision, but her troubled night sight had also disappeared. She stared into the wall, her eyes empty and distant yet with a faint look of wonder.

The father was helpless, angry and suspicious. He was a healthy man who would never doubt the foundation of his own existence. He lacked imagination to envision that life could lose its meaning. The lights had to be turned on in the lighthouse every evening. He tried to explain that he too was grieving a lot, and what had happened was incomprehensible, impossible to grasp. But everybody has their sorrows, and one's work cannot be neglected.

He sat by his wife's bed upstairs and stroked her hair. – You must get up, he said. – You have to try to get up.

She shook her head, slowly, but there was no sadness in her eyes, just a touch of surprise to think that he could suggest anything that stupid. In here it was calm and cosy. If she tried to get up, she would fall into the abyss. Surely he could understand that. No, she would probably never get up again. But she was sorry for him, sorry that he had to tend to the lighthouse. And she turned in the bed, took his hand and lifted it to her cheek, rubbed it back and forth a little. She was so sorry for him that she was in a bad way. He was the one that suffered, poor man.

After having conferred with grandmother Thiede, the father suggested that the minister be sent for. The minister would have to take care of the existential questions, the meaning of life and other such luxury problems. But the Carrot Fairy said no. She didn't have the strength to receive guests, and there was no reason to trouble the nice man.

– What are we going to do with you, Margrethe said and removed the untouched tray from the quilt. – You don't want to help yourself.

As the mother became weaker, she began to talk about her childhood. – I miss my father and mother so much, she said, lying in the bed with her legs pulled halfway under her, her head resting on her arm. Her fine, brown, wavy hair with streaks of grey was combed out and framed her face prettily. Suddenly she looked almost like a young girl.

Margrethe had never known this grandfather and grandmother. To her they had been like black dots far back in the past. – My father was so ambitious, the mother said. – He wanted much more than he could cope with, but he listened to my mother. They were very fond of each other.

They were very fond of each other. Margrethe didn't learn much more than that about the two small dots back in the past. After some time a young man began to appear in the mother's story. He was handsome and full of adventures and stories. He was an easy person to talk to. Then he disappeared again, and now it was the father who showed up, a Thiede who mattered in town and who insisted on having her. – I couldn't get out of it even though grandmother Thiede wasn't very keen on the proposal. And since then the mother had suffered from a bad conscience each and every day because she wasn't able to be adequate, loving and generous enough to this silent man who wanted to have her for a wife. – We have to be good to your father. He deserves that.

Harald also turned up in the story, not the boy, but Harald the child. – He was so fair and radiant, she said and turned her head a little on the pillow. – He was a star child. Sometimes he made me scared when I looked at him.

Nonsense, Margrethe thought. He was spoiled and lonely. Why didn't they ever demand anything from him. Why didn't they shake him out of his arrogance and try to figure out what was wrong with him. But the image of Harald popped up and settled on her thoughts: the angelic child with blond curls and the closed smile.

– Perhaps he wasn't fit for growing old, she said.

– I have grown so old, the mother said and looked up at her. Wasn't there a glint of craftiness in her empty eyes? She snuggled up in the bed like a child would. – I feel so old,

Margrethe. You'll have to take over now.

The mother had loved Harald. She didn't love Margrethe. Margrethe was going to be her successor, the one to take over her functions and be her safeguard against the abyss. For even if she herself didn't have the energy to carry on, the world would have to. That would be her job. When everything was put in order, when all had been seen to, she could disappear, let herself be swallowed up by the sea or the air, become nothing, just the way she wanted it.

I don't want to do it, Margrethe thought. She cannot make me do it.

But Margrethe Thiede stayed at the lighthouse.

10

And now Margrethe Thiede rides her bicycle back and forth between the lighthouse and the town just like in the old days. She rides into town to teach at the primary school and a couple of extra classes at the secondary school, and she rides back to cook dinner for her father who hasn't hired a housekeeper yet. The mother is lying quietly in bed just waiting to die. She has shrugged off all her responsibilities, become smaller and smaller, a little child who needs looking after and having her wants satisfied.

– See to it that we have fish today, Margrethe, she said although she didn't want to eat anything herself. – I know that I have given you too much of a burden to carry, my big girl, my good girl. But she didn't mean it. It was an empty phrase from the time when she still lived within the boundaries of the ordered world. That's the kind of thing people said then. They didn't take the liberty of making demands on others. Now Margrethe must take over from her mother. Somebody has to do it. – And have you remembered to bake bread? We usually do that on Tuesdays. And the cheese with caraway. Your father likes that very much.

Her words had no energy. Even to the mother herself, they had no validity, they were just an old echo from a former life. But Margrethe could not afford to doubt. She had to care for the whole place.

Sometimes Margrethe felt a violent burst of irritation. She resisted the pressure put on her. She had her own life to live and didn't want to submit to this moral blackmail. She refused. Then she looked at her mother who had pulled her shoulders up around her chin like a little girl, and she was filled with remorse. It won't last long now, Margrethe thought. I can hold on for a little longer.

Her books have been sent back home. They are lying open on the table in the attic room where she has moved in for the time being. But she doesn't look at them much. She found the tapes with the voices of the two little men – where was Sem's voice? Oh yes, he was dead just like her mother was dead now. She corresponds a bit with the professor. When she returns, and of course she will return, she will soon be able to study for the exam. But she cannot leave yet, not until things have fallen into place.

The days go by. The months go by.

There, on the grey country road, Margrethe Thiede is on her way. Clouds loom along the horizon in the west, and a gust of wind forces her off her bicycle. Just then she sees a figure walking along the edge of the road, equipped with walking stick and cap, tall and upright, a little awkward. He greets her, and suddenly she remembers. It is Carl Holm, of course. She knew that he had come back to town and is employed at the shipyard as an engineer. He designs ships.

Carl stops walking, hangs on to his cap and waves his walking stick about. She remembers his short pants and his strange bony face with the longish, delicate ears. He had been part of the picture but more like a shadow in the background. She has always liked Carl Holm, in fact.

He crosses the road and walks towards her not knowing what to do with the walking stick, wondering whether to give her a hug or extend his hand to her. He is somewhat overdressed in his tweed jacket with the pipe sticking out of his pocket. Dressed up like an engineer.

She laughs at him a little, and he laughs back, not quite knowing what to say. Perhaps they were childhood friends of sorts. They have something in common, but it is difficult to pinpoint what it is.

She holds on to her bicycle, pushes it back and forth. The wind tears her trenchcoat open, and a corner of the coat gets stuck in the chain. He bends down, drops the walking stick, tugs on the fabric that gets more and more entangled in the metal links, gets oil on his fingers. She puts the bicycle down and bends over next to him.

– Actually I was on my way out to visit you, he says and yanks the coat from the chain. It is torn at the edge. – But I see that you are going the other way.

– It doesn't matter, Margrethe says. – I was just going to a meeting at the school. It doesn't matter. And she turns the bicycle around and pushes it back towards the lighthouse. His walking stick is still in the way, and she suggests he switch hands.

– How are things with Lily Lund? he asks. It would have been more appropriate had he asked about herself first, Margrethe thought.

– We write to each other now and again. She is married and has two children. She seems to think that it is all very difficult to handle.

– And Egon is getting richer and richer. He wants to renovate the pub, did you know that?

She nods. She isn't done with Egon yet. He is an abcess in her gut, and one day she will cut it open.

– Do you see any other old school mates?

No, she didn't. Most of the old students from the secondary school had moved away. In fact, she saw more of the colleagues at the primary school where she had begun teaching.

The conversation flagged. What would they talk about once they had reached the lighthouse and she had made the coffee. She didn't think there was any cake left, but perhaps the father had some snaps. He had begun to drink a little in the evening. Maybe it would cheer him up to talk with Carl.

Margrethe Thiede began going out with Carl Holm, and people in town were talking about it. The two of them went to concerts and lectures. They went for long walks on windy autumn days and later in the snowclad landscape, and Carl spent time at the lighthouse engaged in sensible man-to-man talks with the father who liked him because he was so calm and interested in the workings of the lighthouse and all the practical details.

One day during the pale season of spring, he took Margrethe to the shipyard and into the room where he did his drafting. Through the window she could see the fish-packing buildings and the masts in the harbour. Further out was the big pier where the naval base was located.

– First you have to mark off the buoyancy centre, Carl said and pointed at the sheets of paper covered in thin lines. – That's the point of gravity of the volume of water that the ship displaces. The point of gravity of the ship itself must be placed in a vertical line exactly above the buoyancy centre, otherwise it would capsize, you see. After that you can begin drawing an outline of the framework of the hull. The hull is curved of course, so you have to slice it up in different planes.

– The frame, Carl said and pointed, – is the ribs of the ship. And the keel and the double bottom form the spine. Do you understand?

Margrethe Thiede stood in the middle of a streak of sun by the window with the many small panes. She didn't understand very much. But she fell in love with Carl as he sat there talking about his ships, his head bent over the table. The nape of his neck looked so fragile. His delicate ears lay flat and tidy against the scalp covered by his thin hair. She felt like holding him, feeling his rib cage and his spine.

– You always have to compromise somewhat, he said and sat up straight. A faint expression of pain was showing around his mouth. – The slender ones are the prettiest, but you have to make them wider so they won't capsize.

– Yes, Margrethe nodded and stepped a little closer. Through the closed window the sun lit up a beam of dust particles. His voice carried with it a certain tenderness when he talked about ships.

– Think of the strain a ship like that is under. One moment a giant wave pushes the bottom of the ship, and the next moment it hangs suspended, the bow and stern each sitting on a crest of a wave.

– Yes, Margrethe said.

– And the tension in the hull. Sometimes tension is produced in the welding process. It has happened that all-welded ships have broken into two.

– Yes, Margrethe said standing close to him. She lifted his hand away from the papers and placed it on her waist. It resisted a little, unaccustomed to this new location. Then it relaxed, and she felt the pulsing of the blood in his fingertips against her hip. Slowly he turned around in the chair and pulled her down. She closed her eyes, and the fairy castle with all its flickering lights and fluttering people sank into the ground and disappeared. Perhaps it didn't exist at all, perhaps it was only something she had dreamt.

The father got himself a housekeeper, a second cousin who had moved back to town after her husband had died. She looked like three balls stacked on top of each other, and below the bottom one, which was also the largest, her short legs moved swiftly about. She rearranged the furniture, told the father off when he was in her way, shooed him away and prepared interesting meals based on recipes in the weekly magazines. He preferred the old and familiar ways but got used to hers, and he even thawed out a little when she had been scolding him. Grandmother Thiede, who had made the arrangement for the housekeeper, was not amused and blamed her son for not putting his foot down and getting things back in order as they used to be. When she came for a visit at the lighthouse, she followed the woman's movements with her critical, watchful eyes. But she had grown old herself and didn't have the power she used to have. And one day she, too, had to submit to death. She didn't like it a bit even though the pastor came and sat down by her bedside and guaranteed that a better life was awaiting her after this one. She resisted tooth and nail for several days. Seizures took hold of her, her body would go rigid and then curl up, and she would bang her head against the bedframe while Margrethe and the nurse, who had been called in, tried to keep her still. But at one point when she was conscious and her son was visiting, she managed to signal to him that she had something important to say. It was about the silverware. It was not going out to the lighthouse the way things were handled there now. No, Margrethe was going to inherit it. So, after the funeral, the cabinet with grandmother Thiede's silver was moved down to the house where Margrethe and Carl were going to live.

So now grandmother Thiede is dead and gone, just like auntie and the Carrot Fairy and Harald. Many die in this town. But if you calculate the deaths in percentages, and some people do that, it amounts to a lot less here than out there in the real world that surrounds the town and stretches across the land and the sea for miles and miles, flickering restlessly and waiting to be put in order and narrated. Out there many more people die. They die more haphazardly. And meanwhile life goes on, as it must.

Life goes on and the wheels are kept in motion.

Just like the wheel that Margrethe Thiede Holm – that's her name now – is turning while trying to thread the machine properly so the needle will be able to push through the floral curtain material. She swears a little, brushes her hair away from her cheek, sighs and smiles to herself. She has never been good at sewing. Miss Iversen with her yellow hands hadn't exactly inspired enthusiasm for needlework in her students.

She has borrowed the sewing machine from the school, under the table, so to speak. She has looked at many different fabrics before choosing the brown one with the pink flowerbuds. Right now she is sewing the curtains, and in a little while she will be hanging up the curtains in her and Carl Holm's newly-built house of yellow brick with a terrace where they can drink their morning coffee at the garden table. Inside in the sitting room, grandmother Thiede's cabinet with the silver, a writing desk, a sewing table with an armchair, and the old grandfather clock from the lighthouse are set off against the standard furniture. The smell of emptiness and newness are still in the air, but soon the smoke from Carl's pipe will settle in the curtains and the food on the stove in the kitchen will be steaming. The smell of Carl and Margrethe will begin to be noticeable. The house will become a home.

Margrethe has obtained a full-time job as a supply teacher at the primary school where she teaches mostly the upper grades. But in reality she likes the youngest students the most. They are keen to learn, they hang on to her with their sticky hands, look up to her and demand final answers. In the schoolyard they play singing games, the one about the pretty maiden for whom the monk spreads out his blue cape, and then the one about the emperor who at his great white castle calls everyone to account. The children walk hand in hand in a circle or stand in a line behind each other, pulling until they tumble over on the grey pavement. Above them the autumnal sun-filled air quivers, but there is already a touch of cold in the atmosphere. She has too little to give the children, she always thinks.

She prepares herself carefully for her classes. For her, teaching is a new experience, and the school principal was kind enough to get her the supply job. Still, there is time to spare. What to do with it? She looks in the old text books, weighs the tapes with the little old men's voices in her hand. She found them on the top shelf in Harald's room. It was a strange thing with the old men. They lived in such a simple and manageable world. The sun rose, and the sun set. The axe cut Sem's hand, and the axe itself was bandaged. Their present time spread out and covered everything that just kept happening. Is it possible that things in life can keep on happening? Margrethe sighs and puts the tapes in a wicker trunk in the basement.

During the night she dreams about children, their heavy heads pulsing under their downy hair.

Carl goes to work and comes home from work. They enjoy each other, in the big, new double bed where he is a caring but unimaginative lover. Margrethe would like to coax him into pretending something that makes them different from what they are during the day, in real life. She visualizes the scenes in her head while leaning over Carl's head, letting her tongue slip into his delicate ear: a harem where the sultan chooses his nightly bride, a dark room where a stranger enters and grabs her. But Carl is so shy. He only wants to be himself, and she doesn't have the courage to tell him about her fantasies.

It is also impossible to have an argument with Carl. He turns off, becomes silent, shuts himself inside his own world.

He complains a little about the conditions at the shipyard. There are no big orders, no big challenges. Most of them just want rebuilt ships – they're cheaper. Now they have started making low rectangular sterns of aluminium that reach below the waterline. They are not pretty but practical. Carl works hard on the crew's quarters. Things have to be comfortable for the fishermen when they are out to sea.

Once in a while they discuss politics. Carl sees threats all around the horizon. Over in the south east by the large pier where the harbour has been extended, the warships lie in wait, carriers, cruisers, destroyers. Aren't those vessels becoming outdated?

They lie in wait with their conning towers and spinning observation antennae, their air defence and torpedoes. What are they waiting for? They stand out like ciphers against the sky. But are ships not built to be used?

They talk about it in the teachers' staff room as well. – If the whole situation exploded, it would harm the civilian population, says Margrethe's colleague. The civilians will always be the ones to suffer. A town with a naval base is predestined to suffer.

– But it must be possible to do something to slow down the development, Margrethe says eagerly. – I don't think we're interested in committing collective suicide. She has joined the new peace movement, signed various protests and participates in demonstrations.

Carl doesn't say anything. He reads the newspapers, slowly and thoroughly. In the evening he reads spy novels. He doesn't join her at the political meetings.

Margrethe, on the other hand, makes new friends and meets former acquaintances at the meetings. Mats Mathies is there, slightly more hoarse and a little heavier. He hasn't always familiarized himself with the agenda, but in the name of the cause he makes himself and his horse-dealer face available, along with his cart and some paintings of ships on stormy seas. He donates five of them to lotteries. That's not much to ask when you're up against the armament industry and big business and all the other threatening and faceless words. Margrethe and her colleagues from the staffroom read heavy books and report on them at the meetings. – They are beating around the bush. We have to learn more about the concrete details, she says. But it is all so complicated, and, anyway, why do things happen in spite of the fact that no decent people wish them to happen.

Once in a while a young man dressed in a leather jacket comes to the meetings. He is not very talkative, and the others keep him at a distance. They say that he works for Egon.

And in the horizon the warships lie in wait, grey and foreboding. Sometimes there is also a submarine at the quay. The captain, who is a foreigner, frequents Egon's pub. This much they know from Mats Mathies, but no one knows why it is in the harbour. That remains top secret.

The captain stands down by the quay and surveys the ships. He is a tall man whose hair falls away from the gnarled crown of his head. He has dark protruding eyes and looks concerned and self-conscious.

Margrethe lives in the yellow house with the terrace. She loves Carl, who is sitting bent over at his desk. She feels very strong and very helpless at the same time and dreams about children, their heavy heads pulsing under their downy hair.

But no children come. What is she to do now?

She studies cookbooks and prepares small delicious dinners for everyone. For her father and his housekeeper, for the colleagues at the school, for the president of the shipyard who is jovial but worried about the economy, for Lily Lund and her husband, Berre.

Because Lily Lund had come back to town.

11

Lily Lund had tried her best to be a good wife and a good mother over there in the big city. She really had, as far as Margrethe understood. But of course, she was also a little lazy by nature.

Lily Lund had once entered a pact with destiny: Let me suffer all the pain I can bear if only I may paint ten paintings that are worth something. But destiny had cheated her. Instead of pain, she had been given joy, a good husband who was brimming over with ideas that even paid off at times, and two wonderful children. What did she have to complain about?

She had had a secret dream, then, that she hadn't been brave enough to confide in anyone. She had dreamt that she had been admitted to an insane asylum, not just admitted but integrated, taken in as a resident, so to speak.

It was a fragile wish and a rather special one. She didn't talk about it since people would have considered it insane although not to the point where it could be certified.

She imagined the great calmness that would saturate her life if it held only one fixed point, a bed in a bare room. She imagined the routines, the prepared meals, the locked doors that kept the outside world away, the many new and interesting acquaintances, some of them possibly a little dangerous but never so dangerous that the white-dressed helpers couldn't take them away if they came too close. And always just acquaintances whose grief and pain didn't concern her in a deeper sense.

And she imagined how she would sit there on a chair in front of the white bed and look out the window where a naked branch would strike against the glass, and she would sway in time to its slow rhythm while all the colours that were hidden behind her eyes would be freed at last.

Her husband, whose name was Bent but was called Berre, had found her a part-time job in a canteen, and every day when riding the bus to work she brought a newspaper that she studied carefully. She marked all the food items that you shouldn't buy because they were sprayed, polluted, poisoned, carcinogenic or because they were imported from countries whose politics were objectionable. Every day after work and the return bus trip when Lily Lund stood in the supermarket among the piles of fruit and vegetables – the nubbly orange and yellow ones, the magically shiny green and red ones kept under cellophane and plastic – she tried to remember everything she had read. Was plastic and cellophane dangerous as well?

– That was good, Lily Lund's husband said and wiped his mouth with the paper napkin. – But you don't boil the potatoes long enough. They were almost raw.

– Why can't we have burgers, Lily Lund's two children said. Regitze had a good appetite, but Lars played with his food and refused to drink his milk. Should you force children to drink milk?

There were always crumbs left on the table and on the floor after all the meals. She removed them, but tomorrow they would be back again. Different crumbs in different patterns, dust on the surfaces, a refrigerator that had to be emptied of stale food and cleaned, bed linen that had to be washed. Never anything definitive, always the same.

– Come now, let's help each other, Lily Lund's husband would say on the weekends. – And afterwards I'll take the children out. Then you will have time to paint a little in the meantime.

She found a couple of canvasses in the closet in the small room, looked at them and put them back again. She had no technique. She had a nice little talent. Why should she paint. There were already so many who painted, and anyway, it was too late.

And here was Berre back with the children already for it had started to rain. He had unbuttoned his jacket and shirt and carried Regitze close to his chest. There she sat like a princess, warm and content, while Lars stood beside them and scowled. Lars was a mother's boy, and he and Berre were jealous of each other. Lily Lund knew that.

She was responsible for other people. And she poisoned them. She didn't know what she bought for them to eat, but she was certain that she gave them poisoned food. The water that they drank from the tap was also poisoned, and so was the air that they breathed on the streets where cars were whizzing by. When she opened the window to air the room, a fine dark shadow of soot fell on the window sill.

– Would you like us to move? Lily Lund's husband asked. He didn't object to them moving, but he had grown to like this apartment. He had bought a designer table and put down the linoleum tiles in the kitchen himself, although they could easily afford to have professionals do it, so now they had a very elegant kitchen-dining room. – I wouldn't mind moving to a smaller town. There is a car repair shop for sale in your home town. We could start with that. I have a few other ideas that I would like to try out in a fishing port like that. Would you like to move back?

– That won't work out, Lily Lund said. – It's expensive to move. Lars has just begun primary school. And will I be able to get a job?

– If that's want you want, that's what we will do, Lily Lund's husband said and consulted the newspapers, made phone calls and arranged things. Lily Lund didn't really know if this was what she truly wanted. But all of a sudden they had moved and now lived in a rowhouse on the outskirts of her childhood town. – Just for the time being, Berre said. – Soon we will buy a detached house.

Everything was done with care for Lily Lund. She now had what she wanted, so why couldn't she be happy?

She got a little job at the art gallery, stood behind the counter at the entrance and sold tickets and postcards, herself a painting with her mother-of-pearl skin and her reddish golden hair.

– It tastes good, her husband said when she served fish that she carried in from the narrow kitchen where there was no room for a dining table. – But there are too many bones.

– Why do we always have to have fish? said her children and ran outside to play in the windy street. They made wheels of coloured cardboard, cut triangles from the centre and bent each triangle so that the wheel would fly down the street carried by the wind.

– Come here, sit by me now that we finally have some peace, Lily Lund's husband said and pulled her down on his lap. He loved her. She was the princess who had let her hair down once from a tall window. She was his conquest, silent, mysterious, lovely. And there was no doubt in his mind that he would build her a castle.

But that's not at all how Lily Lund was. At least she didn't think so herself. But if he wanted to believe it so badly, it was his problem. She deceived them all, poisoned them with mercury from the fish, with smoke from the cooking, from scorching the meat. She poisoned them with the stench of despondency that oozed from her pores. She deceived him although he was too busy to notice it. She infected him if he touched her, and the best thing for both him and the children would be if she wasn't near them.

– Nonsense, Margrethe Thiede said when she came around in the evening to visit her friend. Lily Lund's husband had to work up the business at the garage and had a lot to do. He often went over there after dinner. In addition, he had contacted a man who did experiments with the treatment of waste water from the fishing industry and wanted to extract components that could be used as cattle feed. Oh yes, he was a busy man, and one day it would all materialize.

– Let's go for a little walk, Lily Lund said. – The children are bigger now. They can stay by themselves. I'll ask the neighbour's daughter to look in on them.

Margrethe Thiede and Lily Lund walked down to the harbour, past the cold storage plant, the smokehouses, the large siloes and out to the pier. The lighthouses twinkled in the shiny black water, a red twinkle, a green twinkle. You could see dots of light far out that slowly came closer, and hear the gentle chugging of the fishing boats.

– They're saying: Home to mother, home to mother. That's what my father told me when I was a child.

But Lily Lund wasn't interested. She walked with her head down and stared straight in front of her.

– Why are you so dissatisfied with everything? Margrethe asked. – You don't seem to have any reason to be.

– I'm not dissatisfied. I just don't think I'm suitable for anything. I was afraid after all.

– Afraid of what?

– Afraid of being myself, whatever that means. I didn't have much baggage to take along from home.

– I thought it would have been an advantage, Margrethe said. She was thinking of her own childhood home with the structures and boundaries and then of Lily Lund's apartment reeking of cabbage. The mother gone, the father on the chesterfield. Was he depressed or lazy?

– You always appeared so arrogant.

– I don't think I was, Lily Lund said and put her hands in her coat pockets. – I was scared stiff.

When they had reached the town again, Lily Lund would almost always suggest that they go for a pint of beer at Egon's pub. Margrethe didn't care much for the place. She couldn't fit Egon's pub into her own view of the world. It was like a misty island, a floating mirage outside the reality she was familiar with. Here sat the trolls with tufts of hair sticking out of their ears, pulling money out of their breast pockets. Here sat giants and dwarfs, the town's tycoons, the sly and the bold shrouded in tobacco smoke, trying each other out. They didn't fist fight like they had done in the school yard. Only on rare occasions had Egon been standing at the bar, grunting in time with the blows and knowing when to call on the bouncer. But they fought nevertheless. Who is the biggest. Who is the best. With whom should I ally myself. Who wants to support my big projects. One fellow had property that wasn't ready for housing construction but could be ready if the new road was to go west of the town and not to the right of the viaduct. Another had plans to start a factory but the water treatment plant was too expensive. And was it even necessary. The smell of trash fish shouldn't bother folks that much. Oh yes, it would bother the tourists and also the fellow who wanted to build a beach hotel and who had trouble with the nature conservation board.

Of course, ordinary people who just wanted to grab a pint and complain about this and that frequented the place as well. But generally speaking, Egon's pub had developed into a club for those who wanted to control the town. A few of the city council members were seen there too – Margrethe knew this from Mats Mathies – and they listened and made shady deals that didn't pass close inspection. These deals lay in wait until one day they reached council hall with their long tentacles. And suddenly a large project had been approved, a conservation regulation redefined, a suspension obtained, a new factory built. Perhaps it was good for something, but not in the long run. They discussed this at great length in the teachers' staff room. And when townspeople said: – Things are happening without our knowledge, they were told that the documents had been available to the public at the city hall for weeks, and why hadn't anyone thought of objecting in time.

– And there is something to that, Lily Lund's husband Berre said and looked up at Margrethe with a challenging look. He enjoyed a lively discussion.

Margrethe was standing at the end of the table in the dining-room area of the large terrace room serving soup with grandmother Thiede's soup ladle. Across from her Lily Lund, wearing a gauzy grey dress, sat between Lars and Regitze. She scolded Regitze who for once didn't like the food. Berre asked the girl to come over to him, put her on his lap and ate the pale green soup with one hand while holding on to her with the other. He could manage it all: gesticulate with his body so the girl almost slid off, pull her up again, put a spoonful of soup into her reluctant mouth and keep on talking. Margrethe liked him. He wasn't a big fellow but a real man's man who had a faint odour of rust and engine grease about him. She glanced at Carl who was entertaining himself with Lily Lund. His hair was thinning out on top. Between them sat Lars who followed his mother with his eyes. He was too much of a mother's boy but otherwise a lively child.

– No, you have your heads up in the clouds, Lily Lund's husband continued. – It's in the city council that things are happening. You just have to make sure to elect your councillors and then keep a tight rein on them. And you shouldn't get too hysterical about your conservation cases and other local issues either. If we want the town to develop in a sensible direction, not much harm will be done if a lone chimney blocks the view.

— You have no idea what you're talking about, Margrethe said. – If you give them an inch, then! Now they are going to prime the big lots west of the town for construction. And who do you think has bought them? Certainly not the front man whose name is on the contract. No, they say it's a consortium headed by the big-time contractor, the one who was almost convicted of bribery. He couldn't care less what he throws together, as long as it makes money.

– Egon knows him, Lily Lund mumbled. She didn't say much otherwise.

– Yes, there you go, Margrethe shouted. – He will get his permits, no problem.

Carl was rocking back and forth in his chair. City politics didn't interest him in particular even if the minor decisions reflected the major ones. The big decisions were made neither at city hall nor at Egon's pub. He tried to explain that. The big decisions were made by the invisible ones, those who sent their messengers through the silent corridors to meeting rooms and conferences where they carried out their orders. The big decisions had been agreed upon in advance, and Berre and Margrethe and her friends who believed they could make a difference played blind man's buff and were fooling themselves. He attempted to exlain all that but got lost in the words, couldn't articulate what he meant. Meanwhile Margrethe began impatiently to collect the dirty dishes with help from Regitze who had left the table.

– Egon is just a little mafia boss, he concluded dispirited.

– Yes, Egon keeps his gorillas the old-fashioned way, Berre said. – In foreign countries the mafia has begun sending out banking transfer forms. Modern times!

– Who knows if any of those bills and invoices we get so many of in the mail are from the mafia, Margrethe laughed and changed the topic. Sometimes Carl said the strangest things, she thought.

Berre began talking about his new project. Now he wanted to invest money in a little company that experimented with the waste water from the fisheries. You could strain it and skim off the fat. But this engineer fellow that he had begun working with had developed a new system. While the waste water was still red with blood, he added some of the substances that were normally found in the food chain with the result that the proteins in the water turned into flaky particles. Afterwards you'd have to infuse bubbles into the water that would rise to the top and carry the particles along so all the proteins could be scraped off. And now he had found a method to coagulate the proteins. Finally the whole thing had to be boiled and centrifuged and sold as dry cattle feed that eventually would return to the food chain.

Margrethe thought it sounded both like a fairytale and a complicated process, but Carl nodded and understood it all.

And by the way, Berre had a used car, a good one that he thought they should have a look at. Wasn't it about time they acquired a car?

That's how people make smalltalk, smalltalk with many small words that form patterns in the spaces between the big words, patterns that close the spaces.

Regitze fell asleep on the chesterfield with a blanket as cover. Lars was reading a magazine and looked at his mother now and again.

Lily Lund said nothing. She would have preferred to sit in Egon's pub, on a misty island that floated above or below the world.

12

Egon had a finger in everything and money in most things. Light sparkled in the bottles on the long counter in the pub, and lamps threw a soft light above the tables in the small separate booths where people could talk in privacy if they so desired. But patrons could also sit at tables in the open floor space and absorb the goings-on around them.

On the other side of the pub was the discotheque with its glass surfaces, shimmering neon tubes and coloured lights that kept changing. One minute poisoned-green tongues of fire would be licking the girls' legs, the next minute pomegranate-red flames would make their cheeks glow. Things were lively in here, bodies were sweating and grunting, legs were kicking. – Exercise is good for young people, Egon said while pouring draught beer from the keg. He himself had begun to use a cane due to his bad knees, although it only made him look more impressive.

– Egon is one of our town's great sons, the city politician said and introduced him to an official from the navy. – And he can keep a secret.

Behind the discotheque was a room with low armchairs placed in a semicircle around a stage. Here Egon's ladies performed, long-legged Lola and the dark-haired, buxom Rosita. They wriggled in circles around each other, slowly taking off their clothes, first gloves and scarf then their dresses and finally their brassieres and panties that were thrown high up in the air and perhaps landed in the lap of one of the men in the first row. Afterwards they would turn around, sway their hips and point their asses towards the audience, then finally move towards the back curtain and disappear.

Egon also gave the local beauties a chance. They would giggle shyly and be all thumbs when unbuttoning their blouses. A lot of people liked to watch that. And discretion was used when admitting patrons to the backroom.

But at the other end of the hotel complex, for it wasn't just a hotel any more but also a complex, was the nice restaurant with white table cloths, candles on the tables and a lounge pianist who played popular classical music in a lighter vein. Guests could order the three-course menu of the day or, if they could afford it, à la carte dishes with foreign names. Oh yes, the whole place was at Egon's feet even if his legs were sore and swollen.

– Do we have to go in there again? Margrethe asked when she and Lily Lund stood at the entrance to the pub. Lily Lund shivered a little and pushed the door open. Through the tobacco smoke they could see Egon standing at the counter. He winked at them and nodded towards an empty booth. One of his waitresses dressed in a black skirt and white shirt-front took their order.

– Last night I dreamt I was in a madhouse, Lily Lund said. Everything was painted dark green, the people too. There were no other colours but dark green. It made everything seem more manageable. I have the same feeling when I'm in here.

Margrethe felt uncomfortable. She thought of Lars and Regitze whom Lily Lund loved. Of course she did. You loved your children, but did Lily Lund love her husband as well?

131

– He is sweet, Lily Lund said and smiled. – He is so busy taking care of everything, including me. And when he senses that something is wrong, he thinks that he can comfort me with his body.

– And can he?

– Sometimes, Lily Lund said. – But in reality he is just a stranger.

– Why are you so fascinated by Egon? Margrethe asked. – Egon is a sociopath.

– And what does that mean? – You know so many words, Lily Lund said.

– He has no conscience.

– No, that's true, Lily Lund nodded. – He has no conscience.

– He was probably born that way, Margrethe continued. – But the fact that no one looked after him doesn't help. He had a bad childhood.

– Did he? Lily Lund asked and sipped her beer. – It probably doesn't matter very much, anyway. Egon doesn't care. He doesn't believe in anything but himself. Sometimes I wish that I could be just like Egon. He has that special talent. He is disgusting, but he is also wonderful, can't you see that?

And there he came, the wonderful Egon, moving between the tables taking long and slow strides. He whispered something to a young man in a leather jacket. But wasn't he the one from the peace movement? He, Egon, sat down for a moment by a table, snapped his fingers and someone put a tray with a beer in front of him. Then he got up again, moved slowly a few steps ahead and stood like a dark shadow behind Lily Lund. His furry white hand cradled her neck. She leaned back a little, shuddered slightly from his touch. Beauty and the beast. Was Egon a beast?

He sat down heavily next to Margrethe, reached across the table, took hold of Lily Lund's hand and examined her fingers one by one. – You are so thin, Lily, he said in his rough voice.

She smiled at him. One of his eyes looked straight at her, the other stared in the direction of Margrethe, contemptuously, she thought.

– How is your husband doing? he continued. – Can he manage everything with the repair shop? If he is pressed for money, he should come by and talk to me.

Lily Lund nodded. She didn't say anything; neither did she withdraw her hand.

– I'll phone Carl, Margrethe said and made a gesture to Egon that she wanted to get up. – He can have a glass of beer and then walk us home.

But they didn't pay any attention to her as she walked over to the passageway where the telephones were. She might as well have been invisible.

Carl arrived shortly after and pushed himself through the crowd to their table. In one of the booths the foreign captain with the protruding eyes was talking to the man in the leather jacket – whatever they had to talk about was anyone's guess.

– But look who is here, Egon shouted. He let go of Lily Lund's hand and waved with his hand through the tobacco smoke. – Come and sit down with the ladies, Carl, I have to go. And he continued his round in and out of the booths and around the tables, a handshake here, a comment there: – That property. No, hell, it is supposed to be a parking lot. We have enough nature here in this town. – Rosita? That's her business, but something can probably be arranged after the performance. A new girl is arriving next week. – A sludge pump? Just phone the contractor and pass on greetings from me. Then you'll get a better deal.

Wasn't he like a sludge pump himself, that Egon. A bottom feeder. He sucked up the rotten dregs from his surroundings, thrived on them, let them seep into the larger organism that in turn transformed them into power. He didn't suffer from frustrated ambitions or a tortured life of the soul. That's what Margrethe was thinking. And how could Lily Lund look at him as if he were an enchanted prince.

Carl was watching Lily Lund, who sat with her chin resting on her hands and was looking straight at Egon's back. Margrethe didn't understand Egon. And she didn't understand Lily Lund. Who can understand Lily Lund?

It is late afternoon, and Margrethe Thiede and Lily Lund and the children go for a walk along the beach. The sun is glaring. When a cloud covers the sun, the gulls appear suddenly black.

Lily Lund climbs out on a jetty and sits down on a rock. – Watch out, Lars says. He climbs down behind her and wants to hold on to her. The waves throw light and shadow across her face down there and dissolve her features. Autumn has begun ever so slowly. There are small pockets of coldness in the air, but the sea smells of sun-drenched seaweed.

– Don't do that, Margrethe shouted. She stood on the sandy strip further in, holding Regitze by the hand. – Don't look at your reflection in the water.

– Why not? Lily Lund asks and turns her head in the direction of the beach. Then she gets up, stands on the rock for a moment, sways a little until she finds her balance and begins to walk back. Lars follows her, ready to grab her should she trip. – Why can't I look at my reflection?

– I don't know, Margrethe says. – Oh yes, now I

remember. It was something Jaffe had told her. If you look at your own reflection in the water, your soul will fly away.

– I've done that so often, Lily Lund says. – I probably don't have a soul any more. Do you remember your mother used to say that the soul was a butterfly.

On their way home they meet Mats Mathies with his cart. The sun is low on the horizon. A flight of cormorants fly across the sky.

– Stupid birds, Mats Mathies tells the children who have lined up by the cart to admire its treasures. Regitze gets hold of a necklace that she refuses to let go of.

– Yes, stupid birds, Mats Mathies continues. – If you whistle after them, they'll turn around in flight. Abroad they use them for fishing. They place a ring around their neck, so when they catch a fish from the water, they cannot swallow it and are forced to surrender it, thank you very much. Yes, it's a matter of knowing the tricks.

– Are you selling anything? Margrethe asks. She would like to buy the necklace for Regitze, but wants to get something for Lars too. He doesn't seek much attention for himself.

– The season is almost over by now, Mats Mathies says and holds a small picture up: a full moon floats above a ship that leans heavily to one side between huge greyish-black waves. He passes it on to Lars, takes off his broad-brimmed hat and wipes his forehead. The area around his chin is no longer clearly defined, but the stubble is still black, and his small eyes have a green and cunning sparkle in them. – This one here I have sold twenty copies of. Vacationers like to be reminded that the sea is not altogether idyllic. And how are things going with your painting, Lily?

– Not so well, I guess. I'm too lazy, she says. Now I spend my time at the museum four afternoons a week

135

selling postcards.

– In the days when I was young and traveled abroad, Mats Mathies continues, running his fingers through his long hair, I visited a lot of art galleries. I remember that I was fascinated with a painting of this artist who shoots at the canvas with a pistol. I was looking at the picture that was nicely hung up with its five bullet holes, thinking: That man must be a desparate man. But then, after I had visited eight museums that all had one of his pictures with bullet holes on display, I realized that he must keep normal working hours after all. He gets up in the morning and simply loads his pistol. Then he shoots and afterwards he tells his wife that she can bring out the lunch. Yes, it's a matter of knowing the tricks.

– I don't know them yet, Lily Lund smiles, and withdraws from the conversation. Meanwhile Margrethe buys the necklace and the twenty-first copy of the picture of the ship in the stormy night sea.

One day Lily Lund was gone. One day, or rather one night. Berre phoned Carl and Margrethe to ask if she might be at their place. He had come home late from the garage, and she had already been asleep. But now, this morning when he woke up, she was gone, the quilt was pushed back and the bed cold. All her clothes were still on the chair, so she must have left wearing her nightdress and a coat. Surely she would return shortly; he just wanted to hear if they had seen her.

Margrethe went down to see him a little later in the morning when she had a couple of free periods. The children sat at the dining table with a carton of oatmeal between them.

– Daddy has completely forgotten about school, Regitze said and smiled. – You'll have to go anyway, Margrethe said and sent them off with a note explaining the delay.

Lily Lund's husband paced the floor and was ashamed that other people were involved in his domestic problems. – We never argue, he kept on repeating. We never argue, but then she doesn't ever say much.

– I'll phone Egon.

– Egon? He spun around and gave Margrethe a hostile look. What did Egon have to do with his wife?

– But you know that, she said in a reassuring voice. – She often talks with him. We were old school friends.

No one answered at Egon's pub. The phone kept on ringing in the empty room. At the hotel, however, Margrethe got hold of a sleepy hotel clerk. Yes, the owner was in, but he was sleeping and had left a message not to be disturbed.

– Wake him up anyway, Margrethe said.

But Egon knew nothing. He was out of sorts and rather curt. She could hear women's voices in the background. – Shut up. Go to Lola's room, she heard Egon shouting. He returned to the telephone. – Girls from hell, he said. They can put a man to work for the whole night, damn it. They have been here since we closed up. Lily? No, she wasn't at the pub last night. She has probably just gone for a walk. Phone again if there's anything I can do.

In the afternoon after she had walked up and down the residential streets, making inquiries in the shops and at the train station, and had gone out to the pier, Margrethe persuaded Lily Lund's husband to call the police. He wasn't very keen on the idea. – She'll be back, he repeated. – She'll be back in a few minutes.

Margrethe liked him a lot. But it was strange how completely blind he was to the possibility that his wife might have had some problems. He didn't want to admit that something was wrong with her. Maybe it was because he was a man's man.

– Could she have travelled somewhere? The detective constable asked. – Does she have acquaintances in other places? Did she have a relationship with another man? Was she depressed? Had she attempted suicide at any time in the past? Are there any signs of foul play?

– No, Lily Lund's husband shouted. – No, no, no. – She has gone for a walk. She'll be back in a few minutes.

But Lily Lund didn't come back. A description of the missing person was issued, the spruce plantation was searched, the harbour was dragged and the naval base was contacted for information. There were no tracks. Lily Lund was gone.

Margrethe brought the children to her own house. Carl got up from his writing desk and told them bedtime stories. Regitze was a pretty little girl, mild-mannered and self-absorbed. She would crawl up on his lap and cuddle up to him. Later on, after Lily Lund's husband had sold the garage, established himself in another town and found a new woman who was friendly and well-balanced, the girl went back to stay with her father. She preferred living with him and had no problems adjusting.

Lars stayed with Margrethe and Carl. He was a moody and contrary boy, afraid of becoming too attached to anyone. He became the wound in her heart.

13

And time passed. The days flew by just like Lars' and Regitze's cardboard wheels that used to whirl along down the streets forced by the wind. Nothing special happens. All the ordinary things happen.

Glimpses. Pictures that appear and disappear. Margrethe's father, who has retired from the lighthouse and has moved into a little house on the outskirts of town, stands by the staircase and clings to the banister. Then he falls down and is dead, very quietly and without any fuss.

The housekeeper has also died, by the way. She had been injected with some stuff into her bloodstream once when she had x-rays taken. It wouldn't go away again and attached itself to her liver and emitted rays that made cells divide the wrong way. It was a bad and prolonged death. But since she was from out of town, no one grieved much for her.

And there is Egon with his wife at an opening ceremony at the town hall. Oh yes, he has married. Something he thought up at a very convenient time. Now he is strapped into a dark suit, and she is beautifully dressed in a white skirt and white jacket with a big golden brooch pinned on her lapel. She is fingering her necklace. She is just for show, but is also expected to produce heirs. That's the reason he has acquired her.

Carl goes for walks at the harbour dressed in his brown tweed suit. Carl settles at his desk and works on the design of a new fishing boat, a new type that is prettier and more slender. Who has the courage to buy one like that? In the school yard the children sing about the monk who spreads out his blue cape during the long summer days, and about the castle that is white as chalk and black as coal.

And the captain of the submarine stands on the pier and stares out past the ships with his strange protruding eyes.

Lars was the wound in Margrethe's heart. She had never had trouble establishing contact with other people, so why couldn't she reach him? He didn't like school much and seldom played with other children. The books that she had found and given to him he put down again. He would sit in a corner of the sitting room with his shoulders hunched, unapproachable, his body all rigid. But when somebody mentioned his mother's name, he would get up and walk out and close the door behind him.

She herself thought that she understood his problems well. But understanding wasn't enough. She didn't know what to do with him and couldn't get him out of his silent shell. She tried to appeal to his reason. She would lose her self-control, fly off the handle and then cry. She attempted to cuddle him and hide his face and defiant eyes in the folds of her blouse. He remained rigid, put up with her embrace but showed no reaction. She couldn't coax him into smiling or provoke him into a fit of rage. He disappeared in front of her eyes, shrank, evaporated. He existed, but not for her.

– Come out, she shouted at his closed door. – Come out and talk to me a little.

But Lars didn't hear her. He sat by himself and played his heavy, thumping rock music that she didn't care for but wanted to understand because he liked it.

– Can't you talk to him, Carl. It's important that he talks about Lily. His grieving is not natural.

– You're much better at these things, Carl said and rubbed his hand up and down the sleeve of his tweed jacket. – I think we should leave him in peace, and eventually he'll come around.

That's how Carl was. He put off problems. He was passive and avoided taking risks. Margrethe thought that he should borrow money and invest it in the shipbuilding yard and become a co-owner. Carl puffed at his pipe and didn't think there was any rush. For the time being he was quite comfortable being an employee. He wanted to design ships and stay out of the administration.

– You're a coward, Margrethe shouted. – You would have a much greater say over your own work. Look at Lily's husband. He takes risks.

And so he did. Berre's new business, extracting cattle feed from waste water, already had a sister company that oversaw the sales destined for a bigger marketplace. It also handled licence agreements with foreign countries that would be able to produce and sell his system for a certain percentage of the profits. Life around him was still noisy and exuded energy.

– Would you rather stay with your father? she asked Lars. He shook his head. He preferred staying with Carl and Margrethe.

– Yes, but what are we going to do with you, Lars? she said. – You have buried yourself like a mole.

He turned around, went to his room and turned the music up.

As time went on, he thawed out a little. He grew up to be a handsome, blond boy, somewhat thick-set, but supple like his father. When he turned fourteen, his hair got curlier and the girls began to chase him. He didn't pay attention to them. But he was able to smile once in a while. Sometimes he would regret it and quickly change to his usual gloomy expression. But he had demonstrated that he was capable of smiling, which couldn't be explained away. He treated Margrethe with a certain air of friendly protectiveness although he didn't hide the fact that he found her caring tiresome. He kept more to Carl and went for long walks with him in the evening. The two of them evidently had something in common.

One day he approaches Margrethe who is busy with a pile of exercise books in front of her. She has been doing some pushing and fibbing lately and has used all her connections to have Lars declared fit for admittance to the upper secondary school.

– I'm going to quit school, he says. – I want to fish.

– You can't do that, Margrethe shouts. She jumps out of her chair and knocks over the books, which tumble down onto the rust-brown carpet. – You are going to get an education. You owe us that much.

– I don't owe anyone anything, Lars says. – I've signed on, on Kathrine Laura.

It is Carl who has designed Kathrine Laura, and he has made a good job of it. – She's nicely curved, says the skipper, who has signed Lars on as his youngest crew member. – She dances on the water.

Kathrine Laura dances on the waves that look like corrugated silver in the patches where the sun breaks through. She has class. She is a sugar princess, slender, a little temperamental, sweet. The skipper is also special. He could have rebuilt an older ship, gotten a stern trawler with a new shelter deck and conveyer belts to empty the trawl directly into the hold. But he wanted Kathrine Laura. And he laughed the first time she pitched and dipped her bow into the water.

– Yes, you've made a good job of her, the skipper says and slaps Carl on the back. – I'm almost as much in love with her as I am with my own wife. There is nothing more beautiful than standing in Kathrine Laura's pilot house and watching the sunset. I always feel I should take my cap off.

– Perhaps he could try it out during the vacation. It won't hurt him, Carl said hesitantly.

– For the summer, then. Afterwards you can decide what you want to do, Margrethe said.

And so Lars signed on, on Kathrine Laura.

Down at the harbour a submarine has appeared again. It comes from abroad where it has been rebuilt at a civil, state-owned shipyard. After the trial runs it will be delivered to a military dictatorship on the other side of the globe. Over there they always need submarines.

The captain with the sad, protruding eyes pats the hull of the sub. He is uncertain of whether it should be considered a civilian ship or a warship. He does his duty. He does what people at the foreign shipyard tell him to do and what others above those in the shipyard command them to do. They say in town that it isn't just submarines that he tests.

One late summer day shortly before noon, Kathrine Laura disappears in clear weather. Only a lifebuoy, an old wooden-soled boot and a few pieces of wreckage were found floating among the oil slicks.

She had been lobster fishing with two other fishing

boats, Notos and Maja. The skipper on Notos, an older, sober-minded man, was in the pilot house, and when he looked astern he could see Kathrine Laura pitching in the waves. He and his first mate had often talked about the aura of luck that seemed to surround that boat. Her trawl was always full, he later said at the inquiry.

Anyway, he was in the pilot house and leaned over to check the radar, and when he looked out the window again, Kathrine Laura was gone.

After that he scanned the horizon, for he couldn't understand that she would have taken off without reporting it. And sure enough, there she was, astern of the port beam. She was heeling over sharply, and the pilot house was dipping into the sea. When he called her, there was no answer. However, he did make contact with Maja all the while watching through the window of the pilot house how the sail went down. He shouted for his first mate who was down in the cabin, cut away his gear and made for Kathrine Laura.

He couldn't understand any of it. A fishing cutter that had sprung a leak would remain afloat, for a while anyway. But a minute later, the bottom of Kathrine Laura had disappeared in the sea. It was almost as if she had been dragged down, he said at the inquiry.

Many participated in the search rescue that day. A surfaced submarine and its escort ship were among them. After dark, when everyone returned to the harbour and had given up any hope of finding the drowned crew members, for surely they must have died, the skipper on Notos noticed that there were fresh scratches on the submarine's conning tower as if scraped by wires.

On the pier stood Carl and Margrethe along with all the others who had come to hear if there was any news. The lights swayed in the wind, faces were briefly illuminated and then disappeared into the shadows. The skipper's wife is there too. She has tied a large scarf over her thick hair and is holding her coat closed around her belly. In there, in the darkness, lies a new child. Out there, in the darkness, is her husband. – Why are you coming back already. Why don't you continue till you find them? she yells.

– Yes, why not? Margrethe repeats. She can only repeat things. There are no more words left in her.

– In seventy-five fathoms of water, mumbles Niels Buus who is standing beside them, his hands buried deep in his pea jacket. He has such an energetic chin, is a big shot at the auction office and is on his way up in the town council. Niels Buus is a fighter and lacks the talent for letting injustice go unchecked. Always good for a strong opinion and always ready to defend it. Why does Margrethe suddenly think of Niels Buus' chin while standing there on the pier.

– They need a special diving team, he says and looks straight ahead.

The police are also there. The crew from the submarine is questioned, but as usual no one knows anything.

At home Margrethe smokes one cigarette after another. She who has never smoked before. She cannot sleep, she cannot sit still, she cannot stay in one place for long. She is full of heavy grey lumps of grief that won't dissolve into tears. – It's my fault, she says. – Why did I give him permission. She imagines seeing Lily Lund, pale, her hair like flames around her face. I tried, Lily. I tried to dissuade him. But Lily Lund looks at her silently and reproachfully.

– Why were you so passive. Why didn't you support me? she screams at Carl's back. He is sitting with the plans for Kathrine Laura. His hands are shaking while he leafs

145

through them. Did he place the point of gravity in the wrong place. Did he design Kathrine Laura to be too slender. Is it all his fault.

– Stop it, Margrethe shouts and shakes him by the arm. – Stop tormenting yourself. It was the submarine, you know that. It ran into her trawl and pulled her down because the wires wouldn't snap. It was the submarine. It'll be clarified at the inquiry.

14

The inquiry is a draw. It becomes necessary to replace the courtroom at the police station with a larger hall at the town hall, and it is already packed. Carl and Margrethe arrive late. He has lost weight during the past week. His tweed jacket hangs loosely from his shoulders.

They work their way up the aisle in the middle of the hall. Carl has his head lowered. Margrethe nods to friends and acquaintances. There are faces red-eyed with weeping, empty faces, angry faces. Voices are humming, falling and then rising again. There is so much to talk about, so much no one understands. Why do they use the designated areas that from time immemorial have been used for lobster fishing as a site for trial-runs. Why don't they do the runs in locations where there is very little fishing. And why are the designated areas not known to anyone.

'No one' and 'anyone' mean us. We know who we are, but who are 'they'? 'They' are unpredictable and ambiguous. They make the decisions, for someone must have made them. But they become invisible as soon as accountability is called for. They disappear, evaporate until they condense and form a dark cloud somewhere else on the horizon where they let new decisions rain down on our heads. Who they really are remains unknown. Do they simply use the fishing boats as exercise targets in order to find out how close they can go undetected? There ought to be a local skipper from one of the fishing boats on board. Guessing from their manoeuvres, they haven't the faintest idea of what's going on when a cutter has a trawl line in the water. And why aren't we informed about when the trial-runs take place. They – and this would have to be another unknown party – could at least ensure that we were notified about their positions. The Navy's Operational Command knew all about it in advance, of course.

The air is thick with questions. So many questions. And why are we so powerless.

The skipper's widow is sitting there. She looks straight ahead and doesn't see any of the people that crowd around her to express their condolences. Condolences? What kind of expression is that. It doesn't mean anything, but perhaps it protects against all those things that cannot be said. She nods a 'thank-you' but is beyond consolation. She will have to distance herself from her grief and think about compensation now. She is carrying a child in her belly and has other children to provide for as well.

Extra chairs are set out. Carl and Margrethe find a couple of seats on the left side of the aisle. Officials from the Ministry, insurance representatives and other experts are sitting in the front rows. Each one is an individual in his own right, but in the present situation they all look alike.

Margrethe nods to the president of the Fishery Association. At least she knows one person here.

The sun is shining obliquely through the upper windows high up under the ceiling. She closes her eyes. Where is Lars now? Will he ever be washed ashore?

– They won't deal with the question of blame today, Niels Buus says and sits down behind her. She turns around to greet him. This is what Lars could possibly look like in twenty years. Cleft chin and bushy eyebrows above dark blue eyes. Niels Buus always thrust his chin out, but his mouth is curvy and soft. – Yes, it's hard, he says and nods

148

to Carl while patting Margrethe on her hand. He is so warm. Margrethe can feel how the palms of his hands are burning. But Lars is cold. Touched by death with its icicle hand.

Carl hooks his arm under hers, and she turns around again. Carl also needs to be comforted.

In a row further ahead she eyes Egon's broad back. Egon knows the submarine captain who frequents his pub whenever he is in port.

– Who are the four men sitting up there, Margrethe whispers over her shoulder. – They look like foreigners.

– That's what they are, Niels Buus answers. – I think it is the representative from the shipyard and his two solicitors. And they probably have an interpreter with them.

The interrogations begin. The skipper from Notos is the first to sit in the witness box. He had noticed the escort ship when he started the engine and swung around to the position where he had last seen Kathrine Laura. But he knew nothing about the submarine. It seems impossible to obtain information about certain things.

– It's outrageous, Niels Buus shouts.

– Silence in the court room, the judge says and bangs his hand on the table.

Then it is the other skipper's turn, the one from Maja. He is very emotional, blows his nose and begins his account by saying that he cannot stop thinking that it could just as well have been him and his crew that were now on the bottom of the sea. But slowly he regains his composure: – We were three fishing boats in the same area and were in contact with each other both visually and by radar. That's necessary when we fish so close together.

But what about the submarine. Didn't it have contact

with anybody? Wasn't the escort ship supposed to warn it about fishing boats in the waters so it could get around them and possibly come to the surface. Are there no rules for that?

The captain of the submarine doesn't know anything about rules. That's what he says when it's his turn to answer questions at the witness box. The interpreter is by his side and answers a little hesitantly in the beginning. The judge has informed him that he can refuse to explain anything that would result in charges against himself.

But the captain wants to testify for all the world to see. One of the solicitors waves the interpreter over and approaches the Bench. He wants to point out that questions might arise that will demand further discussion behind closed doors for reasons of security or business protection. It is all legal jargon.

The captain is actually a good speaker, which becomes quite clear when the interpreter starts translating. He acts civilized and modest, looks straight ahead with his sad bulging eyes, never losing his composure. From his days at the sea training school he knows about bottom trawl and pelagic trawl. No, he is not ignorant of the methods used for lobster fishing these days. Neither has he had any accidents before during all those years that he has done trial-runs on submarines to test their capacity.

The area was assigned to him by his own navy in agreement with the Danish Naval Command. Whether the fishermen know anything about the runs, when and where they take place, is not his responsibility, he says and opens his arms regretfully.

Normally a submerged submarine has no contact with the surface, he explains. The submarine telephone is used as little as possible because it interferes with the sonar and navigational systems. He doesn't believe the otter doors from a trawler can be heard, unless the submarine doesn't move at all and the sonar conditions are good.

He is so articulate. Watching him, you almost begin to feel pity for him as he tries to explain himself.

He produces the log and the engine book. He has also brought the records of manoeuvres. But the transcript of the sonar is kept in a box at the shipyard back home. It cannot be surrendered before the security people and the client have assessed it. The representative from the shipyard can confirm that.

Now the captain is being asked to describe what actually went on that morning when Kathrine Laura disappeared, as far as he knew.

He speaks at great length about the first trials of the day, about speed, course and trimming, all in technical terms.

Margrethe isn't listening any longer. Images pop up in her mind. The submarine that twists and turns down there in the deep sea while altering its course and changing its speed. And, up above, Lars is standing in the sun on the deck of Kathrine Laura.

– I was standing next to the sonar engineer when I heard a noise, the interpreter translates. – There was nothing unusual on the sonar screen, no signs of fluctuation that could be read as a ship being in the vicinity.

– And then? the judge asks.

– I asked the first engineer. He couldn't identify the noise either. But as chance would have it, he had just looked at he trim controls and noticed a minor fluctuation. We thought that it was perhaps a broken side light. But I ordered both engines to be cut out.

Behind Margrethe's eyes Kathrine Laura begins to heel over. Now the pilot house is dipping into the water. Where is Lars? Has he already been swept overboard.

– And then? the judge asks.

– It must be pointed out that the ship stopped while it was accelerating. The speed at the time was increased from four to nine knots.

Carl gives a sudden start. Niels Buus nods pensively. Margrethe stares into space. Now the sail is dipping. Now the boat heels over completely, and the bottom disappears in the waves.

– We took a sounding and kept our distance from the ships that the escort ship had on its radar. Then we began to surface. When we had reached the level where we could use the periscope, I scanned the horizon and discovered that a whip aerial on the tower was broken. We concluded that this must have been the cause of the noise.

– Were there other signs of damage on the submarine? the judge asks.

The captain hesitates and says something in a low voice. The interpreter translates: – We received a radio report and took part in the rescue search for the disappeared fishing boat. At one point I leaned over the tower and saw that paint had been scraped off.

And the captain leaves the witness box. He appears to be a man of culture and duty. He only does what he has been told to do. Margrethe straightens up and follows him with her eyes when he sits down on his seat in the sun. Now Lars is lying deep down in the darkness.

The first officer on the escort ship, a small fiery man, abdicates all responsibility. It is the captain of the submarine who is in charge. As one can imagine, it would be impossible to report all surface ships to the submarine. In that case you would be on the phone continuously.

– What will happen now? Margrethe asked as they worked their way towards the exit. – Will they lay charges?

– For involuntary manslaughter, Niels Buus said and let her and Carl pass in front of him. – I don't think so. The question is whether the shipyard will surrender the sonar transcript and acknowledge their responsibility.

At the door Margrethe brushed against a jacket sleeve. She shuddered slightly when she saw that the jacket belonged to Egon, who smiled contemptuously at her with his right eye.

The next day there were demonstrations at the harbour. A small bus stopped at the pier where the submarine was. A group of young people jumped out and began to spraypaint slogans on the hull: OUR COLLABORATION WITH COUNTRIES THAT SELL WEAPONS TO MILITARY JUNTAS COSTS THREE ... They didn't get any further before the police arrived, arrested them and drove them off to the police station where they were charged with vandalism.

The captain of the submarine was not charged. The judge followed the reasoning of the shipyard, which claimed that he couldn't be legally responsible for the accident. And no one thought of charging the shipyard and its employers or the Naval Command that hadn't given warning of the trial-runs. The case would be settled amicably and decently, and the families of the deceased would of course be compensated for their losses. The sonar transcripts were also surrendered although the shipyard made a lot of fuss over it, claiming it to be an exception, an act of kindness, and that it really should have been treated as classified material. No one mentioned whether it could be used as evidence.

Margrethe Thiede knew the demonstrators. They had been at her peace group, and she had often met them at various meetings. She hadn't been present at the demonstration. She sat at home in the chesterfield with her arm around Carl rocking him back and forth. – I was the one who said it to Lars, he kept on mumbling. – I was the one who talked to Lars about it.

Niels Buus hadn't been there either. He had gone to meetings held by the Fishery Association and the Fishermen's Union and helped out with tightening up the resolutions that were going to be sent to the Ministry:

We demand that trial-runs be moved to locations where there is no fishing. During the transition period we insist that precise information regarding the designated areas and times of the trial-runs be given. The captain of the submarine must be briefed on the local methods of fishing and know how trawling of various types of fish is done.

– It's so obvious, Niels Buus said. – Why did three men have to die before we thought of this.

Margrethe was on her way home from school and had met him on the street. – My demonstrators want to have the submarines removed altogether, she said.

– Don't be naïve, now, Niels Buus said and squeezed her shoulder lightly. – But it is a filthy business. Perhaps there is something to the rumour that they use the fishing boats as practice targets when trying out their instruments. They come much too close to the boats.

The newspapers wrote that it was a complicated affair, with political and nationalistic undertones. The foreign submarine was civilian because it had been rebuilt at a civilian shipyard, even if it was state-owned, and only later would it be sold to the military junta, where it hadn't been received yet. The reader was made to understand that during the testing it didn't fall under the Navy's jurisdiction and therefore couldn't be ordered to obey the Navy's rules for trial-runs. The Minister of Defence would have to disclaim any responsibility for the incident and point out that the relevant authority was the Minister of Finance.

That's how the case was perceived outside the country. But at home there were problems as well that caused Niels Buus to doubt whether the resolutions had been sent off to the right Ministry. Seeing that the accident had taken place in international waters, the case wasn't the responsibility of the Ministry of Fisheries but rather that of the Ministry of Transportation where the department dealing with ocean traffic recommended that an escort ship immediately notify its submarine when other crafts are in the vicinity. However, since there were no special rules concerning submerged submarines, no demands could be made in this case. One could only emphasize the need for a general practice for domestic crafts.

– It's all gibberish, Margrethe said. – Why did they stress that the sonar transcript was classified material? And is there no law that prohibits arms sales to areas with political unrest?

She thought a lot about things during this period, thought and thought, so as not to see the image of Lars all the time, Lars, white and cold, far down under the waves among shoals of fish.

But what do the dead care about politics and legal quibbling.

There was no body to bury so there was no actual funeral. Instead, a memorial event was arranged with flags and representation from the town's associations. Many came, Regitze among them, a big pretty girl who cried inconsolably in Margrethe's arms. And along came Lily Lund's husband who was now another woman's husband, although he was his own man more than anything. He was grieving, too, but of course he hadn't seen much of Lars the last few years.

– I've never been able to understand that boy, he said. – He didn't like me. He clung to his mother, but then she began acting strangely and pushed him away.

– He resembled you in many ways, Margrethe said. – If he had been allowed to live, the two of you would probably have discovered that you have much in common.

EVERYTHING HAPPENS

15

What happens when you fall in love? How does the feeling take hold of you. Like a sneeze, some people say. Others claim that it comes to you like a thief in the night. The thief sneaks his way in, yet the sneeze explodes with a peculiar suddenness. It's not easy to make out. The two theories have apparently little to do with each other. Perhaps they are both valid, each in its own way.

But not for the young. Being in love is a climate for the young. It is a heavy warm atmosphere; the air is full of fiery-hot specks of dust. The young have a flair for it. They know it is lying in wait for you, and whoever is the object of the infatuation is really unimportant, except that a certain chemical correspondance is necessary. The object is the love sensation itself.

What happens later, then, when you are getting on in years? Why, for instance, did Margrethe Thiede fall in love as a so-called middle-aged woman who had given up on childbearing – she had plenty of children at school – and was prepared to spend a quiet life with her good husband Carl. And why was her chosen object – for in this case we are indeed dealing with a clearly defined object – a married man with two young girls and a career to look after. It was an impossible love affair, impractical in all ways, and yet it happened like a sneeze or a thief in the night.

She stood in front of the mirror in the bedroom and looked at herself. What did she really want with her life? To live it. Yes, she wanted to live her life. She wouldn't allow grief to turn her to stone. Her blood wouldn't let it happen. With her hands she cradled her breasts, which pressed against the folds of her blouse, pushed them upward and stared at her own image, feeling lost. A tall, strong, dark-haired woman with a soft face and solid legs. These legs were going to carry her for many more years.

Carl was getting thinner on top, and in body too. He couldn't get past Lars' death and talked sometimes in riddles about the rights of the innocent that were disregarded and about justice that would be reinstated after the big conspiracy had been exposed. When she tried to press him for clarification, he retreated, smiled apologetically and retired back into his silence. He withdrew more and more, went on his solitary evening walks and refused to talk about the things that preoccupied him.

At the shipyard they thought he was an eccentric, a slightly comical character with his tweed jacket, pipe and odd opinions. She realized this one day when she came to pick him up and found him amidst a group of workers, whom he was trying to engage in a political discussion. He was excited and awkward, and they were laughing at him. She could sense it, although no one was directly impolite. She swept her hair off her cheek, nodded hurriedly to the men and dragged him off. What was he thinking? It was obvious that they didn't want to have anything to do with him.

– We have to see other people, Margrethe said. – It's not good to stay put and get lonely.

She herself was never lonely. She had her colleagues, her friends from the peace movement, the children. She had been offered teaching at the secondary school again, but it was the primary school that interested her.

– We have to see other people, Margrethe said, and sent

out invitations to a party: the new manager of the shipyard, a couple of colleagues from the school, one accompanied by her husband, the other by a boyfriend, a few of the young people from the peace movement. – Please, don't make too much propaganda, she warned them. – It's somewhat old-fashioned. And oh yes, she also invited the new member of the town council, Niels Buus, and his delicate wife who laughed too loudly, was overdressed and had a frightened look in her eyes.

Margrethe did her best, set out the glasses and the china from the cabinet, polished the Thiede silverware and added damask napkins to the table setting, all starched and with a monogrammed T done in satin-stitch.

– It's nice making use of the old things, she said, suddenly cheerful, surrounded by food smells as she popped in and out of the kitchen to the sitting room where Carl was. She polished the crystal glasses and tapped them carefully against each other, listening to the fine ringing sound that rose to the ceiling and disappeared under the chandelier. – Listen Carl, she said. – Listen. It's such a long time since we last used them. But Carl didn't know what to do with himself in the middle of all this activity and followed her around, becoming a nuisance, until she finally gave him the tasks of making a seating plan and opening the wine bottles.

After everything was done, the soup eaten, the roast served and consumed to much applause, she leaned back in her chair and drank a toast with the guests. She could feel her cheeks flushing. It was a great success, no one felt left out. Eyes were twinkling, and the conversation was lively while the Thiedes' silver forks made their way to and from the dinner plates and the mouths. Carl hinted at his theories of the big conspiracy, but carefully, halfway in jest. They laughed with him, not at him. He was the host and therefore had the right to provide a little eccentric entertainment. – Yes, yes, the new manager said. – Soon housing construction will move forward again. Niels Buus could inform them of where and why land properties were being primed for construction. The two female teachers felt more doubtful about all this optimism and thought that one should be sceptical. And the young man from the peace movement pointed out in a friendly and non-aggressive manner that it had happened before that illegal construction was carried out and that town planning had to be changed as a result. – Yes, there have been a few ugly affairs, Niels Buus said, but he thought that those days were more or less over. And he told stories about the louts in the town council and their internal fights, while the manager was of the opinion that there were so many restrictions now that free initiative hardly had any room to move. – That's what we need in order to build. And Niels Buus' wife suddenly said something that made them all laugh, and the voices kept humming along without interruption.

Then it happens that Niels Buus leans over the table with his glass lifted and says in his low voice: – You have dimples, Margrethe.

It doesn't come across as a statement of fact but as a new discovery. He says it in a serious voice with a touch of surprise. And she feels herself blushing; the warmth fans out across her chest. She drinks a toast with him, and the entire table with its centrepiece and platters and talking faces disappear. His eyes burn into hers. Only his eyes exist, only this warm breath of air that brushes against her cheek.

And afterwards? Nothing. Nothing special. She gets up to clear the table and serve the dessert. Her friends from school offer to help, Niels Buus' wife too. But she declines, places the dishes on a tray, puts them away in the kitchen, takes out the homemade ice cream with fruit from the refrigerator and scoops out cold, brightly coloured balls that she places on the small glass dessert plates. She does it in a mechanical fashion, hardly looking at her hands. No amount of coldness can affect her. She is burning under her loose silk dress, and the air is studded with fiery specks of dust.

Later on, after the coffee, she suggests that they dance. Why not? The table is cleared and pushed to the side, the record player is turned on. Was it one of Lars' records? No, an even older one, a tenor saxophone that spins a golden veil of notes to fill the entire room. The floor space seems so large. The chesterfield and the easy chairs are in the corner where Carl is sitting, talking with the manager. Their mouths open and close between clouds of smoke. But Margrethe approaches the manager and asks him to dance. He is a little shy and has trouble finding the rhythm. The golden veil flows and expands, the chesterfield becomes a small rectangle far away. The old silver candlesticks from the Thiede family gleam distantly on the bureau.

Margrethe is dancing. Her dress swirls and fills up the whole room. She dances with the manager and then with the husband and the boyfriend of the colleagues from school. She catches a glimpse of Carl who moves around slowly with Niels Buus' little wife. Margrethe is dancing and just waiting for the moment when Niels Buus will come and take her by her wrist: – Now it is my turn to dance with the hostess. And suddenly a feeling of great calm comes over her.

Carl shuffled back and forth helping her clean up. He was quite satisfied with the evening. The new manager was not an uninteresting man, but he didn't understand much about ships, more about money. And Niels Buus seemed to know everything that was happening in town. Now there were apparently people who wanted Egon elected to the council. But Egon himself believed that he could pull strings more easily from where he was right now, or so they said. The young people from the peace movement had not made a strong impression on Carl. They appeared a little scruffy. – And why were you so frantic, Margrethe. – Everything went well, after all.

Margrethe rinsed the dishes and put the silverware away. She kept on hearing Niels Buus' voice in her ear, a low voice that whispered that she had dimples.

Two days later she ran into him at the harbour. They talked about the party and the new cold storage plant that had purchased refrigeration and freezer systems from another company.

They stepped out on the pier where the ocean spray washed over the rocks. It was a grey autumn day, small raindrops sparkled in Niels Buus' hair. A couple of fishing boats were chugging away between the small lighthouses on the piers that were already flashing their green and red lights. Shrieking gulls were following in the wake of the boats.

Margrethe was shivering a bit.

– Are you cold? he asked and turned towards her. He had been facing the harbour. – Do you want my jacket.

She shook her head.

– Then give me your hands. We'll put them in my pockets and keep them warm.

She was standing very close to him and could smell the wet wool from his pea jacket.

– If I kiss you now, he murmured, – then the whole town will know about it.

– You should try and broaden the terms of reference for your peace movement, Niels Buus said later when they sat in the cafeteria having a cup of coffee. – Peace will never happen as long as there are people around. And most likely they'll figure out on their own what kind of weapons they don't have any use for. It was more civilized in the olden days when people used their fists.

– Those days didn't last long, Margrethe said. – People have always been good at inventing. And what about those madmen who don't think beyond the trigger button that will start the whole thing.

– They'll be done away with. There's no use for them any longer. Now the fighting is based in technology and economy, and it has become more dangerous for the losers although it looks less bloody.

– I don't understand what you're saying, Margrethe said. She couldn't quite see his face in the dim light above the brown table top. Other people with trays in front of them could be made out in the semi-darkness. Niels Buus knew some of them and nodded. For them he was a person; for her he was a voice carried on waves of air. He was warmth and smell and sound, and she wanted to breathe in the air that he breathed out.

– Why don't you get a little more involved with local town planning, he said. – And try to do a follow-up on the water treatment plant that we have adopted. You would be able to do something sensible then. Your group knows too little, and you think too much in the abstract. Not much will come of that. And if you're at home tonight, I'll pop in with some documents.

– Are you allowed to do that? she asked. – To show me

the documents.

   – Well, not really, he said and thrust his broad chin out.
– But we need pressure groups.

   – You're a fighter. You don't understand how to compromise.

   – Is that how you see me, he said and got up.

Carl went all the way out to the spruce plantation and back on his evening walks. Once in a while he would also drop in at Egon's pub and sit in a corner and listen. At Egon's pub many of the things that were going on were worth listening to.

   And Margrethe had visits from Niels Buus. When he rang the door bell, her heart grew, bumped against her rib cage, thumped like a piston. Then it fell back into place and found its normal rhythm again. Almost.

   Picture slides: Niels Buus is sitting in the chesterfield leaning over some documents that lie on the low table in front of him. His reading glasses balance on his nose. He is pointing with one of his hands, the other is placed on the armrest close to an easy chair where Margrethe is sitting leaning over as well. You can only see her brown hair. It is shining in the light from the standard lamp and appears newly washed.

   Next: Margrethe has settled in the chesterfield with her legs pulled up. Niels Buus' hand, which previously was pointing at the documents, is now placed on the back of the chesterfield, the other hand rests palm up on his thigh. The reading glasses, two wine glasses and a bottle are on the table. It looks like port.

   Next: Margrethe and Niels Buus lie on the chesterfield, rather awkwardly as it isn't very wide, Margrethe farthest in, her head resting on her arm. Niels Buus' hand, which was previously turned upwards, is now hanging over the edge of the chesterfield and reaches for some support on the floor. The other hand is behind Margrethe's back and hidden from view.

Next: Niels Buus is lying on the rust-red carpet, his upper body against the chesterfield and his legs still up on its seat. He is holding Margrethe around her shoulders and is pulling her down. His face is hidden by her hair. The table is pushed aside. It looks as if the bottle is swaying. Sheets of paper are scattered on the floor.

It's absurd, it's comical, it's terrible. – No, not here. Someone is coming. Carl could return any time.

Afterwards they sat in the chesterfield again or rather: Niels Buus was lying with his head in Margrethe's lap and reading out loud from the documents that she ought to study and understand. She could feel the weight of his heavy head with the curly hair. In bygone days there was once a smith who made drinking vessels from his enemies' skulls. Or was it from the skulls of his enemies' sons? She wanted to drink from him. She wanted to exchange blood and juices with him. She wanted to melt into his skin, and he was never to leave.

– Yes, you better leave now. It is late. Carl is coming. Your wife will worry.

– Yes, he said and got up unwillingly, then sat down again. – Yes, I must leave.

16

During this period Margrethe seemed to be rather giddy and reckless. She felt like hugging the whole world and holding it tight against her body. She had so much affection to give, affection for the friends, for the children at school, for Carl. She patted him on the cheek. Good old Carl. He had such fine, delicate ears. Behind his lined forehead thoughts were bouncing back and forth. He had lost almost all his hair on top. What was it he was pondering so intensely. What was it that worried him.

Then she would suddenly see Niels Buus in front of her, and Carl would fade away.

She walked around in a golden haze. Golden haze, golden daze. I want to be where you are. When I see you, I can't say anything, my voice disappears, my hands become numb. What do my hands want to do? Hold you, touch you. My pores melt into yours, your blood throbs in my blood. Throbs, throbs. And the others? There are no others. Who would they be? There is only your voice. Your voice is a burning light brushing against my skin. I'm mad. I'm happy. I'm alive.

A friend of Niels Buus' from out of town had a small summer cottage far out in the dunes. That's where they had their trysts. Inside it was raw and damp. A snow storm was roaring, and the cottage was creaking in the wind.

– Why me? she asked. Niels Buus was squatting in front

of the fireplace, trying to light the fire.

He turned around and looked up at her. Behind him the flames were licking the logs. – You are a good-looking woman. There are many people in town who would have liked to catch you, but they didn't have the courage, I think.

– And why not?

He turned back, grabbed a bar and poked at the logs. – You are so wise, Margrethe. You are a good teacher. Actually I don't care much for women who can think. I can do that myself.

– Fool, she said and kneeled beside him and passed her finger across his soft lower lip. – May I be allowed to think just a little bit?

– Yes, if you have brought bread and cold meat and want to serve it for me.

– Then you must promise me not to play with the crumbs from your bread, she said and pulled his hair. – It irritates me.

Later they sat in front of the fireplace wrapped in blankets. It was snowing heavily outside. The wind blew the snow against the windows in gusts, and the woodwork was creaking.

– Now we'll be snowed in, he said. – We'll have to stay here forever. Do you think we could manage that?

His face seemed so young in the glow from the fire, young and a little tense.

– You couldn't, she whispered. She leaned against him and kissed him at the base of his throat. – You are too restless.

– What do you tell your wife? she asked while they stood in the open doorway looking out at the storm. The tracks from the car were still visible.

– I lie, he said and took out his car keys. – I have to.

Margrethe lied too, but Carl didn't ask many questions anyway.

In the evening the phone rang. Carl answered. – There was nobody, he said. – It has happened a couple of times lately. Perhaps we should report it.

The next time Margrethe answered. She heard a couple of deep breaths, a loaded silence. It sounded like a child was calling in the background.

– Do you sleep with your wife? she asked Niels Buus. It was in the late afternoon, and they had decided to meet and go for a walk in the dunes and down towards the sea.

– That house out there at the edge, he said and pointed, – they should move it, or the next storm will grab it. It also prevents new dunes from being formed as long as it stays there.

– You know so many things, Margrethe said. – Do you sleep with your wife?

– No, that stopped a long time ago.

– Did it?

– Of course it didn't. We live together. We have children together. We got married too early. She never had an education. I can't go anywhere before she has had an education.

He spoke in spurts. His breath was like steam in the frosty air.

– Does she know anything about us?

– I don't think so. I'm lying to her, of course, but she isn't stupid. She could easily go places if she was just given the opportunity. When the children get older, she wants to train as a secretary. We have talked about that.

– What are the two of us going to do, Margrethe said.

They had reached the top of the dunes. In the clear air they could see far out to sea even though it had begun to grow dark. The sun had already set, and red and ivory-coloured clouds were fanning out in streaks across the violet sky.

– I don't know, Niels Buus said and began to walk back along the path. – I can't figure anything out any more. Now they want me to enter national politics, too. That's what the members are talking about in the voters' association.

– Then you won't be able to go solo any more. Always being good for a strong opinion and always ready to defend it. You will become a man of compromise.

– It won't necessarily be that bad, he said and smiled. If I don't have any red on my palette, I'll use green. That's a pretty colour, too.

– You'll look good on television, Margrethe said.

He stopped and slid his hands under her coat. – This is something to hang on to, he said. – It's nice.

– And then you'll be moving, she whispered against his throat.

– Maybe. It depends on which constituency I'll be getting. I'll probably be doing a lot of traveling. Then we can see each other in different cities.

Margrethe didn't answer.

In the supermarket Margrethe saw Niels Buus' wife. She was better dressed now, more subdued, more stylish. Some would even say that she was attractive.

Margrethe greeted her. Niels Buus' wife looked the other way. They kept their distance in the aisles, but at the checkout they happened to stand in the same queue.

– You have a lot of groceries, Margrethe said. She thought her voice croaked.

– I have children to feed – and a husband. They eat a lot, Niels Buus' wife mumbled and turned her back to Margrethe. Margrethe could sense the anger and fear that oozed out from the woman's back.

– Don't think ..., she said in a low voice. – Don't be afraid.

– I'm not afraid of you. You're old after all, Niels Buus' wife said and stuffed her purchases into her bag.

Was it true, was Margrethe really old? She was older than Niels Buus. She hadn't thought of that before. Her body was firm and smooth, full but not old. Her hair was shiny, and she had dimples. When she was waiting for her lover – that's what it was called, my lover – she felt nervous like a schoolgirl. How could she be old?

But there was no future, no tomorrow, only a here and now.

She saw it all and yet she saw nothing. She could see the pores in Niels Buus' face, the strength in his glasses when he put them on to read, every stitch in his knitted sweater. But when she thought of him, she could no longer make his face hang together. And Carl was a blurred spot far out in her field of vision.

One day the school principal called her into his office. – I wasn't sure if I should show you this, he said and placed a picture in front of her. – But I think you better take a look anyway.

It was an ugly picture. Margrethe's face cut out from an old snapshot – where did that come from? – and glued on to a drawing of a shapeless body of a woman with huge pendulous breasts.

There was no writing. No message. No verbal insult.

– It's a thoughtless joke, the school principal said. – Guys down at Egon's pub are the types that would dream up this kind of prank after having imbibed too much. I've heard about similar cases.

– Can't the police do something about it? Margrethe said. Her voice was shaking.

– The police. Well, perhaps. But what can they actually do? You wouldn't want to have too many people involved in that kind of thing.

Margrethe had to agree with him there.

17

So far Margrethe Thiede had had firm ground under her feet. You don't think about that expression as long as you have it – firm ground under your feet. She stood firmly on her legs, solid legs, good for standing. The ground is sliding from under me, she had sometimes thought to herself, but more because it was a common phrase rather than something she could feel with her body, feel under her feet that carried those solid legs. Oh yes, things had happened around her, awful things, unbearable things even. But she had had to bear them anyway. Reality had held her grounded, and it, too, was solid. She had chosen a path through it, and no cracks had opened up, at least none that were big enough to signal any danger. She had not fallen into the abyss, not been knocked off the ground. Basically, people have a great talent for surviving. Basically, I'm a healthy person, Margrethe said. And she said it as if she knew the ground under her and trusted it.

But now the ground was shaking beneath her. Why had it not happened much sooner? She had experienced much sorrow, after all, sudden deaths and disappearances and now finally this heady and highly inconvenient love affair that certainly had no solid ground to build on. Why was it happening now, then?

The cause – for there was a direct cause even if it only acted as a catalyst for a process that had already been set in motion – was in itself insignificant. All that happened was that some valuables that Margrethe hadn't even known she was attached to had disappeared, gone forever, to emerge in all probability in another and less definite form somewhere else in the world. That's the way it goes with people but also with things and everything else to which we attribute constancy and permanence. All that remains are the images we have created of them somewhere in our brains, and even they will fade, lose their details, become blurred and melt away.

The Thiedes' large silver ladle, for instance. At the base of its handle was a finely engraved leafy pattern and further up a corresponding pattern of interlaced lines coiled around the oval surface. But what did the coiled lines look like, and how big was the oval surface compared with the surrounding pattern?

Margrethe could visualize the ladle. It sparkled in its silver brilliance. It poked its head into the soup tureen and emerged again filled with steaming soup. But the pattern further up the handle was covered by grandmother Thiede's old shrivelled hand or by her own hand while she was serving soup and passing the bowls on to Carl and to Lars, to Lily Lund and Lily Lund's husband Berre who were guests at the table, to the manager of the shipyard, to a young woman who laughed too loudly and whose dress was too gaudy, to a voice that flowed through the steam from the tureen and rose to her cheeks where it settled as a glowing, rosy blush. 'Snow White and Rose Red' was the name of one of the Carrot Fairy's stories. Why was she thinking about that when she was supposed to describe a soup ladle.

A soup ladle. That particular soup ladle. Its place had been in the top drawer in the heirloom cabinet that safeguarded the Thiede silverware. Stacks of trays covered in blue velvet, filled with regular forks and cake forks, soup spoons, dessert spoons, teaspoons. Why weren't they called coffee spoons? It would have reflected more accurately the norms and habits of those places where the spoons were used.

It had all been there, bright and shiny, when she had pulled the trays out in the past. The bottom trays had been less frequently in use, for who needed all that silverware. It was only a nuisance and reserved for more important occasions where you would want to make everything beautiful and impressive and maybe demonstrate – subconsciously – that there was security and resistance in your life, a kind of composure that you weren't willing to lose even if a low melting voice flowed through hot steam from a soup tureen.

There, in the top tray, then, the ladle had been hidden when it wasn't in actual use. And now it was no longer there. There was nothing in the trays in the cabinet apart from an old battered tea strainer whose thin layer of silver coating was partially gone. It ought to have been thrown out a long time ago; it couldn't be used for anything, neither for the making of tea nor for the establishing of composure. It was in no way representative.

One Sunday morning when Margrethe came downstairs in her dressing gown and opened the door to the sitting room to continue her way to the kitchen to put the kettle on for coffee, she found the room turned upside down. The drawers in the bureau were pulled out, papers were strewn all over the floor, books were missing from the bookcase, cushions thrown into the corner by the grandfather clock, cabinet doors opened, the trays pulled out halfway and all the silverware gone. The open veranda door was banging against the door frame in the wind. The burglar or burglars must have escaped that way. How he or they had entered was another story that Margrethe discussed with Carl and later with the policeman who had answered the call without much enthusiasm.

A window in the kitchen had been unhinged and carefully placed in the sink. Was it possible that it had been left ajar? It must have been since there was no apparent damage. Or could one imagine that a sharp and flat implement, the blade of a small axe, for instance, could have been worked in between the frame and the window bar and thus lifted the window? The last suggestion was highly unlikely, but nevertheless, a small axe with a black handle and a greyish shiny blade was lying in the middle of the kitchen table.

The window was now an empty frame. A stray curtain swelled in the wind, then went limp but was soon flying from one side to the other. And the light from the empty square was reflected in the axe blade that shone menacingly on Margrethe's incredulous face when she leaned over to look at it. She and Carl had been sound asleep upstairs, even if it perhaps couldn't be called the sleep of the innocent in her case, and meanwhile a man with an axe had walked around in her sitting room, had touched her things, messed them up and removed them. She felt as if she herself had been touched by something unclean that couldn't be washed off. Someone had permitted himself an intimacy that was totally unacceptable. Why hadn't she woken up, why hadn't she gone downstairs and surprised this man, seen who he was so she could give him an identity. Now he was just a faceless shadow, the man with the axe. Dread.

– Gone downstairs, the policeman repeated. – You should be grateful that you didn't wake up and think up all that nonsense. Rather unpleasant things could have happened to you. And he sprinkled powder on the axe blade and put it in a plastic bag without giving them too much hope of solving the burglary. – There are a lot of things happening in town these days. Perhaps it is organized. And they sell the silver south of the border where it is melted down.

He walked towards the front door, turned around just before opening it and looked at Carl with a smirk. – So, when will we next have the pleasure of a visit from you, he said. It was as if he didn't take the incident seriously.

Carl gathered the papers from the floor and inspected them carefully. He kept going back to a black letter case with a golden lock that had been forced open, took out some documents, counted them and put them back in the case.

– What is so important, Margrethe asked and leaned over him to have a look. He closed the case and returned it to the bureau drawer. – Nothing. Nothing in particular. It's just that it means something to me.

The days went by, and there was no news from the police. Margrethe had never thought that the Thiede silver played any role in her life. You can get attached to people but not to things. Now it was all gone. The ladle with the pretty leafy pattern etched around the oval surface, gone, melted down. The nice old crafted piece now a small lump of silver. During the night she dreamt of the man with the axe, who would enter the bedroom and slash Carl's fragile skull with the shiny blade. And she dreamt of spoons and forks, twisted together in a intricate silvery lattice fence that would surround her on all sides. And she was standing behind this trellis, protected and confined, until the forks and spoons suddenly dissolved and turned into grey dust, grey fear, grey fog that rose like steam from the abyss. And she sank into the fog where nothing is important, where all things are of equal importance, of no importance, are futile, without any interest.

The days dragged on at a snail's pace. Margrethe went to school and taught the children. She no longer recognized them, and they looked at her with hostile eyes. She felt that the older ones were laughing behind her back. Maybe they knew something about the picture the school principal had shown her. Perhaps they despised her, and why shouldn't they. She was despicable. Men with axes and empty faces had been in her sitting room, thrown her things about, ignored her existence, although she had been sleeping just above them. She had begun to wake up during the night and go downstairs to settle accounts with him, the faceless man. Some place deep down in her subconscious she knew that this was foolishness and delusions, that the burglar most likely was a poor chap who had thought the house had been empty and who had escaped through the veranda door because he had heard a noise from upstairs, that the fear that was paralysing her was caused by other things entirely. But she refused to listen to her subconscious and to see through herself. She couldn't see anything anyway. She was opaque, a metal lump, only mass and dead weight.

Niels Buus had left town. Or rather: he had enrolled in a sort of course along with the children and the wife who had also gone back to school, people said. The house hadn't been sold but temporarily rented out. And how Niels Buus could afford an experiment like that was anyone's guess. But of course, he was studying to become a politician, and someone had probably invested money in him.

Margrethe knew a little more than that but had no one to confide in. She had talked to Niels Buus on the phone and had also seen him in another town in a small hotel room on the very top floor of the building. There was only one window in the room, on a sloping wall, and he had been sitting there in the semi-darkness on the bed, his head resting on his hands. She had lifted herself onto her elbow and passed her hand over his white back, over the small bumps formed by the muscles. They wanted to give him a secure constituency. They expected a lot from him, and he would most likely be quite busy. And she had understood everything he said. This was only an episode in his life, wonderful as long as it lasted. Now it must come to an end. – I am going to join new expeditions, take part in new conquests, he said, and you can now set forth on your quest for happiness or whatever it is you feel compelled to seek. It was an old echo. Of what, she didn't remember.

– I'll phone, Niels Buus said and began to pull his shirt over his head.

An episode. It had been wonderful. It was already so far back in the past that it no longer was the simple past but the past perfect. During the night she dreamt that she gave birth to a marten. It was crawling about, scratching things. Its muscles were moving under the fur. She wanted to push it back into its own bloodfilled darkness where it belonged. But it escaped from her hands, nipped at them with its sharp teeth and looked up at her with its clear curious eyes. She could smell its scent. When she woke up, she could still smell it. But later in the day, she couldn't smell or feel anything. She was a dead weight, a lump of grey metal.

And where was Carl during all this. He wasn't there at all. He would pat her awkwardly on her shoulder. Thin and stooped over, he would brush his teeth in the bathroom. He would cough that raspy cough of his and lie down to sleep, his back turned towards her. In the daytime he would walk around and pick up signals with his long delicate ears and make inquiries. Bent over, shuffling his feet, he would listen. Carl was everywhere but not really present. What was it he listened for on his solitary walks when he initiated conversations with people in his awkward way?

You look somewhat pale, my girl, Mats Mathies says and leans over in Margrethe's direction with his big stomach. They sit on the bench at the pier and look out over the water. Mats Mathies' corduroy jacket is greasy, and his long hair looks as if it has been dipped in an old barrel. But he is concerned about Margrethe. – You ought to be an earth goddess, he says. – That's what you are meant to be. And it doesn't suit you to be thinner.

Margrethe smiles weakly. Unlike Carl, Mats Mathies is present, he hasn't become a stranger. His horse-dealer face with its slanted eyes swims towards her, stops and bobs up and down in the sunlight, then withdraws to join his body again, the greasy jacket, the stomach that bulges out like a balloon over his trousers. It's a blue balloon that gives way to a patch of smooth brown skin, as the lower shirt buttons are missing. And further down below the stomach, his short legs stand firmly planted on the ground.

– You're not feeling all that well, are you? You're not your usual peppy self. What about a little change of air, my girl. And his small eyes twinkle cunningly close to her face while one of his hands pinches her upper arm tentatively. – My goodness, the bones have started to pop out. That's too early. It'll have to wait till the cemetery. You better try and get some more padding again. And he pulled his hand back and slapped himself on his fat stomach.

The school principal spoke about traveling and a change of air too. – We can easily get a supply teacher if you can produce a sick note, he said. – You don't have to be so conscientious, Margrethe. – We can all see that you are unwell.

She was not conscientious. Not that. She worked like a robot and attended to her routines. If they disappeared too, the whole thing would crumble. What would she get out of traveling when the world had lost its smells and colours.

– Curiosity, that's man's gift of grace. That's what keeps us alive, Mats Mathies said and sat down beside her on the bench at the pier. – Pull yourself together now, Margrethe. It is not like you to get stuck. Think about the peace movement. It's not doing very well either these days.

But whatever he said was lost on her. He was just a kind dwarf and understood nothing.

It was Egon who finally managed to get through to her. Why Egon who was her enemy and opponent? Well, that's exactly why.

Carl went for his long solitary evening walks in the musty autumn darkness. He preferred to be alone. Although tall he would walk with a stoop and stride down the empty evening streets until his cap and tweed jacket disappeared from the lights. Carl was never really present. What was going on inside him?

– Carl? He is over at Egon's pub, letting them ridicule him, Mats Mathies said. – He is too good for that kind of thing. But you probably don't care.

No, Margrethe did care, a little bit anyway, even if Carl

had withdrawn from her and found his own whatever it was. She looked at the back of his head and stroked him gently. She had to protect Carl.

– I'll walk with you, she said one evening and put on her coat before he had time to protest.

– Where do you usually go? she asked and took his arm. He answered evasively. Here and there, usually, to the harbour perhaps, or out to the spruce plantation.

They walked to the harbour where the fishing boats were unloading at the pier. Crates full of fish on ice were moving along on large conveyor belts, moving on and on under orange lights that were swaying in the wind. Margrethe grabbed a green net that was lying in a heap. The threads looked like spiderweb but were as strong as steel wires and cut into her fingers. Further down the pier a crane lifted its narrow lizard head. Suddenly she thought it looked like Carl.

They stood and watched, a middle-aged couple looking on while busy men in their oilskins were puffing, lifting things, giving directions, shouting and once in a while laughing.

Carl and Margrethe were not talking. There was nothing to say. Of course, one could mention that the new fish crates of metal were uglier that the old wooden crates, or that the green net here was very likely used for catching flatfish. But why use words that would only fall into the void and disappear without leaving behind a single scratch or other trace.

Afterwards they went over to Egon's pub-cum-disco-theque that sparkled bright and metallic with its black tables on steel legs under the shining lights, but where you could still find a dark and quiet corner along the wall to sit and keep silent together.

It was obvious right away that Carl was no stranger here. – The Stick is here, someone shouted. – And with a lady.

Margrethe Thiede looked around. A couple of young fellows that had graduated from the senior form a few years earlier nodded shyly to her. She thought she recognized other faces as well, faces that had aged, lined faces. She hadn't been at Egon's pub for a long time. In the past she used to go there with her friend Lily Lund who would sit across from Egon and let him pat her slender hand, Lily Lund who had no strength to overcome the normal stress of daily life even though that is the only safeguard against perdition.

Margrethe shuddered and moved closer to Carl. He was tense, his upper body was leaning forward, his face turned towards the open space of the room. He was trying to pick up all the sounds and signals with his delicate ears as if at a listening post.

And here came Egon, the mountain troll and ruler of the land of chrome. His steps were heavy, he had grown bigger. His hair had receded from the temples with the result that his meaty face with its fine features now appeared even more massive. Had Egon ever been completed, she wondered, had his limbs been properly chiseled and freed from the block. Or he was an Earth Climp, that Egon, not at all suitable for the princess with the golden hair in whom he had once confided, and to whom he had whispered secret words with his small cruel mouth, words that Margrethe had not been allowed to hear.

He approached their table and slammed his fist down on the black surface so the beer glasses jumped and Carl straightened up with a start.

– Well, don't we have fine guests today, he said and

pulled a chair over and sat down astride it. – Of course, we see quite a bit of Carl in here. He is practically a regular, our mascot. But it's a long time since you were here last, Margrethe. You look pretty miserable, by the way.

His one eye looked down past Margrethe's shoulder, the other observed her with a sly and secretive smile. What made Egon laugh? He didn't have just two eyes, but many. She could feel them crawl all over her body like tiny creatures. She rose from her seat to shake them off, and suddenly she felt light, freed from her own weight. A strong, warm feeling of rage began to shoot through Margrethe's body.

– Yes, that Carl, Egon continued, sounding friendly and nudging Carl on his tweedy sleeve. – Do you know that we call him the Stick, or sometimes the Tin Soldier, Margrethe? We're in the habit of using nicknames down here, you know, but we don't mean to be unkind. It's because we like you, Carl, Egon said and looked from Carl to Margrethe in his jolly way. – Down here your husband has to put up with a good deal, Margrethe. And he does, but without taking offence. In turn, then, he gets to sit at the regular table and listen to the big boys when they talk business. You like that, don't you Carl.

Carl smiled apologetically, and his head dropped between his shoulders. Like a turtle. For a moment he resembled an old man.

An old man. My man. No one was going to give my husband nicknames.

Egon snapped his fingers and ordered snaps from the waiter. A tubby woman with pitch-black hair passed on her way to the bar. Carl nodded as if he knew her. Margrethe startled. Wasn't it? Yes, surely it was Rosita who had once taken her clothes off on Egon's stage. Now she was called

185

something else. Karen. Karen Jepsen she was, and didn't have much to show off any longer. She had married a fisherman, and people said that he beat her.

Rosita stopped, came back as if she wanted to say something. Egon grabbed her roughly by her upper arm. – Get lost, he said in a low voice. – You have no business being here.

He filled Carl's glass and his own. Margrethe covered her glass with the palm of her hand.

– Do you know anything about how Niels Buus is doing? Egon asked. He asked so innocently all the while watching Margrethe with his sly eye. – They say that he is about to become a politician at the national level. Which is a good idea. Then he won't do any harm here in town.

Carl cleared his throat. He had raised his head again but wasn't listening. His attention was focused on Rosita who was standing at the bar arguing about something.

Egon's face was dancing in front of Margrethe. His eyes were lit up, his small mouth gurgled air with a whistling noise. – You are a pest, she shouted, stood up and swept the glasses off the table with her arm. – Do you remember when I slapped your face. That could happen again.

Egon's face retreated. His lower jaw dropped, and his eyes became suddenly watchful even though they looked in two different directions. Silence had descended on the room.

– Steady now, Margrethe, Egon said. – That's just like you. I was under the impression, though, that you had become more reasonable over the years.

But Margrethe marched past him, pulled Carl from the bench, pushed her way through the room while unbelieving eyes and gaping mouths followed her to the door. She tore the door open, and outside the autumn wind greeted them.

– What's the matter with you. Was that really necessary, Carl shouted and tried to keep up with her while she hurried down the street. She struck out at him, hit the air instead, slammed her hand against one of his arms, stopped running and turned towards him. – You are such a wimp, she screamed. – Why do you put up with it. She could feel that she was about to cry. – What have we done to ourselves?

He put his arm around her, a little hesitantly. – You don't understand, Margrethe, and you don't have to. But something important is happening. Very important. Don't spoil it for me.

They walked silently side by side the rest of the way home. But the silence was no longer empty.

– Why can't you tell me what it is that you're brooding over? Margrethe asked when they reached the garden gate. The sky was cloudy, the wind tore at the trees. The garden path was full of fallen leaves.

– Not yet, he said and brushed her hair from her cheek. – You'll find out when the time is ripe.

When the time is ripe? Would she ever come to understand Carl.

The following day she told him that she wanted to go away. She would pay for a supply teacher herself. Surely they could afford that.

– I have to figure things out, she said. – I have to find out what I'm all about.

She wanted Carl to come with her. Yes and no. He also needed change and had never gotten over Lars' death. Why had they never talked about it? Why had they never talked about the grief and instead allowed it to seep into their relationship. It was after Lars' death that Carl had become strange. Or was it earlier?

– I can't go. There are things that I have to take of. It is not going well at the shipyard either. They seem to want a younger man instead.

– Should I stay? Margrethe asked. – Do you want me to stay? We could travel together later, then.

No, Carl didn't think she should stay. But she had to promise to come back home again.

Where else in the world could she go after the journey was over? Margrethe promised to come back to Carl, but first she would have to come back to her own self.

Many people in town found it curious that Margrethe Thiede took off by herself like that, away from her husband. Some of them were speculating that she would go and see Niels Buus, but that couldn't be true. Niels Buus had bought a house in his new constituency and was living there with his nice little wife who had begun some sort of education. She had always been odd, that Margrethe Thiede.

18

She travelled by train and followed by and large the route that she and auntie had taken years earlier. There were so many places that she had never had the opportunity to see, either then or later. She stopped here and there in cities where a sudden impulse, an ocean view, a church spire, or a domed building would entice her to get off.

After she had managed to drag her suitcases down the steps of the train, or had them handed to her through the window of the compartment, she would stand in the middle of the pile and begin to unfold a small luggage cart. She would pull out the handle, place the suitcases on the cart and fasten them with elasticized ropes. Then she would pull the cart down the platform until the suitcases began to shift, the handle collapsed and the ropes loosened, and she would once again stand in the middle of the pile with the now broken cart beside her. She never succeeded in making it to the tourist bureau without some mishap, and therefore she wasn't able to obtain information about suitable hotel rooms, places of refuge or points of departure for excursions to the domed building, the church spire or the ocean view. In a way this appealed to her. Here was a practical problem that had to be solved by herself or by one of the passers-by that had gathered around her to comment on the cart's mechanism. But in one small dark hotel room whose stone floor smelled of antiseptics, she unpacked the most necessary dresses and shoes, transferred them to a newly purchased canvas bag and gave the rest to the chambermaid. From now on she wanted to travel light.

She tried to make herself understood to porters at the train stations, to doormen and waiters. These were casual conversations that due to her limited vocabulary would address only practical matters or simply be friendly comments. In the beginning she accepted the hotel rooms that were offered to middle-aged women who travel alone, small dark rooms with a view to a fire wall or a construction site. But after a while she learned to gesticulate, to deplore, to demand or even to smile in order to get what she wanted. She felt that she became another person, more theatrical and merrier when she attempted to speak this other language.

At night she would dream about the dead. She also dreamt about Niels Buus, who was now dead to her, and about Carl. In the dream she was angry with Carl. He disappeared down some steep stairs ahead of her, hurried down the brownish red steps that led from domed churches to open, empty squares with fountains where water was gushing from the gaping mouths of devils with distorted features. She ran after him and called his name, but he didn't turn around. His long back disappeared around a corner in the white sunlight. She kept on running through alleyways where houses would lean towards her as if offering her their empty shuttered windows. In an open gateway Harald and Lars were playing chess with their heads bent over the board. A strange misty light enveloped their faces, and she had trouble making out their features. It's a good thing they have found each other, she thought in the dream. And that Lars has risen from the sea.

Lily Lund walked slowly past her, her reddish golden hair hanging like a cape around her shoulders. She moved like a sleepwalker, looked straight ahead with empty eyes.

She held a child in her arms, but she carried it awkwardly. Its heavy head had dropped down unsupported by her elbow. It'll fall, Margrethe shouted, the child will fall.

But it is Egon's head that is lying in the middle of the pavement. It is rocking back and forth, the eyes squinting. She attempts to step over it, but Egon's rocking head turns into a fish with a small mouth that tries to nip her. She can feel its slimy skin between her calves.

Go away, she shouts in her dream. I want to wake up. When I wake up, you are dead. But she can't wake up.

Two yellow-brown girls are dancing in front of her. They are called Skin and Bones. And Niels Buus is standing at the bottom of the alley in bright sunlight. She wants to reach him, but the moment she begins to run towards him, the alley stretches out endlessly, and he is standing even further away in the bright sunlight.

Suddenly she is back at the lighthouse. The Carrot Fairy calls her in from the yard. It's time to clean up her room because it's full of spoiled food. The whipped cream in the bowl smells rotten, the soup ladle sits in a tureen whose content is covered in greyish green mould. She turns on the tap at the sink. Sand pours out of it.

Clean up, the Carrot Fairy says. But how can she dispose of all this decay. It has to go somewhere.

Bury it, Sem says. He is standing with Kam and Jaffe in front of the cottage with the hollyhocks. Bury it, then it will turn into something else that can be used again. Next, she is far out somewhere in the dunes, kneeling in the sand and digging with both hands.

In the morning Margrethe Thiede woke up in the hotel room where sunlight had entered between the slats of the shutters. She woke up with her legs entangled in the sheet, not quite knowing where she was. She stayed put and tried to hold on to her dreams, dozed off again and found herself in some city standing by a river. The sun was shining in the rippling water in which stalls displaying scarves and blouses, golden necklaces, colourful fruits and old books were reflected. She picked up a book and began leafing through it. It was about herself. In the book she was standing by a river. The sun was shining in the rippling water, and she picked up a book from a box and began reading it. In the dream and in the book in the dream, and in the book that the book in the dream spoke about, Margrethe Thiede was standing by a river while the sun was shining in the rippling water in which stalls displaying scarves, golden necklaces, colourful fruits and old books were reflected.

She began thinking about the language in which the dreams spoke to her. It was a strange language. Images and fragments from real life were combined in new and odd ways. Time expanded in all directions or shrank to a compact form. Was it a more truthful interpretation of the impressions, colours, smells and shapes that flowed past her during the day and whose elements she believed she was able to describe in words. When we talk to each other about the world, we interpret it through ordinary language, the language we have learned, she wrote in her notebook. But do we experience reality differently? When we believe we are speaking about the same thing, do our points of reference in fact spring from different experiences? What was Carl's sense of reality?

But during the day, the reality of the foreign cities wrapped around her in a reassuring and concrete way. She began exploring things with increasing curiosity. When she returned to the hotel and the hotel porter politely inquired about her adventures, she would explain herself in her limited vocabulary. And he would nod as if he recognized it all.

One evening at dusk she was standing in a room decorated with wallpaper in a rose pattern. The room had a view to a small patio where a couple of lamps were gleaming peacefully above shiny white-painted tables. On the wall between the windows was a reproduction of a painting she recognized from art books, a young woman, an earth goddess that carried flowers and fruits in her arms and a hat loaded with fruit and large bunches of flowers on her head. Her childlike doll face with its dark shadows under her pale eyes peeked out from under the hat. Her big, pregnant belly was wrapped in a magnificent dress of brocade. But in the folds of the brocade shadows lay hidden. This fertility fairy and adorned child-woman, who was carrying all the riches of the earth, was also carrying her own death. One could see that.

Margrethe Thiede looked at this picture for a long time and then turned towards the mirror that was mounted in an ornamental gilt frame. She looked at her hair, at her bangs above her heavy eyebrows. And she looked at her face that still had plenty of soft hollows. I have dimples, she thought to herself.

The next day she traveled on to a nearby city that was famous for its old buildings and great art treasures. She found lodging just outside the centre of the city in a light and spacious room high up in a hotel. However, it had one disadvantage as the bathroom was separate from the room, located on the other side of a corridor leading to the fire escape. In the middle of the night after she had fallen asleep without having anxiety dreams, she was woken up by a noise coming from the corridor. She swung her feet out onto the cold stone floor, ran over to the door, flung it open and stepped out into the corridor that was dimly lit by a naked light bulb in the ceiling. A short gentleman wearing a striped silk robe was rattling the handle of the door leading to the stairs. He was using both hands, kicking the door panel and pushing with his shoulder.

– The other way, pull the handle towards you, Margrethe shouted. She ought to have expressed herself in the foreign language, but she didn't think of it.

The man let go of the handle and turned towards her. – Margrethe, he said. – It was a good thing you came. My room is on fire.

She stared at him with a confused look while still half asleep. His body was twitching slightly under the silk robe, his greyish brown hair had fallen down and covered his forehead. Then she recognized him. It was the professor.

There was no fire in his room, of course. A reddish glow from a neon sign across the street was showing through the shutters. Margrethe opened them halfway and could spell out an advertisement for a brand of coffee on the sign.

– I must have dreamt something unpleasant, the short professor said seemingly unconcerned now. He treated Margrethe with whiskey served in a water tumbler while inquiring about her journey and what had brought her to this city, to this hotel and to this very corridor by the fire escape. He remembered her very well although their correspondance the last few years had been reduced to an occasional postcard. And hadn't she thought of taking up her studies again. It was never too late. He for his part had taken early retirement in order to see more of the world, to eat his way through the world, so to speak, as he had taken an interest in gastronomy late in life. It was also a kind of research, as food was a reflection of culture. His next project was going to be about language and food, quite a topic to tackle.

Dressed in his pyjamas and silk robe, he was raising his glass good-humouredly now the scare was behind him and he had run into Margrethe so unexpectedly. It was her turn to talk. He wanted to hear her entire life story.

Her life story? But there was no story to tell. It was all so trivial, so insignificant. In reality she had never done anything special, just turned to the tasks that lay immediately in front of her. Her troubles had never originated with her. They had arrived unannounced, unsolicited, and her life had crumbled away.

– No moaning, Margrethe, the professor said. – Life is tough, but think of the alternative. And he told stories about his marriages, terrible stories but also terribly funny stories so that Margrethe had to laugh and wonder whether he might not regret his frankness the next day. After all, the professor had previously observed a certain distance between them.

They were hair-raising, these stories, and calculated to be so. Margrethe swept her hair up in the back with the back of her hand and felt suddenly conscious of her wearing a nightgown that, although decent, was low-cut in appropriate places. She had seated herself on the straight-backed chair in front of the desk, herself somewhat straight-backed, balancing the whiskey glass and quite surprised by this familiarity that had developed between her and a pyjamas-clad gentleman in a foreign hotel.

– Come over here and sit by me on the bed, the

professor said. – Make yourself comfortable. I hardly pose a threat to your virtue. Although, who knows, he added and smiled to her. – Life demands that we take some risks. Come over here and I'll tell you how I got rid of my second wife, the one you knew when you were a student. You do remember her, don't you? A pretty girl in her own way. I was a disappointment to her. She was under the impression that there was more substance in the academic world. She embarked on slimming diets to punish me. I think she wanted to demonstrate how enervating it was to be married to me. All this happened later, of course, after the first hectic year when I fell for her. She represented a new world of elegance, was always painted and laquered, the daughter of a landowner, a conquest. In the beginning she fascinated me. In those days I always wanted to make conquests.

– Your wife seemed very striking, professor, Margrethe said. – Very correct. I don't think she cared for all those students that were brought to the house.

– Please, don't call me professor, the professor mumbled absent-mindedly. He was deeply involved in his story, and Margrethe was just an audience. For some reason this irritated her.

– She didn't want a divorce so we continued living as a couple although once in a while I .... Well, no need to get into that now.

– And then what? Margrethe asked and shifted on to her side, resting her upper body on her elbow.

– We were visiting her father, the landowner, who has hunting rights that he leases out. We go for a walk on the property, and perhaps somewhere in my subconscious the thought occurs that all this could one day be mine since I apparently can't get rid of her. I don't know. There are so many roles you don't get to play in your short life. And then you can only hope that you choose the right thing. Now, let's have another drink.

And he poured out the whiskey and pushed a pillow towards Margrethe while scratching his chest. She could see his grey curly chest hairs through the opening of his pyjama jacket.

– Now imagine a large green meadow at the edge of the wood where my wife and I are strolling along, he continued. – She is a little ahead of me, wearing a light brown coat, I am behind her wearing rubber boots and a wind breaker, the closest I could get to sporting a landowner's get-up. At the edge of the wood we notice three figures wearing caps and carrying hunting equipment. We didn't think anything of it since we hadn't been informed that it was inadvisable to walk around in certain parts of the property. The three of them disappear into the woods, and shortly after we too stroll into the deep, silent calm below the shadowy greenery. We, too, are silent as we had more or less ceased to communicate with each other. My wife stops and bends down to pick a flower with her back facing some oak scrub. I arrive a little behind her. The light is filtered through the tree tops, and there she stands, bent over, while light and shadow flicker above her. A shot rings out. My wife drops to the ground, hit, as it later turned out, right in her rear, fortunately in the fleshier part. I run towards her. From the other side of the oak thicket I hear excited voices, and from behind the branches the three gentlemen equipped with hunting gear step out to inspect their fallen game. And it is at this point that according to my ex-wife I delay the entire rescue operation by pulling out a notebook from my pocket and begin to interview the unlucky huntsmen. What did they think they had seen, and what colours and what shadow effects had caused them to conclude that my poor companion was legitimate game? We discussed these questions heatedly for some time before we thought of making a stretcher of sorts to transport the victim back to the estate.

The professor had moved further up in the bed. He sat with his legs crossed and his back against the headboard. He held the whiskey glass in his hand, and his eyes began to look glassy.

– I don't deny in the least, he said and yawned, – I don't deny in the least that from her perspective my behaviour must have been hurtful in addition to the hurt she had already suffered. In any case, the incident triggered off, so to speak, my large dissertation on concept formation. I assume you have read it, or else you ought to. Before its publication date, my wife and I were divorced. Anyway, her backside has been honoured with a place in the history of research. That's something! And now I think I want to sleep. He put down the glass on the night table and rolled over on his side.

Margrethe swung her feet out over the edge of the bed. – You are welcome to stay, the professor mumbled half asleep. But she loosened the blanket, covered him and tiptoed carefully out the door to her own room and her wide bed.

That night she dreamt about three hunters all wearing big white hats that were pulled down over their heads. They walked along the green edge of the forest pointing brown shotguns ahead of them. The sun was setting in front of the trees and turned into a small golden ball that came rolling towards her. In the dream it didn't seem particularly odd to her that the sun was setting in front of the trees.

Afterwards she was Snow White lying in the glass coffin while a group of little men were dancing around her, thumbing their noses at her, mocking her and shouting that she was boring. Boring. Boring. None of the dead were in her dream, but she herself was almost dead until she managed to sit up in the glass coffin and spit out the poisoned apple. When she woke up she could still feel the cramps in her stomach, but then she remembered the dream and thought it banal.

The professor insisted on showing her the city. He dragged her through narrow streets that opened onto squares and piazzas; he ran ahead and pointed out statues and sculptures, lectured to her, endulged in himself and offered her all his vast knowledge. – Magnificent. Glorious. You don't have to look at the fat youth over there in the recess. He is poorly proportioned. Sentimental rubbish.

– It says in the guide book that it's a masterpiece, Margrethe Thiede said, prepared to fight.

– That guide book must have been written by an idiot, the professor declared and dragged her away.

He was funny, and he was intolerable. Marble faces were staring at her from all directions. She wanted to pause in front of them in silence. Perhaps they wanted something from her. Who was to know. But the professor talked continuously. – Do I tire you out, Margrethe, he asked and continued talking without waiting for an answer. Suddenly she remembered how his use of language had struck her as being peculiar back in her student days.

One afternoon after an interesting and solid lunch that was to be part of the professor's new research material, they reached a newer section of the city with wide streets, expensive shops and art galleries. – Now we want to see something modern, we are tired of all the old stuff, the professor pronounced and pointed at a building removed a short distance from the street and nestled among trees. – They have an exhibition in there that was nearly closed down. It violated public morality, whatever that is supposed to mean. A phrase that in fact implies the concept of so-called private morality which can be doubtful in any case, as we know. 'The nature of morality, as with most other sciences, changes its shape every hundred years.' And now you are supposed to confirm this with a nod and look enthusiastic. You don't know enough quotations. They always come in handy.

Margrethe was getting tired. She stood on the stairs leading to the museum and tried to push one of her shoes off. Perhaps she had a blister on her heel.

– Come now, they are closing in fifteen minutes, the professor shouted and flung the door open.

The rooms were cool and white. After having been outside in the bright sun, she couldn't see anything at all, but then her eyes adapted to the semi-darkness, and she could make out the pictures.

Silver Print, Platinum Print. A white leg crossing over a black leg. A white profile behind a black one, the eye in the white profile open, the other one closed. A white Adam's apple resting on a black shoulder. A white hand curved around a black cock. Large threatening pictures, a closed world. Beauty without humanity. The labels underneath read Dan and Ben.

Dan and Ben viewed from the front and the back, with chains around their waist and down between their buttocks. Ben curled up inside an oval frame. He pushes his shoulders up against it, tries to break out, but he is closed in. And a young man wearing a leather vest, sitting on a chair, chains dangling above his naked knees. His hair is curly around the temples, his eyes are shining. The artist's self-portrait. Roy Vige. Silver Print.

On the back wall in the last room hangs a picture of a young woman. She is posing with her thin arms folded across her chest and looks at the world dismissively and defiantly. Her face is empty, porcelain-like, mysterious-looking under her heavy hair. Lily Lund. Platinum Print. I'll make you famous, Lily Lund.

Margrethe Thiede looked at the picture in the cool semi-darkness. She forgot the professor who kept on talking next to her. She was playing hopscotch with Lily Lund on the sidewalk outside the apartment, Lily skipping on one leg, pushing a blue and emerald-green glass stone gently with her narrow foot, the other leg bobbing up and down behind her. She is walking in the spruce plantation with Lily Lund, and the wind lifts Lily's heavy reddish golden hair. Why were you so arrogant, Lily? I wasn't, I was scared stiff. Oh yes, you were arrogant. Life was not good enough for you. You don't understand, Margrethe. I couldn't handle the normal stress of daily life. I tried but it was too hard.

And Lily's hand covered by Egon's furry fist.

It seemed as if Lily Lund was leaning out from the wall and smiling to her, a faint smile, tired and forbearing.

– I knew that girl, Margrethe said and turned towards the professor. – She disappeared. I think she must be dead.

– First there is me outside the fire escape, the professor said later when they were enjoying their dinner in a small eatery so exclusive that it was only known to the initiated. Margrethe had preferred to sit somewhere outside but ought to feel honoured to belong to the initiated, and besides, it was getting colder. – First there is me outside the fire escape, and then your best friend in effigy, so to speak, elevated to art. Whether his art is everlasting is not for me to say, but he is an excellent photographer. You must be overwhelmed, Margrethe, he said and motioned to the waiter to let him know that it would be fine to serve the next course and another carafe of wine. – Life is inscrutable and has many surprises hidden up its sleeve, just like language, by the way. It makes up a considerable part of our life, and to an extent it structures life for us. Have you ever thought about that, Margrethe?

Yes, in fact Margrethe had thought a great deal about that. The professor's language gave his life a certain structure and covered it in a transparent membrane so he could see everything but didn't have to worry about being too close to things. On the other hand, perhaps the opposite was the case. Perhaps the professor's language had been shaped by his life experiences and was able to keep things at a suitable distance. He was a nice man, for sure, but she sensed that he found it inappropriate and a sign of poor upbringing if people showed their feelings and spoke in a straightforward manner. Once he had talked about his impoverished childhood, but it was in a mocking tone, she recalled. Suddenly she pictured him as a little boy, for he must have been little once upon a time, a little boy who wanted to explore the world and label it with names. Had he pondered, even then, how you could use words to push things away from you.

– Tomorrow I will continue my journey, the professor said and skewered a deep-fried shrimp with his fork. – I could have asked you to be my traveling companion, but I have other plans. Our meeting has so far been a great pleasure. You have grown older, but you still have substance and a good appetite. Let's order some dessert now. And my bed is at your disposal again tonight if you should feel so inclined. Don't look at it as a request but as a reasonably neutral offer from an older man with a good deal of life experience. We will remain friends whatever you decide. And now I will give you my home address.

When she returned home one afternoon at the beginning of winter, Carl was waiting for her on the platform. She could see him when the train turned around the last curve before the station. The wind had lifted his thin hair, and the sun was shining right through it. She couldn't make out his facial features. He was drawing circles on the cement with his walking stick, and although she called him from the window, he didn't notice her before she had eased the luggage down the tall steps of the train car. She kissed him on the cheek and held her arms round him, but he drew back a little as if he couldn't remember who she was. Then he hugged her, awkwardly, and grabbed her canvas bag and the big bags with the gifts and began walking ahead of her towards the car. She talked non-stop, asking questions and chatting to prevent silence from separating them again. He answered in monosyllabic words as if he was thinking about something else. In the car, she sat down behind the steering wheel as she normally did. She felt that everything she said sounded hectic, forced, wrong. But by the time they were back home and sitting at the table that he had taken great pains to set nicely with flowers, candles and sliced ham from the butcher, she began to feel that she had reached him again.

She told him about the trip, about the exhibition with the photograph of Lily Lund and about the professor, leaving out certain details that were insignificant in the present context. And she mentioned that she had a new idea for a long article that she wanted to write. She was really looking forward to getting started on it.

Nothing special had happened in town. Oh yes, Rita, the woman next door, had looked after him just as they had agreed. He definitely hadn't suffered any hardship. And the shipyard had received a couple of new orders. She sensed that he was happy to have her home again. And yet he appeared somewhat distant. He wasn't completely present when he spoke.

When they were in the bedroom, he turned towards her. She put her arms round his tall body that had grown so thin. She herself was filling out once again. She had eaten well on the trip.

– There is something else you should know, he said addressing the dark room. – They have found Lily Lund.

– What are you saying? She leaned over and shook him by his shoulders. He lay there quietly, hardly moving.

– They have found Lily Lund's remains, he repeated. – She has been dead for many years. I would rather not talk about it now.

– But you must. I have to know what is going on. Her voice was shaking. She dug her nails into his shoulder blades.

So then he told her, unemotionally, in a flat voice. The following day she got the rest of the details from Mats Mathies.

During a storm with heavy downpour a portion of the cliff in the spruce plantation had given way. A couple of trees stood leaning over the top of the cliff, clinging on to the edge with exposed roots. And there among the roots and further down in the mud that had slid down, they found bones that, according to the medical examiner, came from a youngish woman.

Most of the collapsed cliff had been dug out, and a skull had been found a short distance from the other remains. The discovery of the skull had naturally been a great help in identifying the deceased. There was no doubt that it was Lily Lund who had been lying in that cliff for many years, most likely since the day she disappeared. The bones were cut up in a strange way, Mats Mathies said. He had obtained this information from a friendly acquaintance of his that worked in the police force and who on a few occasions had insisted on finding out whether Mats Mathies in fact was allowed to sell pictures from his cart. It looked as if she had been cut into pieces, Mats Mathies said. And it had taken quite a long time before her husband had been given permission to bury her as the skeletal remains first had to be examined to establish the cause of death and the possibility of a murder being committed. It would have to be a murder. A corpse can't cut itself up. Perhaps it was someone from Lily Lund's past or a stranger she had met by chance. All the people that were possible suspects had alibis except for Lily Lund's former husband Berre, and no one could imagine accusing him of killing his wife. Now the police had started all over again with the case, but no one thought they would find out anything after so many years, save Berre who had been furious and written to the newspapers accusing the chief of police of being incompetent and doing sloppy work.

– Why didn't you send for me? Margrethe asked.

– I didn't know where you were, Carl said. – And what could you have done.

By the way, Berre and Regitze had stayed with him for a couple of days. Regitze had grown into a handsome woman, soon to be a professional nurse. Now she also wanted to train as a midwife. Who would have thought that of the little spoiled girl. And things were going well for Berre who was thriving with his new woman. He had entrusted the auto repair shop to a manager and built yet another factory with a water treatment plant.

The dead remain dead. You grieve, think about them and then forget about them again. Once in a blue moon they will appear in your dreams.

19

There were still a few weeks left of Margrethe's leave from the school. She used the time to organize a work room for herself in Lars' former room. In a corner of the cellar stood the old wicker trunk that she had brought with her from the lighthouse. It was covered in dust and smelled musty. Among books and old notebooks that she had never unpacked, she found the tapes with the recordings she had once made of Kam and Jaffe. She held them in her hand, feeling a little lost. They looked odd those ancient tapes, antiques already, recorded at speeds that were no longer used. Then she thought of the old machine that she had used for the recordings and wondered if it perhaps was still somewhere in the school. She rang the caretaker who believed that he had seen an old monstrosity like that in the upper attic. He promised to dig it out for her some day when he had time.

She began to teach again. The children were singing in the school yard. And Margrethe Thiede's life slipped into its habitual routines, but in her spare time she started making inquiries into the whereabouts of the three old men.

The municipal archives were of no help to her. It was difficult to find any proof whatsoever of the three little old men's existence. She recalled how she once upon a time had believed that they were the ones who had let the girl in the Carrot Fairy's story find the wild strawberries in the winter snow.

She didn't know their real names. No one seemed to

know them. Apparently they had never paid taxes, never voted in any elections or troubled the authorities in any other way. The officials at the town hall shook their heads in response to her enquiries. No, they didn't know anything about these three old men. It was possibly due to an error made a long time ago before their time in the office. Those men that she kept on referring to had fallen out of the system or perhaps never been in it. It was unfortunate, and it was extremely unpleasant for them as well to think of this as a possibility. But that's how things were.

Death certificates. Surely, there would be death certificates somewhere. Margrethe Thiede knew approximately when Kam and Jaffe had died and could calculate more or less the year of Sem's disappearance. But the burial authorities couldn't find any registrations of deaths that were likely to be those she was looking for. Had they walked into the sea? Or had they found a hiding place where no one ever came?

There were of course still people who remembered when the short dark men came to town with their catch of herring, mackerel and eel either to sell or to barter. Oh yes, they were quick with their fingers, were good carpenters, cheap and didn't get involved with the tax department. But it was difficult communicating with them. Their language was peculiar, and they didn't always show up when they were supposed to. Otherwise they were reliable enough, they completed what they had started and didn't behave like certain other tradesmen that never kept their promises.

A woman on the outskirts of town had befriended them and had occasionally invited them in for coffee on their way back to the cottage. Her eyes lit up especially when she spoke about Jaffe. Once she wanted to give him a mirror, but he had refused to take it. He evidently thought that you could lose yourself if you looked into it. No, they didn't use mirrors, and they didn't own many clothes. – But otherwise they were nice and clean when they came to visit me, she said and told Margrethe how they had smoothed out the chair cushions when they got up to leave. – As if they were afraid to leave any impressions behind them, she said.

Margrethe searched her own memory and thought of the time when Kam had been angry at Jaffe and put sharp stones in his footprints. She had been sitting outside the cottage playing with the dog. Jaffe had come home from fishing and had complained about a tool that had broken. And that it was Kam's fault because he was the last person to use it. Shortly after that, Kam had come out from the cottage. He began walking down the path until he found a clearly outlined footprint which he then proceded to fill in with sticks, sharp stones and bits of broken glass from his pockets. He winked at Margrethe while doing it. But she was busy with the dog, which had pulled on the red ribbon in her braid. But then Sem, the eldest and most reasonable of the three, came running out. He shouted angrily at Kam, removed the sharp objects and carefully smoothed out the footprint.

She couldn't quite manage to get a good grasp on her own memories of the old men. They had no history. An older fisherman could confirm what she had already heard from auntie and grandmother Thiede. His grandfather had told him that they came to town when they were little boys, accompanied by a dark-skinned woman, a gypsy, they thought. You never knew what these people were up to, and that was probably why no one had bothered to register them. – How old were they? she asked. The two older ones were around three or four years old. The youngest was in her belly.

But Mats Mathies had actually known them, she discovered one afternoon when she and Mats were sitting on the bench at the pier. He and the men had partied together, drinking, and he thought they were jolly old fellows, although strange in many ways. They were saying that you could rub fatigue off with a stone, and afterwards they would take some leaves and remove the fatigue from the stone. – I tried it too, but it doesn't work on me, Mats Mathies said. – They had their own ideas about things, and here in town they were barely considered human. But your mother was good to them. I remember that clearly.

– Do you know anything about how they died? Margrethe asked.

– It must have happened when I was down in the south country with my cart, Mats Mathies said. – I asked about them when I returned. Yes, Sem had disappeared already before that time. No one had heard from them, and the cottage was empty and looked deserted.

– There are no death certificates, Margrethe said.

– No, here in town they were barely considered human, he repeated as if it would explain everything.

– And now you want to find out more about them? he asked and pulled two bottles of beer out of a plastic bag. – Don't you want a sip of beer. It sharpens your thinking.

Margrethe declined. She sat with her hands resting on her knees, looking straight ahead. She was cold. There was snow in the air.

– I understand how you feel, Mats Mathies said. – It is sad the way things are going in the beer industry. They changed the recipe a few years ago. Before that time there were vitamins in beer. You could practically live on beer.

Didn't you notice how building activities suddenly reached a crisis situation. It was around the time when they removed the vitamins. All the workers came down with deficiency diseases, and now the houses are collapsing as well. It is rotten, he said and wiped the foam off his mouth with the back of his hand. His face had begun to take on a glazed look. He drank too much but was seemingly never drunk.

– Tell me everything you can remember of the three old men, Margrethe said and pulled her scarf further up around her chin. – Let's go home to my house and have a cup of coffee.

– Or a small glass of snaps, Mats Mathies said. – It helps to fight the cold.

He didn't have much to add, though. In his opinion the old men had become slightly dotty from living so isolated from others. From time to time, after he had had a profitable sale, he would drive out to their place with beer in his bag. Kam had also produced a bottle of snaps on a few occasions. Then they would drink all night. Jaffe could tell fantastic stories, wherever he got them from. They were good drinking buddies even though they weren't very well informed about what was happening in the world. They appeared uncomprehending about so many things. He remembered coming to blows with the hot-tempered Kam one day. Kam went crazy and slashed at his hand with a knife. Blood spouted, but then Sem interfered and told Kam to clean and bandage the knife while he took care of Mats Mathies' wound in the same manner. He was quite amazed that the knife received the same treatment as his hand, but the wound actually healed in record time.

Margrethe nodded. She remembered a bandaged axe standing in the corner of the cottage.

– Yes, a little dotty they were, Mats Mathies said. – But nevertheless, they often uttered sensible things in their strange language. Their words were in a way closer to things than our words are, do you understand what I'm saying? They didn't drag them through the whole web of words that we use.

– You mean that they weren't so abstract, that they didn't generalize so much, Margrethe said.

– I don't know if that's what I mean, damn it, Mats Mathies said, irritated. He emptied his glass of snaps. – Speak so I can understand you.

– But they were heathens, he added and poured himself another glass. Margrethe took the bottle and carried it out to the kitchen. – They were afraid to look at themselves in the mirror because they believed their souls would disappear.

– Did they ever talk about their childhood? Margrethe asked and sat down on the chesterfield again.

– Not to my knowledge, Mats Mathies said, still annoyed with her.

– The eldest two must have had some form of language. When you are three or four years old it is possible to express yourself. There must have been a language of communication between mother and children.

– Yes, in any case they spoke oddly, Mats Mathies said pensively. – They were capable of expressing themselves the proper way, and they had attended school for a short while, from what they were saying. But when we were alone together, you had to keep your wits about you to understand them. I don't think they ever learned to write, but Kam and Jaffe were damned good at numbers, and Sem and Jaffe could tell stories. You never heard them say anything about the mother. People were saying that she was a loose woman, but not many have actually seen her. She was not given to much talking. Oh yes, old Ane Petrine up on the hill. She says that she was scary-looking, a small dark thing all shrivelled up. And suddenly she was gone. Perhaps she was like certain animals that take control of the situation when they sense where things are going.

Margrethe drove to the school to pick up the tape recorder. The caretaker carried it out to the car for her. – It is an antique, he said, – let's hope it works.

But it did, and after she had threaded the tape and fastened it properly to the reel, the old men's voices jumped out at her. The sound quality was poor, and there was much crackling, but the voices were unmistakably those of the old men.

It took her several days to transcribe the material although it didn't seem like much on paper. It was unsatisfactory, haphazard. In those days she hadn't known what to ask. Did their language have rules, she asked herself. Or was it just a question of it being a primitive and helpless version of the standard language that they had acquired from people in town and from the old village school which they must have attended. But even in the old school registers their names were not to be found.

She was on a journey now, descending deep down into the past, forgetting Lily Lund, forgetting Carl, although she still cooked the meals, tended to her teaching and functioned normally. She was obsessed with her project.

Oh, it felt so good being down there in the past in front of the cottage with the hollyhocks and the humming bees. It seemed as if the sun was always shining then, but it couldn't have been so, naturally.

Suddenly she remembered a whole lot of things. She

came straight from school one day and had just learned about nouns and verbs and had decided to share her knowledge with the old men who became her pupils. They wipe their noses on their sleeves, they eat without manners, and they speak incorrectly. She wanted to teach them everything she knew.

– Nouns, she said, – are those that are always present. You can see them, at least most of them. Plant is a noun, and lightning and house. And the verbs are those that tell us something about the nouns, about what happens to them.

They didn't understand this at all and thought that her teacher must be stupid or that she must have misunderstood something. Just look at the hollyhock. It is a plant, but it happens all by itself and doesn't need others to tell it to do so. It grows out of the earth, blooms and dies off again. And lightning, well, that's obvious. Lightning zigzags in the sky and then disappears right away.

– What about houses? she asked in a subdued voice, no longer so sure of her newly acquired knowledge.

Oh yes, houses also happen, but much slower. Houses are built and then they stand there, battered by wind and weather day by day until they one day collapse. But their own cottage is made of good driftwood and is happening very slowly. Everything in the world is connected, everything happens and changes, some things more quickly, but for other things it takes longer. The sun is perhaps an exception. It's true that it disappears every night, but it comes back again in the morning although sometimes it is hidden behind clouds. She could call the sun a noun if it was so important to her. But the sun was far away, and it was also possible that it was happening in its own way even if you couldn't see it. On the whole they found her classification of the world misleading.

Of course, they couldn't have explained their views using these words exactly, but she remembered their forbearance, their politeness, scepticism and laughter. And her own uncertainty when she the next day in school had to analyse sentences and label the different parts of speech.

Mats Mathies had said that their language was closer to things. Perhaps it could be the basis for her investigation to ask herself what he had meant by that.

She brushed her fringe away from her face and turned the tape recorder on, took out a piece of paper and began to write down sentences in columns. The old men were not always consistent. Their language had continuously been influenced by their surroundings, and they had acquired the rules of standard grammar. But traces from a totally different structure were visible in the cracks. It was this structure and its rules, if it had any rules at all, that she wished to reveal. She was unaccustomed to that kind of work and was lacking both tools and terminology. But perhaps it was a good thing, she thought, not having a set system in advance through which she could filter these sentences. She was more helpless but also more impartial, not knowing in advance what to ask.

It is unseemly to eat with your fingers, she heard her own little self-righteous voice saying deep down in the past. I take my fingers and eat the fish, Kam says. He is smiling to her, slyly. Now she remembers it well. She was sitting by the kitchen table in the cottage. Jaffe was standing by the stove, frying herrings, and the dog was sitting on its chair with a plate in front of it. He was well looked after, that dog. And then another situation: Jaffe is repairing a fishing net. She asks him how he does it, and he answers: I take the needle, make loops.

Kam takes the knife, cuts the bread. Jaffe takes the axe,

chops the wood. He didn't chop the wood with the axe. Well, of course that's what he did, just like Kam cut the bread with the knife. But when they retold what they were doing, they let the sentences follow the sequence of events and used a series of verbs rather than prepositions.

There were clearly fixed rules in the data, she discovered little by little. Kam walked to the sea and brings good herring, Jaffe said. At this point when Jaffe volunteered the information, Kam was already sitting at the table eating. She remembered it now. Kam had arrived with the fish and had begun cleaning it. He had thrown the heads and the bloody guts into a rusty pail and then pushed the cleaned fish towards Jaffe who had lifted the stove-rings and put on the frying pan.

Kam came with the fish and cleans it, Jaffe said as if he wanted to explain that the labour was divided and that it wasn't a loss of status just because he had taken over the role of the housewife. But both of these things had taken place before Kam had sat down to eat the fried herring and would normally be relegated to the past as well, although the fish couldn't be cleaned before it had been brought home. They used the past tense to indicate that something had happened before something else, even though this something else also belonged to the past. All of a sudden she could find many examples of this.

The past tense had another function as well which deviated from the standard use. Yesterday the sun shines. Yesterday a strange dog came. When they talked about something that suddenly had occurred but no longer took place, they used the past tense while the continuous actions or those that were repeated were expressed in the present tense. After all, the sun was always shining, every single day, even if it now and then was hidden by rain clouds. The sun was there. And the difference between events that are completed and those that are not seemed to play a much greater role in their language than the normal distinction between what has happened in the past and what is happening right now.

Now, what about these things that you just imagine, the unreal. Did they differentiate between what they wished for or imagined and what actually happened. She wasn't certain that she heard correctly but thought she could make out a little word that was added in hypothetical contexts. I went and find you, Kam said when he had gone to meet her on the path leading to the cottage. Kam went 'te' and find you, Jaffe said the next day. But at that moment Kam had not found her because she was sitting here outside the cottage with Jaffe, and it was Jaffe who was referring to what Kam had been imagining. Was the word perhaps 'to', she wondered? Yes, there were more examples of the same phenomenon.

It was the same day that Jaffe had scolded her because she had loosened her hair and begun to comb it outside in the sun. Not here, he had said and hustled her back inside the cottage. Not here, then storm comes. And it was also the day, she remembered, when he told her the story about the man who had to defend his family against a giant. This giant had suddenly appeared on the beach. Every evening the wife would take her husband's soul and put it in a box, and every night he would fight the giant, but he wouldn't die because his soul had been hidden away, and in the morning it would lie ready to be put back into the man. She didn't have that story on tape, and she couldn't remember how it ended either.

Her head was buzzing. She turned the tape recorder off and went to sleep beside Carl while her brain continued to formulate sentences. How was she going to describe what she had learned from the data.

Several things would suggest, she wrote the next day when sitting by her desk after work, that they acquired the vocabulary of the new language but applied it according to grammatical rules that reflected their own logic, their own perspective on life. From where did they get this logic? From what people were saying in town, their mother was practically dumb. Did they after all have a stronger footing in some first language. Or, is it possible that this logic was already programmed into their brains, that there was a hidden pattern which couldn't be broken due to their isolation in each other's company.

She could remember how she had been on to them once for refusing to say that the dog was a mammal. It was impossible. They couldn't make themselves say the sentence.

You saw a dog. You get scared, Jaffe said teasingly on the tape. A stray dog had frightened her when she was walking along the path, and she had run towards the cottage, her heart thumping. When you see dog, you get scared, he said and laughed. Always scared. She denied it. She was only afraid of very big dogs, and besides, she had been carrying the heavy tape recorder. When you see dog, you get scared, he insisted. And suddenly, while sitting here by her desk, she realized that Jaffe was using the word dog to express a concept. He wasn't any longer thinking of a familiar dog or a certain unfamiliar dog but of the concept 'dog'.

Their own dog was called The Dog. She had slowly gotten used to it even if she didn't like it when it was sitting at table with them. Dog is mammal, Jaffe said and wouldn't budge. In his world, grammatical forms denoting specificity couldn't be applied to concepts. That was logical enough.

Margrethe noted the seemingly incorrect constructions and wrote them down. Through the cracks in the language she felt that she once again came close to the little old men. They were quite capable of talking about things that weren't in their immediate vicinity. They were not stupid. But how far did their world extend? Up into space, out over the sea where it meets the horizon. They kept to themselves and observed all actions as distinct events without trying to draw them together into larger contexts. They took their time, and they never drew far-reaching conclusions when capturing time and space in their language.

I thought that they had difficulties speaking and that their sentences were a primitive and fragmentary version of correct language use, Margrethe wrote to the professor when she sent him her first draft. I corrected them and tried to teach them to speak properly. But what is proper?

Stop relating sentimentally to your old men and stop indulging in home-spun philosophies until you stand on firmer ground, he answered. Stick to the facts that you have collected and wait with the conclusions. Try to find out the mother's heritage.

And don't forget that language is our safeguard against anarchy, he wrote. Of course, it might be true, as you say, that we shouldn't be too arrogant because of all our abstractions and ideas of concept formation. There are many people – not counting the two of us, naturally – who operate within false and mindless language structures. Certain politicians and religious fundamentalists, just to mention a few nasty extremes. Your old men's analysis of reality is quite refreshing, but you'll have to admit that their level of thinking is rather primitive. Yes, what is the proper way? The story goes that when Adam was ready to use speech, everything was just waiting to be labelled: the storm, the elephant, the giraffe. It is a nice story but somewhat simplistic, like most fairy tales. You just carry on with your work, but be critical.

– I thought it was the climate, Carl said when she entertained him at the dinner table with her observations.

– The climate? she repeated astonished. – Well, maybe. We probably shape our patterns and categories according to what we need, and then we forget about the rest of reality. In some places there is no need for words to describe snow, and in other places that's exactly what's necessary.

In the scientific literature that she had started to read, reality nearly disappeared from out under the words.

– That's why it is so difficult to translate from one language to another, Carl continued and leaned back in his chair. He wasn't particularly interested in her project, he went his own way but tried to be kind. – It is completely different with code language. There the two systems must correspond exactly to each other. I've just read about one-time-only code books where only the sender and the receiver had copies of the book. Each page was used once and then destroyed. You had to translate the words to four-digit numbers and add them to the numbers in the book.

– And what, then, if the spy accidentally destroyed two pages at one time?

– Then it would be a case of false information, Carl said and looked suddenly serious. He was still reading spy novels. Margrethe had attempted these but thought they reflected a very limited world view.

At school she had the youngest pupils work more analytically with language. She would read them a sentence and ask them to make a drawing of it. The dog's bite was terrible, she read, and at the end of the class she was given twenty-seven pictures of savagely bitten animals. Some of them hardly looked like dogs. – But could that sentence mean something else, too? she asked. One of the brightest put up his hand. – Maybe it was you who were bitten, he said. – But then she should have said: The dog bit me, and its bite was terrible.

What would the old men have responded to that? She didn't have any sentences like that in her data. In reality, you had to think your way through a lot of processes before you could make that dog bite a person that didn't even appear in the sentence.

Margrethe tucked her greying hair behind her ears, slammed the doors behind her and was energetic just like in the old days. She borrowed books from out-of-town libraries and involved all her surroundings in the project.

– Do you know why so many inventions have been made in other parts of the world but first developed and applied in our part of the world? she asked Carl. No, he didn't know that and asked her to pass him the potatoes.

– You see, it is because we have a certain understanding of the world built in to our language with nouns, adjectives and verbs. We believe that everything takes place in time sequences that point outward and that can be divided into past, present and future. We believe that time is an absolute entity and that things can happen simultaneously.

221

– And of course they can, Carl said. – Here at dinner time almost all people in town are eating at the same time, more or less. That's the most practical arrangement, anyway.

– Who says that their time is the same as ours, Margrethe said, ready to lose her temper. – Why are you so certain that time just marches straight ahead and that cause and effect follow one upon the other.

– It seems to me that I have often experienced that, Carl said and helped himself to another portion. He ate well but in spite of that never gained any weight. Margrethe had decided that she wanted to fatten him up. She didn't fancy looking like a big bulge next to a skinny man. But it was of no use.

– And what is it you want to say with all this? Carl asked a bit subdued. He was listening but wasn't really interested. There was nobody in town that she could talk to about the things that preoccupied her.

– It is metaphysics, Margrethe said. – We perceive reality in terms of certain categories. They are the ones that have created our stress and rushing around, our dynamism and our time-oriented culture and science where we think we have to exploit our environment. It hasn't always been like that, you see.

– Perhaps it is the climate after all, Carl said and wiped his mouth with the napkin. He understood nothing and wasn't very dynamic, anyway.

She wanted to find out to what extent the children were conscious of the fact that they were speaking in words. – How many words are there in this sentence, she asked: – Jens ate eight cakes.

– None, said Jens who sat in the first row. – For I ate them all.

Reality and words. Words that attempt to gather all that we sense and see and transform it into abstract concepts. She felt uncertain. What kind of experiment was it anyway that she had embarked on. The children didn't mind playing along with it, but they didn't understand what she wanted from them. They smiled at her and pointed at their foreheads to indicate that she was a bit dotty. The children moved through her life like undulating waves. They grew bigger, left the school or disappeared into the upper forms. They greeted her politely, sent her a postcard and were gone. Why hadn't she ever had her own children? What was wrong with her? Why was she unproductive? Perhaps it was Carl who didn't want to have children, but it wasn't his fault. It was her own fertile body that only wanted to bloom for its own sake, that refused to give nourishment to something foreign. Egon had a son. The boy had been sent off to a boarding school, and they said that he didn't do very well.

Carl, if I don't have you, I have nothing. She dreamt that she was nursing him. He curled his long body up in her arms and drank greedily. I want to have children, Margrethe said in the dream. But she only had Carl and the three little old men that had lived their lives without leaving any footprints behind and now only existed in her consciousness. When I die, they will disappear without a trace, completely erased.

She wasn't just buxom any longer. She felt that she was becoming more matronly. Looking like Juno, the school principal said politely. – You mean fat, don't you, she interrupted. – Carl is losing weight and I'm gaining in spite of us eating the same things.

In the teachers' staff room they wanted to know how the

dissertation was progressing. Yes, it was going to be published in a scholarly journal, and she was going to give a lecture in the Language Society where the professor now was presiding. He called the Society his sandbox. The professor had suggested and arranged it all for her.

In the teachers' staff room they were proud of her, or pretended that they were. Margrethe Thiede complained that she didn't know enough. And while this was true, it was also a way of staving off hubris.

It was impossible to obtain information about the old men's mother and her origin. Although all her superstitious beliefs had probably had a lasting effect on them, it was unlikely that her language had shaped theirs. Margrethe had found rudiments of a long list of strange, but quite logical, grammatical rules. In some respects it resembled children's language that was not fully developed yet, but in other respects it reminded her of the kind of language that second-generation immigrant workers spoke amongst themselves in the past. She had read about this in foreign books. Immigrant workers who came from all corners of the earth learned to speak the dominant language of the new country at a very primitive level. But their children in turn invented a new language based on the vocabulary that was used in their new country but with a special grammar that was totally consistent, and that perceived of time, for instance, very differently. And as a result she had come to believe that language perhaps was pre-programmed, inborn, biologically grounded with traces in the brain that go way back to the time when our ancestors needed language to communicate. Therefore language was also in some ways affected by their attitude to life, she thought. The fact that we later modified it according to our changing needs was an entirely different matter, however.

– We learn language at our mother's breast and later in school, the school principal said categorically. On the whole she could sense how the colleagues in the staff room had begun to look tired and inattentive when she carried on about her theories of the three old men and their language. Maybe she glorified them too much. Their understanding of the world was vague and poorly defined, but that's exactly the reason why they didn't get caught in the traps. They could stand by their words and had no pre-established opinions. They didn't have preconceived notions about people or situations and didn't enter into linguistic areas where they hadn't been themselves, bodily speaking. Which made her think of how prejudiced she herself had been. Yet not nearly as prejudiced as the town itself that rested on a foundation of fixed assessments. The children also brought their prejudice with them from their homes and knew exactly what to think, what to say and how to dress in order to belong.

But she had a difficult time formulating her ideas. Her topic had become too big, too unmanageable. Although it had started with only three little men and a few pages of transcribed notes, it had since spread out to the farthest-reaching corners of the planet.

– It is not like you to be so uncertain of yourself, Mats Mathies said. – If it works it works, and if it doesn't work, it will probably work out anyway.

Keep to the facts, the professor wrote. And stay away from hypotheses that your brain cannot contain. Don't concern yourself with how our low-browed ancestors invented ways of classifying their kaleidoscopic impressions and separating one category from another. It is not your task to solve the riddle of language formation. It will only lead to conjecture and guesswork and has nothing to do with science. Keep to your own little corner, and get as far as you can within its parameters.

The professor's letter irritated Margrethe. He was arrogant and thought that only he had the right to observe things in a wider perspective.

20

Margrethe Thiede was expecting a lot from her own performance at the professor's Language Society. She had bought a new dress at the large clothing store on main street – it was loose-fitting and the fabric was subtly patterned in green leaves on a dark background. When she moved, the pattern would shimmer in delicate folds around her legs. In front of the mirror she gathered her hair into a bun at the nape of her neck to see how it would look with her fringe. She thought her face looked more rectangular. She raised her eyebrows and made faces. Perhaps it didn't look so bad after all.

She had decided that Carl was to come along. He could do with a break away from home. She had neglected him during the period where she had been so preoccupied with her own work, and now he had started to behave strangely again, speaking absent-mindedly or not at all, going out in the evening and checking all the locks upon returning. She needed him, she explained. If things didn't go well, he would be there to comfort her. She didn't expect this to happen, though. She had won her self-confidence back; her presentation might not be as scientifically sound as it should, but at least the data was original.

They were going by train, which Margrethe had decided as well, so she would have a chance to run through her paper one more time. The evening before their departure she and Carl went for a walk, not down to the harbour for once but to the outskirts of town where all the new housing had sprouted up, blocks of flats and small low houses nestling oddly between the tall walls of the tenement buildings. The construction work out there is shoddy. Egon's friend the mighty contractor is behind it, and he has skimped on the materials.

While walking, Carl turns his head abruptly now and again and looks behind him as if checking to see if anyone is following them. The moon is a slender sickle above their heads, and the stars are poking through the frayed edges of the fluffy cloud clusters. In this town it is almost always windy.

A short plump woman with a cardigan draped loosely over her shoulders comes out from one of the low houses. She gestures to them to come closer. No, not Margrethe, only Carl. She smiles reassuringly. It will just take a minute. And Carl lets go of Margrethe's arm and follows the woman into the house.

Margrethe is waiting by a lamp post. Carl's anxiety has rubbed off on her, she thinks she can hear footsteps. Isn't something black and shiny hiding behind the tree by the parking lot, a shoulder in black leather. No, now there is nothing. The street is deserted, only the wind is whistling through the branches. Isn't Carl coming back soon.

There he is, standing in the dark door opening, then turning halfway around and mumbling something that she cannot hear. A woman's white hand is holding on to the belt buckle on his coat, slowly letting go of it, and the door slams shut behind him.

– What did she want from you? Margrethe asks. – Why wasn't I allowed to come in. It was very rude. I know who she is, it's that woman Rosita, Karen Jepsen. They say that her husband is no longer fishing but working at the factory now. Where do you know her from? Are you helping her

228

with something.

– I've talked to her a few times, Carl says. – She is a very unhappy person.

He didn't respond to the rest. He stepped out ahead of her, nearly ran, as if he couldn't get home soon enough.

On the train Margrethe was absorbed in her notes. Carl's edginess was bothering her. He kept opening the door of the compartment and peering down the aisle, but when an elderly, portly gentleman came in and sat down on a seat near the door, Carl moved over to the window and hid behind a newspaper.

On the ferry she lost sight of him. She had figured that they would eat in the restaurant, but instead she ran up and down the stairs from one deck to another trying to track him down. He was standing at the stern of the ship, looking down into the wake. The sea looked striped with green and brownish black lines as if the ship was floating past stones or reefs, but the foam from the wake funnelled out to both sides forming wide streaks. Even further out where the golden sun was gleaming through the clouds, the water was rose-coloured with a touch of grey and appeared soft like silk.

– Come now, she said. – We can just make it, and I'm so hungry I could eat a horse.

They took a taxi to the hotel, and Margrethe changed her clothes. – Maybe it's not a good idea with that bun. But it's just for this evening, loose hair seems too youthful. What do you think, Carl?

– It's nice, he answered without looking at her. – Keep it the way it is.

There was something wrong with Carl. She would take him to the doctor when they were back home again. But she couldn't deal with him right now. She had to concentrate on her lecture.

It was drizzling when they walked through the streets. She recognized the place from the old days. First through the gate, then a turn to the left and finally upstairs to the second floor. On the landings, busts of men with heavy, wise faces were displayed in recesses in the walls. Now she knew who they were. One of them winked at her. Incidentally, they were alone on the stairs. Not very many people could have arrived already.

The professor was standing in the foyer by the lecture hall under a painting of a younger man humbling himself before an elegantly dressed lady and holding out a book to her. Margrethe didn't remember having seen that picture before. The professor approached her with his arms open. His hair had turned white, but it still fell over his forehead when he tossed his head. His yellowish brown eyes were gleaming with a sparkle that seemed to rise from deep within. He greeted them enthusiastically, first her, then Carl, and showed them into the lecture hall.

In front of the rows of chairs was the podium with the microphone. Dark wood panels covered the walls, and along the sides of the room hung gilt-framed paintings illuminated from below by small strip lights. The professor made a sweeping gesture. He had conjured all this up for Margrethe tonight. Tomorrow it might all vanish again.

She stood by the door looking a bit lost and looked for her manuscript in her handbag, making sure it was where it was supposed to be. It was a good thing that Carl had brought his suit, she thought. The professor somehow seemed different in these surroundings, friendly but distant as if he wanted to secure a safe retreat should her lecture turn out a flop.

Now voices could be heard from the stairway. Elderly gentlemen arrived, hung up their coats and entered the hall in lively conversation. The ladies were not as dominating as in the olden days, but a grey-haired woman wearing large glasses approached her and introduced herself. – This is the editor of the journal, the professor said. – She has read your article.

– Unfortunately there was no room for it in the current issue, the woman said. – But we're counting on including it in the next one. We also need a translation of the summary. Perhaps you would prefer writing that yourself.

A couple of young men came over and shook hands with her. One of them had eyes like stars and a heavy mop of brown curls. He squirmed a bit when standing in front of Margrethe. – One of our hopeful youngsters, the editor whispered.

– And now everyone seems to be here, the professor said, scanning the audience and looking at his watch. Margrethe didn't think that very many people had shown up. Evidently she was not a draw.

The professor introduced her briefly. A former student who had interrupted her promising career to devote herself to her marriage but who had finally thought better of it and had now completed an original piece of research. To Margrethe's ear, it sounded as if he in his subtle ways was trying to be amusing at her expense.

She walked up to the podium. The microphone pointed straight at a spot between her leafy-patterned breasts. She bent her head to speak into the device but found the position awkward and began turning the screw on the pole just below the head of the microphone. There was a croaking noise followed by a hoarse coughing sound. – I think I need some help, she said, thinking her voice sounded frail and girlish.

The professor and a dark-haired young man who had arrived with Starry Eyes jumped up. They grabbed hold of the microphone, one on each side of her, the dark and the white head bobbing up and down right below her breasts while the men were trying to push the device up closer to her face. – Is anyone here in possession of a screwdriver by any chance? the professor said and looked out at the audience.

– It isn't necessary, I'll manage without, Margrethe mumbled. Then she repeated it, this time louder and more determined. She pushed the microphone aside and leaned forward.

– When I was a child, I often visited three old men who lived in a cottage not far from my home at the lighthouse, she began her talk. She wanted to tell it as a story like she used to do at home in the classroom. First they had to know the background, understand the old men and their way of life. After that she could delve into the heavier material.

She could feel her legs rubbing against each other under her dress. The silk around her hips felt nice and light. Yes, she had their attention now. A couple of elderly gentlemen were smiling, admittedly sceptically, but the female editor was leaning forward attentively. And Starry Eyes was taking notes.

Then it was already all over. People applauded. The professor stepped up beside her, thanked the former student proudly and pronounced that there was no doubt in his mind that Margrethe Thiede had worked out a significant footnote to the history of language development. Margrethe smiled, her face flushed. She felt a little embarrassed, thinking that he could have used another word. She didn't want to be a footnote.

Afterwards there was supposed to be discussion, but not much came of it. A few of the members mentioned briefly that the lecture was interesting and that they were looking forward to reading it in print. Subsequently they began talking about their own areas. One member was an expert in place names, and apparently there was nothing else in the world but place names. The world was full of them. But the places meant nothing in themselves, it was the ways in which the names were put together that were interesting. Another wanted to talk exclusively about full sentences and embedded clauses. And meaningless sentences and clauses were lining up and standing on parade. It was all very clever and full of insight, everyone had his own speciality, well-defined and self-contained, but none of it had anything to do with reality, Margrethe thought. Reality was a trivial and sentimentalized word, in principle without interest to the discipline of grammar.

– But the categories that we employ, she said tentatively, – must at some point have derived from our ancestors' surroundings. The categories must have been created from certain needs of theirs.

– It is possible that universal deep structures exist under the surface of individual languages.

– But that's not what I mean either. You cannot just look at language ahistorically. I'm talking about a gradual development.

– I don't believe that you have the background for following my argument.

No, she didn't. They were dropping names and titles that she didn't know, dissociating themselves from certain theories and calling attention to others. Her three old men were fading away and disappearing into the darkness under the ceiling.

At one point she lost her temper and hit back. It worked, she discovered. Some of them nodded thoughtfully.

What the fellow with the starry eyes and the curly brown hair was saying, she didn't comprehend at all. He stuttered so badly that the words got swallowed up by each other. After a while she understood that it was about a frog that could only perceive of movement and non-movement and that would catch flies without experiencing them as anything other than air currents. Had that anything to do with language? Well, yes, perhaps it did. He was now fully engaged in the argument, and at any rate he was not afraid of looking at things within a broader perspective. She smiled in spite of herself. She had never thought about how frogs function. It was probably brilliant what he said. She could sense a certain aura of respect about him.

When she was asked whether she wanted to respond to the comments and add a few concluding remarks to tie up the discussion, she shook her head. All the strangers in the hall only wished to see things from their own point of view. The same was most likely true in her own case. She, too, had been programmed to experience reality in a certain way. Maybe we are all blind like the frog although we believe that we can see. But what really surprised her was the fact that they were so cocksure about their ideas, apart from Starry Eyes who stuttered and possibly thought more about what he was saying. They had no doubts; they had complete faith in their own language that spun reality in a web of clever words that tightened around the world and made it smaller and poorer. That's what Margrethe was thinking, but then she was a little naïve and ignorant about many things after all. Underneath all these words, reality would have to preside, she thought. Incomprehensible and multifarious although you couldn't actually see it. Perhaps she could say something to that effect, but she didn't want to be accused of being sentimental.

The dark-haired man, who turned out to be the secretary of the Society, stepped up to the lectern and announced the next meeting. In four weeks the author Uwe T, who had just returned from a trip abroad, would lecture about language and the novel. Margrethe nodded. She remembered his mosquitoes and cockroaches.

It was all over. The professor was rubbing his hands and seemed very satisfied. – It went very well indeed, he said. – You made them come out in the open and succeeded in shutting the mouth of the windbag. That was excellent. And now we will go out and enjoy a nighttime snack. I understand that you and your husband are leaving already tomorrow morning.

– Yes, Margrethe said and looked around her. Where was Carl? – He left right after the discussion started, the female editor said. – He asked me to tell you. I think he was tired.

She was angry at Carl for taking off. But in the restaurant she was seated between Starry Eyes and the professor, surrounded by food platters and wine bottles, beaming in her new dress. Now she finally felt that things had gone well. They complimented her, inquired about her work and didn't seem to have the need to show off in front of each other any longer.

When Margrethe got back to the hotel accompanied by Starry Eyes with whom she exchanged addresses, Carl was still not there. The night clerk had not seen him. The gentleman had not been in his room, and there was no message.

Margrethe lay down on the bed with a book. An hour later she phoned the professor. – I'm sitting here in my dressing gown enjoying a quiet whiskey, he said good-humouredly. – We left too early, but that was your fault. You insisted on going back to the hotel.

She told him that she was worried about Carl. – In all probability, he has gone elsewhere, the professor said. – He might have found it somewhat tiring that this performance was exclusively about you.

– He has behaved strangely lately. It already started going wrong on the trip coming here, but at that point I was too preoccupied with my own things to take notice.

– You might of course want to make some phone calls to the various casualty departments at the city's hospitals, the professor said. – But if I were you, I would go to bed. He is probably sitting in a small pub somewhere, telling folks about his ships.

Margrethe put the telephone down after their conversation. She didn't know what to do.

Early next morning the day clerk helped her with the phone calls. – Maybe you should try the police stations instead, the night clerk suggested. He was on his way out the door and made no secret of the fact that he knew a thing or two about gentlemen from the provinces who were visiting the capital. Margrethe gave him an icy stare.

The professor called around eleven o'clock to hear if they had left. – Which is a stupid question since your voice has clearly confirmed to me that you are still on the hotel's premises. He didn't think that one could do much else but wait. – You are welcome to come here if you feel like it. But Margrethe wanted to stay where she was.

It wasn't till later in the afternoon that she received a phone call where a composed female voice asked her to confirm her name. Mr Buus would like to speak with her. Her heart began to pound, and her hand was shaking when she pressed the receiver against her ear.

– Carl is here with me at the party secretariat, a voice announced that she couldn't recognize right away. – He came to see me half an hour ago. Apparently he has been walking the streets all night. He seems to believe that Egon's gorillas are following him and that someone is trying to get rid of him. And that's not very good, is it Carl? The voice suddenly sounded jovial and muted as if the speaker had turned away from the phone. Then the voice returned. – I'll get a taxi and accompany him to the hotel. At least he remembers the name of the hotel. We'll have to talk about what to do next. There is a vote coming up in about an hour so I don't have much time to spare.

She went downstairs to the lounge and ordered a snaps. Her body was shaking. She could see the street from the window. A car drove up and stopped. Sun rays were touching the roof of the car at an angle. Niels Buus jumped out, paid the driver, leaned against the door and seemingly tried to persuade his fellow passenger to get out of the car. A leg came into view. The trousers were dirty, sprayed with mud. Then Carl's head emerged. His long neck was turning from side to side. Margrethe flung open the front door of the hotel and called out to him. With Niels Buus at his side, Carl climbed the stairs. He had a small cut above his cheek and walked slowly and stiffly as if each step was painful.

Upstairs in the room he sat down and kept silent, looking out the window. When Margrethe tried to approach him, he waved her away.

– Carl won't tell me what it's all about. He wants to be

237

assured of my confidentiality, Niels Buus said and signalled to Margrethe to follow him outside in the hall way. – I don't think he really trusts anyone.

He closed the door behind them. – There is something very wrong, he continued. – He went to the police, too, this morning and told them a tale about murder and espionage. I have just spoken with them. They have contacted the police station in your town and had confirmed that he has shown up there a couple of times as well, with his cock-and-bull story that they couldn't make head nor tail of.

She stepped closer towards him. – You never called me, she said.

– He's a sick man. It's no longer just a question of him being odd. He's suffering from delusions. You must see to it that he is taken to a hospital.

She placed her hands on Niels Buus' shoulders and looked him straight in the face. It had filled out, become more fleshy. His features were less distinct, but his mouth was still the same, soft, curvy, his lower lip butting out and tightening the muscles in his cleft chin. – And you? she asked. – Do you suffer from delusions, too.

He laughed a little, and his face relaxed. Then he removed her hands from his shoulders and placed his arms around her. She was locked into his embrace. His fingers ran down her back, and it felt more like a threat than a caress.

– If I don't have any red on my palette, I'll use green. Is that what you mean. No, I haven't sold out. Not yet. And he released her again so suddenly that she tumbled back towards the door. – Actually, I have often thought of phoning you. I want to talk to you.

A man passed them in the hallway. She could see him approaching, a dark shadow against the light from the distant window down at the end of the hallway, legs that moved mechanically, step by step.

– I must go back inside to Carl.

– Yes, he said. – Today we have enough on our plate. Here is the name of the doctor that I use over here. He pulled a scrap of paper out of his pocket. – Give him a call. He can help you. And then call me when you know more. If I'm not available, the secretary will take the message.

– Yes, Margrethe said and stepped towards him again, passing her finger over his lip.

Carl was still sitting in the chair by the window. Sudden noises outside caused his long body to shudder. She kneeled in front of him and began pulling his clothes off. His travelling pants were in the closet. A good thing that he had brought an extra pair.

She kissed him on his throat in the hollow where the skin was loose and porous. He didn't show any initiative himself but was silent and compliant when she washed his face with the corner of the towel. She didn't want to consult a doctor she didn't know. Carl was going home with her.

During the train trip she was holding his hand. They didn't go upstairs to the restaurant on the ferry but stayed in the semi-darkness in the train compartment where she would let her fingers slide across the back of his hand and up along his arm, stroking him up and down until the tiny hairs on his hand were standing straight up. Carl stared into space with a vacant look and didn't want to talk. Back on land but still in the train, he dozed off at one point. His head tipped back and looked white in the sunlight from the window. His mouth was half open, and he snored with each breath. For a moment his breathing stopped, air was building up but couldn't pass through, but then his jaw dropped a little and he exhaled. His breathing returned to normal once again.

Margrethe Thiede had let go of his hand and stood by the window in the compartment and looked out at the landscape. Yellow rape fields, green hillsides. In the distance a pair of wind turbines were turning and looked like long-stemmed flowers. Small towns with red train stations slipped by, small houses, blocks of flats. How was life in those towns, what did people do there, what were they thinking. There were so many towns. Suddenly it all seemed like an unfolded backdrop, a curtain that could be unhooked and rolled up. What was behind it?

The sun had disappeared. Out on the horizon the sky was grey but just above it she could see narrow golden bands that gradually dissolved into an ivory-coloured pool of light where the sun would be hiding. A small rain cloud was moving past at a rapid pace. Light was reflected in puddles on newly ploughed fields. Now the golden-red bands became thinner and vanished altogether. The sky was covered by a dark drapery whose bright fringe was touching the horizon.

Carl was still puffing heavily. His head had turned over on its side. His ear was lying nice and flat against his head. Carl's skin looked thin. You could see the shape of his skull through it. He was a sick man. His mother had also been sick, staying up all night and always wearing her beret and singing hymns. Niels Buus was of the opinion that Carl should be taken to the hospital. Suddenly everything fell into place. Why hadn't she paid attention to the many signs earlier. She had become accustomed to him going about his business quietly, seldom saying much, while she herself was running around looking after her own affairs. He had become a sick man. Or was it the other way around. Was it Carl who could see things clearly while her own vision had become blurred due to the myriad of details that she and others believed to be so important. The thought flashed through her mind, but she quickly brushed it aside again.

When they were back home, he sat down by the desk while she was looking for something to eat in the kitchen. – Have I been sitting here long? he asked when she called him. Evidently Carl couldn't remember anything about their journey.

21

Carl. Carl Holm in short pants, his knees turning blue from the cold. Carl who tells Margrethe about the ships' spine and ribs, who draws Kathrine Laura, who goes for walks at the harbour wearing his tweed jacket with his pipe poking out of his pocket. Carl who sits in Egon's pub watching Lily Lund.

What does Carl's world look like, Margrethe Thiede asked. She couldn't penetrate it. Carl's world was mysterious, closed. Perhaps only after his death did she begin to understand parts of what was going on inside him.

In his head Carl was writing a diary. Only in his head. When sitting at the writing desk, he would make notes that he either ripped up or carefully placed in a black letter case that had once been equipped with a golden lock. Later Margrethe read the notes the best she could. The diary was mentioned in them.

Finally ready for action, Carl wrote in his mind's diary. Pages filled with invisible signs were slowly turning in his brain. Can these ciphers perhaps some day be conjured up as proof of faithfulness and loyalty, of stubborn devotion to duty in a world of falsehood and deception?

It's so small. The corner that he has to take care of is so small. He doesn't see any pattern, there is no coherence. Killer angels are lurking in the fog, in the tobacco fog in Egon's pub, in the yellow fog at the harbour where men in oilskin are loading grey fish crates onto conveyor belts. Death's messengers have protruding eyes and furry butcher hands. They wear black leather jackets, follow him wherever he goes and breathe down his neck. When he turns around they have disappeared and left no traces behind. The enemy knows him. But is he forgotten by the One who sent him out, has he been deleted from the filing system and left to fend for himself. Shall I never meet the grand Controller who pieces together all the fragments and shards for those of us who cannot see the whole pattern but only the divisions and the parts.

A walk in the desert, a long, long waiting period, always solitary, always wearing a mask to hide his true face. The large conspiracy against us has its messengers everywhere. They have infiltrated language, encoded it with false signs, smothered the true words. Margrethe has told him that much, but she didn't know what it was all about.

And he is destined to walk among people, walk among the workers at the harbour. The call him the Stick, he knows that. It doesn't matter. It is part of his disguise, the identity he must take on. But where is he himself? Is it possible to wear a mask without becoming the mask.

Do they distrust him? Carl taps the spent tobacco from his pipe and sends them a loving, ironic look. They don't know it, but it is a loving, ironic look. They are the ones he is working for, the ones he is thinking of. The innocent whose rights have been overlooked. Human beings used as fodder on the barricades, guinea-pigs, murdered senselessly, spellbound by trolls, blinded, ignorant of the plot that is aimed against their existence.

It is for their sake that Carl must listen for and catch the signals. At the shiny mahogony tables in meetings with management, at dinner tables with friends or so-called friends. At the old pub that was transformed into Egon's Pub and Discotheque where neon lights cut through the smoke above white tables, no, black tables, loaded with glasses and bottles. Egon who is behind the bar counter, big and bloated with those strange eyes that look inward and outward at the same time. Egon is laughing at him behind his back. Egon is the mafia boss in this small enemy country where music penetrates the eardrums to deafen you and prevent you from listening.

I'm going for a walk. With Lily Lund. We might end up at Egon's pub. Then I'll phone you.

There is Margrethe, large and warm. Margrethe is not to know his true identity. She gets too excited, is too outspoken. Let her play, do her work in the peace movement, in the environmental group. It is of no importance. They will never achieve anything for Death's messengers hold power there as well. But Carl must go to Egon's pub and listen and write his lonely reports. Who picks them up?

Lily Lund. She was a beautiful, mysterious woman. She didn't fit into the lifestyle that she had chosen for herself or had been coerced into. And the nice little husband who believed that he could save the world with his wind turbines and water treatment plants.

Lily Lund was not meant to live in a modern rowhouse with a husband and children, only to leave them in the evenings and sit in Egon's Pub and Discotheque, with her elbows on the table and her chin resting in her hands, her frizzy reddish golden hair framing her inscrutable face. She should have lived in an apartment and used a business as a cover address, a shop selling lingerie or antiques, no, a gift shop. Lily Lund among fine porcelain and silver candlesticks until closing hours after which she would go upstairs to her apartment, lie down on the silk cushions on the divan, ready to make her report.

Did I recruit Lily Lund? Carl asks himself in his mind's diary. He doesn't remember. Suddenly, one day Lily Lund had disappeared, from the rowhouse, from Egon's pub. And Rosita, no, Karen Jepsen was her name, pulls him into her living room and whispers something to him about Lily Lund. She went for walks during the night with Egon while her husband was asleep, Rosita whispers.

Margrethe is waiting outside by the lamp post. She is not to be told anything. The material is accumulating, but there is still not enough to initiate a full disclosure. They don't believe him. He was once at the police station, standing by the front counter and offering them his notes. They leafed through them, shook their heads and handed them back. How could you prove any of this? The police are corrupt, bribed. They, too, are an organ for the great conspiracy. There were other notes. They had disappeared from the black letter case with the golden lock and were never recovered.

And in spite of that, Carl must continue to listen and pick up the signals. In the evenings he goes to Egon's pub and sits among noisy people surrounded by noisy music. It is his duty. During the night he retreats to his room and works out the reports in codes, letters referring to numbers that again refer to letters, folds up the papers into small tight triangles, puts them in his pocket and takes down his cap and walking stick from the coat rack.

And there, there is Margrethe again. Why is she always standing there blocking his way.

Come back in and go to sleep. You never sleep any more.

But I mustn't sleep, Carl writes in his mind's diary. I can

see her eyes in the room, wide open, inquisitive, anxious. She will stop me from doing my work and lure me into her arms. It must not happen. She wants to do the right thing but can only see what is closest to her, just like I used to do in the past. I cannot trust her or anyone else. I am doomed to be lonely, and I cannot allow myself to love. Those who love become vulnerable. I must gather all my strength to penetrate the grand satanic pattern. Therefore all friendships will have to be pseudo-friendships. There is no hope or faith for me in this cramped world. I'm threatened by everyone and condemned to loneliness.

I'm going for a walk, Margrethe. I'll be back soon.

And he goes outside under the cold stars, walks along silent streets, out to the gravel road towards the spruce plantation, the wind blowing in his face, the cap pulled down over his ears. The spruce trees are swaying in the wind, clouds are drifting across the dark purple sky. There is the letter box, the hollow tree stump from the time of the oak forests. It stands alone in the middle of a clearing. Isn't there some movement, a shadow behind the dark trees. No, it is the wind. Carl walks through the grass, drops the paper into the hole, turns around, follows paths that smell of death and decay. Who will find the message. Was there in fact a message? Is it just something he was dreaming.

No, there is no time for dreaming. Finally ready for action, Carl writes in his mind's diary. The long waiting period is over.

They pick him up an early morning. He only needs to bring the most necessary things, toiletries, a dressing robe, underwear, a couple of shirts. Margrethe wanted to come along, but that's impossible. I'm going off to war now. No,

246

don't worry, Margrethe. I'm going on a short journey. You'll hear from me.

The men in the car are silent. He doesn't ask them where they are taking him. For a moment he is suspicious. Could it be a trick. Had the plans been revealed, and was he himself going to be interrogated and tortured. No, there is the Retraining Centre, the nursery where the chosen ones will suck up all the nourishment to prepare themselves. This could be the last day. And how many of us are prepared.

It is a low unadorned building hidden behind trees and shrubbery and surrounded by a tall wall. Further down the road is a high-rise building that seems to contain offices and storage spaces. Which cover address do they use? And the safety measures have left quite a bit to be desired. The thought flashes through Carl's mind but disappears quickly again. There is so much he still hasn't been briefed about.

The spartan room is painted in a yellow-green colour and equipped with a washbasin, a bed, a wardrobe and a small writing desk. You cannot expect luxury, that's what the Control says too when he stops by to look in on the newcomer. He stresses the importance of physical and psychological training, but Carl interrupts him with a smile, and in his mind's diary he takes note of the little smile. If there is anything he has made an effort to do in preparation for this very situation, it is keeping in shape. On the other hand, he needs elementary training in the operation of radios even though he knows how to use the Morse code. But the equipment has probably become more advanced over the years.

And he can reassure the Control of him maintaining full confidentiality concerning his stay. I have informed my wife that I have gone on a journey of indefinite duration and that she under no circumstances may contact me.

The Control nods thoughtfully, takes his glasses off and begins to polish them with the tip of his tie. He is sympathetic but very young, and he will not at the present time, and this he strongly emphasizes, inform Carl of the nature of his mission or the date for his departure into the actual enemy country. Perhaps he doesn't know it. He is a subordinate. Where is the real Control.

Carl goes for a short walk to familiarize himself with the building. From the outside it appeared smaller than it really is. Long corridors extend in all directions. After having taken a few steps away from his own door, he has already lost his bearings, but perhaps this bizarre design is supposed to give residents the opportunity to exercise their sense of direction. He strays into unknown territory where doors lead to halls, offices, kitchens. Strangers pass him and nod briefly. He still doesn't know who the assistants and instructors are and who the trainees that will be working in the field like himself are. In one of the corridors he meets a woman. She is young and shapely but has dark rings under her eyes. He steps aside but happens to brush against her arm when passing her. Excuse me, but perhaps you have difficulties finding your way around here too. She nods and pulls away from him. Even here people pass one another like shadow figures. Here, too, we are afraid and don't trust each other. Remnants of our old unreal lives are still within us. But one day we will meet in confidence. One day when justice has been reestablished.

One day, but when? Each day is like the previous one, training sessions, routines. They wake you up, you tidy your room, you might have an interview with one of the subordinate Controls, then consultations with the instructors after which you practice orienteering and code language by means of newspapers and magazines that are on display.

All the meals are taken in a common dining hall. It is simply a training camp, what else had he expected. He sits next to the young woman from the corridor. She is still dismissive and reproves him discreetly when he is about to get on to dangerous subjects. She is right. But it is difficult not to speak when you have remained silent for so many years.

One of the other residents at the table is almost too gushy, an elderly compact woman with iron-grey curly hair. She calls herself Rita just like his neighbour who took care of him when Margrethe was away on her journey. When was that? Why did Margrethe have to travel so suddenly. Come, let's have a smoke, Carl, says Rita and drags him into the day room. You and I are of the old guard. Apparently she has been a coffee server in one of the large restaurant chains that cater to airline companies, and she is a master in smalltalk. Exhausting. And what is a coffee server. Wasn't it tiresome making coffee exclusively? No, Carl, and she laughs to the point where the ashes from her cheroot drop and scatter over the surface of the table. I made tea and hot chocolate as well, you see.

She calls him Carl. Was Carl his cover name. What am I actually called. What is my real name.

And what could this woman who calls herself Rita have been doing for them. She willingly entertains him with stories about her operations, hip surgery with implanted metal pins. Is that a hint. Is she telling him that she was used as a messenger. If you want to travel, you must have a doctor's certificate, she says and takes a long draw on her cheroot. For you run the risk of setting off the beeper when going through the security check at the airport. Has she been passing through airports with medical certificates and beeping hips and all the while been carrying secret firearms.

She is a joke, a fragment that doesn't fit into any pattern. What is she doing here.

Apart from Rita who is overly joyful, all the other faces around the dining table have the same look. Dark shadows under their eyes, marked by suffering. Does his own face look the same way. He contemplates himself in the mirror above the washbasin. His hair is thin, his nose is prominent. But his temples are not hollow. Thoughts are pulsing behind them, his gaze is sharp, his chin smooth.

He shaves twice a day even though he doesn't need it. They insist that he use an electric razor borrowed from the Centre. The young instructor laughed when Carl inquired whether it in all its innocent disguise served a hidden purpose. It is a parlour game, a trial. They don't tell him anything, he has to figure it out for himself. The razor is lying on the bed in front of him. He has tried to take it apart, but it doesn't reveal any significant secrets.

And all these young people, many of them are women. He doesn't understand them. They walk into his room without knocking first. They laugh at him when he wants to give an account of his experiences. No one here is talking about the grand conspiracy. We don't have to. It surrounds the building like a poisonous atmosphere, and soon, soon we will go into action.

But do these young laughing people regard him as a veteran, a fossil, a relic of the past. Here, too, he senses that he is being observed. Is their helpfulness just camouflage. It confuses him. It confuses me. I must speak with the Control. And why haven't we received any instructions in the use of firearms yet.

The Control scratches his chin. There is something slovenly and informal about his mannerism. He is not equal to the occasion. Maybe firearms are not necessary, he says.

What does he mean. He is an armchair general who knows nothing about the work in the field. Will they send me into enemy country, into unknown territory, abandoned, unprotected. Shouldn't I have some means of defending myself.

His watch is wrong. He has asked the Control to get him a new one equipped with a radio transmitter. The Control declined, referring to the budget that won't allow for purchases of advanced equipment. He insisted that there is, incidentally, nothing wrong with the watch.

The Control is in contact with Margrethe. Your wife is asking about you. She would like to come and visit you soon. That would be wrong. No one from your private life may be privy to any of the information. Margrethe is naïve, gullible, easy to fool, easy to lure into traps. Under no circumstances should she know about his whereabouts. He must forget her and their little false life together that of course also had its moments of happiness. Yes, well, there was even an oasis here and there. But he will have to forget her. It is a necessary sacrifice.

There are three distinct areas: the retraining camp with its affiliation to other camps and connections to the upper levels of the Control. The world of falsehood and deception, created by the enemy, where people are staggering around without being able to find their way out. And then there is the actual enemy territory. He doesn't know where it is located. In the corridors of the power structure, in buildings that scrape against the sky, in subterranean laboratories where they create devices capable of destroying the planet. That's what he thought once. But perhaps it is much further away, some place in the universe which is losing heat and is expanding towards its own extinction.

And these corridors that stretch out like long black

tunnels, they suck him in and lead him to unfamiliar rooms where people with empty faces look at him without seeing him. He is ashamed to have to ask a female instructor to escort him back.

The leaves are falling from the trees. When did I arrive at this place. How long ago was it.

Accompanied by one of the instructors, he takes long walks out through the gate, along the road and up to the woods. He insists on carrying full marching gear and adds extra weight to his knapsack because he still hasn't received his radio equipment. Takes long strides so she can barely keep up. Hopes she will take notice of his fine condition and report on his readiness for action. The woman called Rita has disappeared. They must have needed her to go on a minor assignment that doesn't require thorough training. Strange. He misses her. He never got to know her real name.

He has asked for a key to his room, but the request has been denied him. I must be prepared for everything. Surrounded by people and always alone.

In the room where the yellow-green colour on the walls merges with the darkness at night, the radiator has been turned on. It is annoying. He sleeps best in a cold room, something he and Margrethe had numerous discussions about. He has tried to adjust it, but something is wrong with the radiator. It emits a ticking sound, at times it clicks and howls. At the same time, this constant heat is unbearable even though he turns the thermostat down. He will have to investigate it.

Inside the back cover which you can loosen and

unscrew is a valve placed in a small hole. A little metal object is fastened just below it so the valve won't turn. It looks like a hidden microphone. Are they listening in on him. Don't they trust him any longer.

Now it dawns on him. They have never had complete confidence in him. That's why the training sessions have been postponed and he hasn't met with the upper-level Control but instead been referred to unimportant meetings with this little unimportant armchair general who polishes his glasses and rejects all his suggestions.

But why. What justifies this mistrust and this long trial period where they can't make up their mind about him being either worthy or rejected. What is it in his past that has made him suspect. What guilt and what shame is he burdened with without knowing it. He searches his memory. I'm searching my memory but I'm finding nothing.

He had been listening. He had picked up signals, written his reports and delivered them to the letter box in the clearing in the spruce plantation. Daily life with its routines and obligations had occupied a major part of his day. No one from higher places had called on him. He had never been directly involved in any actions. Or had he. Is there something that I have repressed.

The reports. Had he ever delivered them? He remembers being at the police station showing his notes. But the police are corrupt.

This is hell. The distressing thoughts are tearing at his body. He cannot sleep anymore. The radiator is clicking. Can it read his thoughts too and transmit them directly to the Control at his desk. He is a subordinate, but still he knows everything. Why has this man been put in charge of determining his fate.

And why is he no longer able to think clearly. Did he

recruit Lily Lund. She was sitting in Egon's Pub and Discotheque looking straight ahead, her chin resting in the palm of her hands, her reddish golden hair like a halo around her face. She looked straight ahead without seeing anything. Her face looks like all the others, shadows under her eyes, a sign of painful knowledge. Now he knows. He didn't recruit her, she was an agent. Back then he couldn't see through her. Oh yes, instinctively he could. We are of the same blood, you and I.

Questions. Always questions. For whom did she work? Had she been sent out by my own people, or was she a spy for the enemy. There was a shadow in the moonlight by the tree trunk. Did she discover me. Did she steal my reports.

Lily Lund vanished, her little secretive smile blown away. Why won't his brain reveal what surely must be hidden inside it. The brain is my instrument, my body's cooling system. Who said that. I cannot trust my brain.

Lily Lund vanished. They found her. There is a picture. White bones under the tree roots. Was I the one who killed her. Strangled her from behind, my hand on her throat.

Egon is sitting beside Lily Lund in the pub. One of his hairy hands is on top of the table, the other has crept up under Lily Lund's hair. It is cradling her neck.

And Rosita is calling him from her doorway and pulls him inside into her small, narrow entrance way. You have to know this. I think someone should know. He sent for us that evening, but it was later, after the pub had closed.

Rosita's black hair. And Lily Lund's reddish golden mane. It is shining in the moonlight. The sea is washing over it. Corpses are rising from the bottom of the sea. On the surface float a lifebuoy, a crate, an old boot. But the boat is gone. I drew her. She was my child. First there were just lines on the drawing board, then followed the ribs and the nails and the curved planks. My pride. Lars was standing on the deck. No, Lars and Carl are walking on a gravel road on the heath. Here we are alone, no one is listening. Have you noticed the captain of the submarine. He has radar in his protruding eyes. He receives messages from Egon.

The ribs snap. The submarine pokes its scarred face out of the water. I'm drowning in all this doubting, I cannot breathe. Every submarine has its own particular sound, like a finger print. You can lay down cables with underwater microphones and calculate how close they are. For they are also listening. They are trying to figure out how close they dare to go. Watch out for the man in the black leather jacket. I cannot say any more.

Lars came along to Egon's pub. What happened. Was he not careful? Why was there never any response, no instructions. Did they already give up on me at that point, and why am I here then. This is hell.

Kathrine Laura is dancing on the waves. She is real. She doesn't belong to the enemy territory. But they took her.

It is morning. Here in the pale grey winter light he can see it all much clearer. He was not responsible for the loss of the ship. He is not to be blamed. But perhaps he has been too passive.

During the night he insisted on speaking with the Control but was told that he wasn't available. That is not right. The Control ought to be available to his agent at any time. He is the agent's lifeline, and if the line is cut, you are at the mercy of the enemy. He must know what they are reproaching him for. He wants to know right now.

The Control is polishing his glasses. His small eyes glaze over. He never looks directly at Carl any longer but

255

gazes out the window at the naked trees that sway in the wind. He is evasive, false. You cannot trust him.

No, he doesn't trust the Control any more. He has finally realized that. He has seen through them. He is the victim of a conspiracy of a gigantic format. This entire Retraining Centre is a deception, constructed in order to break him. The creatures that he has thought of as colleagues, as fellow workers serving the big project in different capacities, are fraudulent, artificial beings, robots. They move mechanically, don't look at him, mumble their answers when he addresses them.

One exception is perhaps the young woman in whose company he eats his meals. He brushed against her arm in the corridor and felt the warm blood through her skin. She is real but poisoned like himself. The pills that they distribute every morning and evening have never been simple vitamins or supplements to improve his physical well-being. They are designed to break down his ability to make judgements, to weaken his mental faculties. How much hasn't he already disclosed under their influence.

He gives them a friendly nod when they hand him the pills. No one is to suspect anything. Later he goes to the bathroom and flushes them down the toilet. He must try to convince the young woman to do the same thing.

His thinking is becoming increasingly sharper. The silly attack of remorse and self-reproach caused by this drug-induced brainwashing is over and done with. He now knows that the so-called Control and the so-called instructors are conspiring against him. But they won't succeed in breaking him even if his own people have left him to suffer an uncertain destiny, from the look of it. I have to get away.

The first thing to do is to get a letter through to Margrethe. He can't use a code, but he will have to indicate between the lines that something is wrong and that he is forced to live incognito in a safe house for a period of time. After that he must try to get a message through to his own people. Since the letter box in the plantation has been dead for so long, they must have realized that the operation has been abandoned for the time being. He will send a coded message explaining the interruption and request new instructions. His thoughts are crystal clear. He knows what to do, and Margrethe must help him. She was supposed to be kept out of it, spared. There was a period when she disappeared for him, radiated in a certain way but not for him. Then suddenly she was present again. Never understood the deeper levels of his work, was not meant to understand. But she is loyal, is a good support at the level of ordinary life.

He has obtained an envelope and a stamp but doesn't dare to entrust the letter to anyone. He will have to make plans now, outwit them. The letter box on the corner outside the wall is emptied every day at four o'clock. So, if I postpone my walk till then. And yes, here is the postman on his bicycle. Before the keeper can intervene, the postman has the letter. The keeper is left standing with her mouth open, evidently not knowing what to do. What will she report?

She has made some sort of report. The security rules have been tightened. When he walks down the corridors he can feel how invisible eyes follow his movements. They talk about me behind my back. They have increased the medication and demand to be present when he swallows his pills. He hides them in his cheek and spits them out when he is alone. Is there no one I can trust.

The woman from the corridor. He places his hand on hers when they sit at the dining table. It trembles like a small frightened bird. Then she wriggles it free of his grasp and looks at him with her profoundly painful look. She is real but immersed in a deep fog. Is she already lost.

He has found a kitchen knife that got stuck behind a drawer. He always carries it with him, even to bed at night.

Night time. A scream comes from the corridor. He gets up, grabs his dressing robe that is lying on a chair by the foot of his bed, fumbles with the sleeves and tiptoes over to the door. He opens it a little. The corridor is empty in the soft light from the night lamps, the screams are faint but distinct. In the shadow of the walls he starts moving in the direction of the screams. They come from a room far away where the corridor turns into a dark passageway. Her room.

Carefully he continues walking towards the half-open door and peeks inside. In the glare from the light in the ceiling he can see her on the bed, tossing from side to side. Her dark hair is flopping back and forth across her face, her eyes are wide open and fearful. And in front of her stands a massive, unyielding female keeper holding a syringe in her hand.

He bends down and gets ready to jump. Legs are kicking, a pair of arms are flailing, hands are grasping the shiny needle of the syringe. The white blanket on the bed has slipped halfway down, everything has melted into one single point along with the piercing sound of the alarm that is penetrating his brain. And the pages of the diary are turning, faster and faster, changing into swirling snowflakes that dissolve the ciphers into nothingness.

Carl walks along the moonlit road in the swirling snow that is falling lightly on the big stones at the roadside. His feet leave footprints in the white cover. The dressing robe's shadow is fluttering behind him. He walks tall through the snow with the girl in his arms, carrying her like a bundle, her head against his shoulder, her hair full of bright snowflakes blowing against his mouth. It is Lily Lund that he is carrying. She is heavy. His arms are shaking and he has to stop to change her postion and make her more comfortable. She feels warm and heavy against his chest.

No, cold. She, too, is cold, unreal, no longer a human being, a dummy. And from the darkness between the trees the guards are approaching. Silently and swiftly. Does he see a glimpse of Margrethe. Has she, too, betrayed him. The snow is beating against his face and blinds him. Everything is white, the world of falsehood is blinding him, a huge white deception. He is running in the snow with his female dummy, stumbles, gets back up, falls over backwards. Black dots and bright spots of light are whirling around behind his eyes, pain is shooting up through his neck, and then there is no more, only darkness.

He wakes up again. His head is hurting and buzzing. He can't move, is lying in something soft, and in front of him he sees half a face, the rest is foggy.

Face? Is it a face. The features are blurred, won't hold together. He knows that he should recognize it, but he doesn't have a name for it. Carl has woken up in a world without words.

Margrethe is sitting in front of the bed with her handbag on her lap. Her shoulders slump a little, and the bag slides on to the floor. She reaches for Carl, pats him on his hand, then holds it tight. His eyes full of questions follow her.

– You are in the hospital, she says. – You are lying in a bed, a white bed. And when you get better, you're coming home with me, with Margrethe.

But her words don't register with him. He has been betrayed. They have cheated him of his life, but he doesn't know any longer who they are. He is lying in a white bed, and in front of him is a woman's partial face.

Inside him vague shadows glide back and forth, shapes and forms that he doesn't recognize. Once he had a goal, a big important goal, the most significant of all things. He can no longer hold on to it. It has disappeared in the snow, lost like a bundle that falls out of your arms.

– First you have to get a new grip on reality, Margrethe says and leans over her husband.

But reality is split up in fragments that no longer fit together. He can distinguish the parts but cannot assemble them into whole patterns. He doesn't have any awareness of his body anymore, and he doesn't have any awareness of the words that once formed part of the living world and were tied to it with thousands of connecting thoughts.

This is Carl's situation. He has lived in enemy territory, been abandoned without mercy. It is peaceful being here in a white bed. They can do whatever they want with him, friends, enemies. It is possible that Carl, who doesn't any longer remember that he is Carl, has lost the ability to imagine concepts such as friends and enemies. Everyone has deserted him, but perhaps it isn't their fault. Perhaps they themselves have been deceived, and those people that deceived them have also been betrayed and so on and so forth, repeated a thousand times in mirrors that eventually lead to the big void where nothing is reflected.

But yes, he is aware of something. The woman with the partial face is Margrethe. He tries smiling to her. There is something he wants to tell her, there is something she ought to know before he slides back into the fog where all words and sensations are erased definitively. She must be on her guard, he must warn her. He must tell her that Egon is Death's messenger.

22

Margrethe Thiede Holm was sitting in her armchair with her legs up on a footstool. Knots of blue veins were now showing on those legs. – You look fabulous, the colleagues said in the staff room. – Considering what you have been through. It wasn't true but comforting. And time heals all wounds.

No, not all. The large wound in the back of Carl's neck has fortunately turned into a scar, but underneath the scar the tissue is damaged, and it won't heal. It could have been worse, though. Carl hasn't harmed anyone else, only himself. And now she has him back home.

Outside, the darkness of autumn is pressing against the window panes. Upstairs, Carl is sleeping. He has been sleeping a lot these last months. He is a child that has to start all over again identifying objects and naming them. When she sits across from him at the dining table, she can see how the wheels are turning behind his fragile-looking forehead. He is trying hard. He wants to succeed but he never does.

He picks up breadcrumbs from the floor and hands them to her as if they were precious objects. He becomes anxious when the spoon disappears into the soup, apparently because he can only see the tip of it. She has tried to send him on an errand to the baker's at the corner, but he lost his way even though he only had a few metres to walk. Right and left, back and forth, up and down are empty words to him. He cannot recognize his own house.

She doesn't know how he really feels. He must be

experiencing life as a nightmare. He is unable to perceive objects in larger contexts. To him there is a gap between words and their meaning.

But it will probably work out, slowly, even if he is very weak. – Try talking about his childhood. – The past is often the first thing that surfaces.

She doesn't know much about Carl's childhood. But she begins to tell him fairy tales: in the olden days when all your wishes would come true. And the castle that is east of the sun and west of the moon. That's where you will end up, late or never. Maybe his mother, who wore a beret and cleaned her house at night, never told him stories. But it's as if the old formulas and fairy tales ring a bell with him. He nods and listens: and the green knight gave the king a book for the princess to read. She was only to open it when she was alone, and each time she opened the book, the green knight appeared. But when she closed it again, he vanished.

Margrethe Thiede leans back in the chair, dozes off a little. She is tired. She has been considering reducing her hours at the school, but Carl's small pension from the shipyard doesn't make ends meet even though she has sold the car. While she is away from the house, the woman next door looks in on him and afterwards reports on all the mistakes he has made. They don't understand him. She will not allow anyone to laugh at Carl. He is trying so hard.

She was once a child herself, was tucked into her bed and was told stories. Mother, sit down by my bed and tell a me story. One you make up yourself. A scary one that isn't suitable for Harald.

Oh, it feels good sitting here resting, forgetting about yourself and all your problems, going far back, all the way back to your childhood and the olden days when all wishes came true.

Mother, tell me a story.

There was once a young girl that went out into the wide world to seek her fortune.

What was she called?

Snow White. We'll call her Snow White.

And one afternoon Snow White arrived at an old church located between two parishes, standing all by itself, protected from the wind by a small pine forest.

It was a summer Sunday. The flies were buzzing, and the pine trees smelled sharp and sweet.

Snow White walked through the open gate in the fence around the churchyard. Most of the graves were run-down. You couldn't even read the names on some of the gravestones, only the odd letter was legible. And Snow White was sad that she couldn't say the names of the dead out loud for without names they were nothing, and no one would ever know that they had existed.

Many of the stones sat in the middle of a grassy field. Others were surrounded by tiny gardens bordered with hedges of arborvitae and yew. In one of the gardens lay heaps of withered flowers and wreaths whose ribbons were flapping in the sleepy wind.

The sun was very bright, and Snow White quickly stepped inside the church door. On the wall by the door was a painting of a pastor with powdered white hair, wearing a ruff. Behind him stood his wife also dressed in black, with her folded hands resting on her abdomen, and beside her the children were lined up in descending order from the tallest to the shortest, all of them with sad little adult-like faces, wearing black dresses or suits.

Snow White looked at the painting for a while and then

continued into the church proper. At one end you could see the gleaming organ pipes. The light that entered through the small windows high up on the walls was faint, the pews were painted grey and the stone floor was cool to the touch. Snow White shivered while walking towards the altar where a seven-branched candlestick was standing on a lace cloth that was spread out over a black velvet cover. She paused for a moment to look at the altarpiece where the grieving Mary stood at the feet of the Crucified. His head with the crown of thorns was hanging limply to one side. He looked away, swallowed up by his own suffering and not noticing how his mother was caressing his pierced feet.

Just then Snow White heard a shrill whistling sound and turned around. But the grey church was empty.

On the wall down from the altar was the pulpit. A wooden canopy was suspended from the ceiling above the lectern, and a narrow winding staircase lead up to the platform. Snow White walked around the pulpit and looked at the carved figures on the panels. They didn't represent the evangelists or apostles but knights wearing gilt-edged capes over suits of armour and solid boots in which their feet were firmly planted. Their hands were leaning on long swords, and they looked sternly ahead of them, five knights, all alike except the one in the middle. He didn't have a sword, and one of his legs was missing from the knee and down. But he looked younger than the others and smiled behind his dark beard.

– I was the one who whistled, he said and opened his wooden lips. – I was afraid that you would pass me without noticing me.

– You can't talk, Snow White said. – And why is one of your legs missing?

– The evil queen has cut it off. She takes people's arms

265

and legs and their heads too if they don't obey her. Well, that's her pastime, but it is hard on those who suffer for it.

– Does she live nearby? Snow White asked and looked anxiously around her.

– Yes, not far from here. And if you want to help me, we can go there and get my leg back.

Snow White stretched her hands up and carefully helped the knight to get down from his panel on the pulpit. Then she put him under her arm, supported him with the other arm, walked past the rows of pews and went out the church door.

– You'll have to tell me which way we're going, she said and looked around her in the churchyard. The sun was now behind the pine trees, and a cold wind swept through the grass.

– Behind the woods is a little lake. Follow the path along the shore until we reach the opposite side. From there a road leads to the castle.

Snow White walked through the forest where the trees smelled sharp and sweet. The ground was covered in old cones and dry, brown pine needles and looked speckled in the sunlight. She held the knight close to her and tried to protect his face from being hit by the branches. Through the painted armour and the painted cape she thought she could feel the warmth from his body.

At the lake shore she sat him down against a tree. – You're getting so heavy. I have to pause for a moment to catch my breath.

– We must hurry and continue. At this time the guards will be getting their pitchers of beer and sitting on the steps playing dice. Perhaps we can sneak in without them discovering it.

Snow White put him back under her arm and ran down

the path. His face was reflected in the water, greenish and brave among the duckweed and the rushes. Further out on the lake a dark bird was calling.

– That's her black whooper swan, the knight said. – And now you better take me under your other arm and step into the shade so the swan won't notice me.

Snow White darted off. Finally she reached the other side of the lake where a wide road opened up between the trees. Far away at the end of the road was the castle with its heavy square towers and a moat around it all.

– Slow down now, the knight said. – And when you reach the drawbridge, you must hide my face against your chest so no one can see it.

– That's just as well for I'm getting tired, Snow White said and began to walk at a slower pace along the dusty road in the setting sun while the castle came closer and closer. At long last she arrived at the drawbridge and walked across the wooden planks and into the castle yard where small tufts of grass poked out between the cobble stones. On the stone steps leading up to the castle door sat a pair of giant men in dark leather doublets. Snow White gasped for she had never laid eyes on such creatures before. Their heads were very small; they were almost all body. And they had hardly any necks, so their heads sat squarely between their shoulder blades.

They had put down their lances, and one of them was trying to wrest a pitcher of beer from the other fellow's hands. The liquid slopped over and settled in small puddles between the stones.

– Now, the knight whispered. Snow White quickly slipped past the guards and up the stairs, pushed open the iron-plated door and found herself standing in a hall whose ceiling disappeared high up above her and into the darkness.

At first she couldn't see anything. Then she noticed a dim light coming from a half-open door at the end of the hall.

– In there sits the evil queen and sews, the knight whispered. – She stitches people together. She uses those heads, arms and legs that she has cut off and sews them on to other bodies as she sees fit. Large heads on small bodies with short legs. Those she locks away in cages so they can do her thinking for her. And small heads on large bodies. They become her soldiers. She creates people that she needs for her own use, and then they are barely human any longer.

– But you aren't a human being, are you? Snow White asked.

– In a way I am, the knight said. – And perhaps I can become one again if I get my leg back. That time when she cut it off, she threw it onto a heap of limbs and then went out to inspect her cages. She probably intended to cut the other one off too upon her return. But by then I had disappeared. I used my sword as a crutch and hobbled down the stairs, across the drawbridge, down the road, around the lake, through the forest and into the church. But when I had gone as far as that, her guards were close on my heels. I was standing right in front of the pulpit when I heard them making a lot of noise by the church door. Up there on the panels stood the four knights and looked down at me. I sensed that they wanted to help me if they could, and I thought that one of them nodded towards the empty panel between them.

So then I leaned with all my weight onto the sword, swung my body up and shrunk myself to a wooden figure while the sword fell to the stone floor and skipped down the aisle, clanking away. They found the sword. But they never saw me, stupid as they are. And since then I have been standing up there for centuries. And that's long enough.

That's my story, and now we won't talk any more about it. Stand me in the corner there and go see the queen. She is wearing a veil over her face. This you must tear off, for if her true face be exposed she will lose her power.

Snow White left the knight standing in the corner and walked up to the door, pushed it open and looked into a large room with chesterfields and tables and mirrors on the walls. Through the tall windows she could see the blazing evening sky in red and golden shades.

The queen had hung a body up on a rack and was in the process of sewing on a head that had a woman's long dark hair. She was dressed all in black but for the white veil with silver threads covering her face. In a chair beside her sat the black whooping swan.

Now she bent over, rummaged in a pile of severed limbs and pulled out an arm. She held it up against the body and threw it back again. Snow White approached her cautiously.

– Well now, Snow White, what is it you want, the queen said and turned around.

– See your true face, Snow White shouted and jumped towards her and pulled the veil aside.

The queen's face was as white as mother-of-pearl with a pink glow on her cheeks. There was nary a wrinkle to see, and her full lips were as red as cherries. One of her green eyes was looking inward. The other was staring straight at Snow White with a gaze that went right through her, turning her bones to ice.

– Feel free to look at my face, little Snow White, the queen said. – Many people have desired to do so, and every one of them were left dumbfounded because it is so beautiful. Meanwhile I can have a look at your arms. You have pretty arms, Snow White. Surely, they can be of some use. And she took the scissors from the table and waved

269

Snow White over to where she was sitting.

Snow White didn't want to move. Yet her legs began to carry her over towards the queen. She thought that the knight must have given her the wrong instructions, and now he was standing outside in the corner without being able to help her.

– Come closer, all the way to the table, the queen said and cut into the air with the big scissors. In all the mirrors on the walls scissors were cutting into the air with the queen's white face hovering above them.

Just then Snow White noticed a small fold or slit on the queen's neck. She fixed her eyes on it while approaching.

– Let's see now, the queen said, took hold of the scissors with both hands and began to close them around one of Snow White's arms. – Those bones are delicate and won't be difficult to handle. And she pressed on the scissors as hard as she could yet didn't get red in the face.

At that very moment Snow White's hand flew up towards the slit in her neck. She took a firm grip and pulled hard. The queen let go of the scissors and tried to defend herself but it was already too late. The mask was dangling from her temple, and behind it was her true face, ancient, wrinkled and thin, her mouth like a bluish white line between hollow cheeks.

Her green eyes glazed over and looked dull. The queen staggered and collapsed in a chair half-way on top of the black swan, which stretched out its neck and began flapping its wings. It managed to free itself and flew out of the window into the setting sun.

– That was that, Snow White said and went out to get the knight. – Oh my, is that what she looks like, he said when he saw the queen. – I thought she was supposed to be the most beautiful woman in the world.

– She must be very old, after all, Snow White answered while trying to find his leg in the pile. – Here it is, I think. No, it is your left leg that's missing.

At last she pulled a leg wearing a boot from the pile and placed it next to the knight. It was a bit too large for him.

– Just begin sewing it back on, the knight said. – Lay me down on the table, then we'll make it fit.

Snow White took the queen's sewing kit, bit off a length of thread and began to sew. It wasn't difficult because the wood above the boot had turned into cloth, and while she was bent over the table, working, she could feel how the knight grew and how his skin lost its hard surface and became warm and soft. She did her best, sewing with small stitches, and consequently only a few drops of blood trickled out.

– Now I have squeezed myself back into my old shape, the knight shouted and jumped down from the table, a full-grown man who looked exactly like the wooden knight but was bigger and alive.

– Oh, wait a minute, Snow White said and kneeled in front of him. – A few more stitches, and then it will hold together.

– What about the others, she asked when she was on her feet again, brushing her hair away from her eyes.

– Well, we can let those in the cages out and tell them where the pantry is, the knight answered. – But don't start re-making them, it would take your entire life and perhaps you wouldn't be able to do it right anyway.

– But this one over there will have to be finished, Snow White said and pointed at the dark-haired girl that was hanging on the rack.

So now Snow White was at work once again. When she was done, the girl looked very lovely and smiled shyly while admiring her new arms.

The knight walked over to her and took her hand in his.
– I couldn't have done better dreaming up this girl, he said.
– Her I want to marry because she has never seen me as a wooden man, and she hasn't carried me under her arm either. Then you can set forth into the wide world and seek your fortune or whatever it is you want to seek.

And then they left the room, walked through the hall, across the drawbridge and down the road. The queen was left behind, lying in her chair. Her true face was already covered in spiderwebs.

No, shouts Margrethe Thiede's voice from inside the dream. That's not how it ends. The prince gets married to the princess, and they live happily ever after to the end of their days.

Fortune's roses of delight, In thorny gardens shine so bright, the voice hummed.

That's not my story, that's yours. And you didn't seek your fortune, you sought responsibility. It smells like whale oil.

Someone must do the sewing and piece things together. Someone must take over. All the stories are your stories. You can end them as you wish.

And the mother's voice – was it the mother's voice? – changes to the sound of the wind, appears again together with her face, disappears in the darkness, is suddenly visible again in the light of the lamp, the mother's face with those large anxious eyes of nightfall.

Margrethe Thiede was sitting in the armchair sleeping, her head tilted to one side.

23

Life in town continues. The professor, incidentally, has died over there in his fairy city in a restaurant where he was trying out a special menu. And Carl. He died peacefully in his bed which was a relief for Margrethe after all. She received many nice letters on that occasion, one from Niels Buus, too, although she hadn't had much contact with him lately. But she has heard from Starry Eyes on a regular basis. They exchange viewpoints, and he has thanked her in the foreword of his new book.

A man down at the harbour also died. He was standing by the hatch to the ship's hold and heard his buddy yelling that he was feeling ill. Then he climbed down to help but suffocated from the poisonous gases coming from the fish that were going to be unloaded. How could the fish already be rotting, the cutter hadn't been out to sea that long. The buddy survived, but the rescuer was dead when they pulled him out through the narrow hatch. Some were of the opinion that it would have been more just had it been the other way around, but how can you speak of justice under those circumstances.

– And it could have been prevented, Mats Mathies said. He is sitting in his stocking feet drinking coffee at Margrethe's in the afternoon. He has left his boots outside on the steps. – There was no air pump in the hold and no safety ropes. I wouldn't be surprised if the loading company will be asked to pay out compensation to the widow. But that is of little comfort.

Mats Mathies is now an old man. His stiff hair that barely hides his little golden earring has turned greyish white. But in the summer he still wanders around town with his cart and is making good sales, especially of his pictures. – No doubt, they think I'm picturesque myself. – And they like what I paint, but they don't consider it art. I suppose it is true that I don't spend much time on each picture. I don't want to paint a picture to death. And then they are recognizable. And that's no longer fashionable. In the olden days it was. Then it was fine if you could tell what a picture was supposed to represent.

– Now we have photography, Margrethe answers meekly and pours some more coffee.

– When I paint, my soul is in my work. No one can deny that.

– Then your soul is perhaps not very interesting, old Mats Mathies.

– You have always had a sharp tongue, says Mats Mathies who likes being teased, especially by females. – And have you heard of Egon's new project.

– But I thought that Egon was getting tired just like the rest of us, Margrethe said. They think he will soon have to use a wheelchair. Margrethe herself is still attending meetings organized by the peace movement and the environmental group, is still going to demonstrations and signing protest letters. But sometimes she feels uncomfortable in the company of the others in the group. They are all so young and say the same things she herself said in her own youth. It's all one big repeat performance that doesn't go anywhere. But perhaps it doesn't go backwards either. And outside Death's messengers lie in wait.

– Egon getting tired? Mats Mathies laughs and starts coughing. He hawks up some phlegm and walks over to the

274

kitchen sink to spit it out. – Better to use the toilet, Margrethe shouts to him. But he always does what he wants.

– Now Egon wants to build his own town, Mats Mathies says after having returned to the sitting room. There's going to be a marina and a sea front and a gambling casino and giant hotels. As far as I understand the whole lot is going to be under a plastic dome so they can plant flower gardens and lay down artificial lawns around the swimming pools that will be equipped with water slides. I wouldn't mind trying one of those. And it's a good idea with the plastic. Then we won't have to worry about bad weather and about having to go outside in our humble nature at all.

– Please, have another bun, Margrethe says. – They are home-made.

– If they are the same kind of bombs that they usually serve in the peace movement, I'll have to say no thank you. I don't understand why you people are so warlike when it comes to that. They are the kind that keep the dentists busy. But perhaps you have a drop of the strong stuff.

– My buns are not as bad as all that, Margrethe says and looks for the snaps bottle in the kitchen cupboard. – And the town could certainly use a big new swimming pool. But what you are telling me sounds horrible. In the olden days there were competitions for architects, and the most beautiful project was chosen. And after that tenders were invited for contracts.

– It has already been named, Mats Mathies continues. – It is going to be called Egon's Sea World. And he has financial backers too who want to invest in the project. We know the main contractor who will oversee it all, of course. And they say that the son is going to be the general manager.

– He studied law, she mumbles. – But otherwise he

hasn't really done anything. For a moment she can visualize Egon's Sea World. Enormous plastic coverings stretched out over the town, obscuring it completely.

– But surely he won't get permission to do it, she quickly adds. – They'll never agree to that in the town council. And what about the planning committee?

– The town council? Mats Mathies says and rubs one stocking leg against the other. – They will probably squeeze out a majority vote. Free initiative and employment to many in town! That business has many angles to it when you start twisting and turning it. Those foxy fellows are making backroom deals, says Mats Mathies who looks like an old fox himself. – You just wait and see. Egon will get his Sea World yet unless we do something about it, of course.

– And what should we do? Margrethe asks. Mats Mathies smells of fresh air and old dirt and sweaty feet. She knows that he has a bathroom in his house, but apparently he doesn't use it very much. Maybe it's part of the image he has of himself, that he must be a little dirty. – Should we demonstrate or collect signatures for a petition? We have done that so often. Nothing ever comes of it.

– This time we'll have to reach a little higher, says Mats Mathies. – I think we should contact your old friend Niels Buus.

That same afternoon Margrethe phoned the party secretariat and asked to speak with Niels Buus. – Mr Buus is very busy, the secretary said in her composed tone of voice. But I'll make sure he gets your message. What did you say your name was again?

He called back the next morning. As always when she heard his voice on the telephone she had a sinking feeling.

His low voice that flowed towards her through time and space. Yes, he had to attend a meeting in those parts anyway and would like to visit her on the way. Sure, he would be able to have dinner with her at her place. – I have got a new car, he said on the phone. – It's quite big. Should I park it in front of your house or leave it at the hotel?

– You can sleep here, she said. – We're old people now and don't have to pay attention to town gossip.

– We're not that old, he said.

She had bought fresh fish at the harbour and steamed them in the oven. She didn't want her hair to smell of fried food when he came. The dinner had to be good but not too elaborate. She didn't want him to think that she had done anything out of the ordinary for his sake. Anyway, it wasn't about her but about Egon's project.

– And what do you want me to do about it? he asked and studied the label on the wine bottle.

– It's from the grocer. I like to support the small grocery shops now that so many supermarkets have opened. I tasted it once on a trip but perhaps you're used to other vintages.

– It's fine, he said and poured from the bottle. – I don't think I can interfere with those plans. Similar projects have turned out quite well in other places.

– This one is worse. In Egon's format.

– I have talked to some of the people in the party, he continued. – They think it sounds promising. It will create new employment in town, and the plans are not as bad as you make them out to be.

– You're developing quite a paunch, it seems to me, Margrethe said. – Do you eat and drink too much on a daily basis?

– No more than I need. I work hard.

– And do you still believe that you can achieve things?

– Achieve things or put a curb on things. The latter is also important.

– We haven't seen you in the papers for a long time, Margrethe said. – Don't you need another cause to draw attention to yourself.

– And that would be Egon's Sea World?

– Not just Egon's. All of it. All the mindless decisions that are being made to change this part of the country into a thoroughfare and a tourist reservation. That's what they think we are good for, isn't it so? The centre of the mainland cleared away to make room for a motorway with detours to the coast, and then hotels all the way around on the remaining coastal strip.

He was rolling bits of bread between his fingers. She suddenly remembered how it had alsways irritated her when he rolled the bread that way.

– You are hot-headed, Margrethe, like in the old days.

– If all of us are apathetic, nothing will be put to the test.

– I'll think about it, Niels Buus said. – And now let's move to the chesterfield and drink our coffee and talk about something else.

When the day was dawning and the candles had long since burnt out, they were still sitting there, Niels Buus with his arm stretched across the back of the chesterfield, Margrethe with a blanket wrapped around her legs. She had to hear about his life, about his wife who was now the head clerk in an office and doing well for herself. It hadn't always been easy, and for a time they had separated and lived apart from each other. But now it was going fine. She had become

278

more sure of herself. And that's what it's all about. Being sure of yourself.

– You always were, Margrethe said.

Oh sure, up and down, as it happens in life. He had been introduced to a scene whose rules were foreign to him and that he had had to learn to play. And Niels Buus recounted stories about opponents and about defeats and victories in the political world that was unknown territory to Margrethe. – I was too ignorant when I entered politics, he said. – I thought I could just see my own concerns through. But now I know the tricks of the trade. Now, no one can push me around.

Afterwards Margrethe told him about Carl's last years and how he had tried to learn to write again, sitting for hours working on a single sentence because the words wouldn't reveal their meaning to him. – Sometimes he would pretend that he understood what people said, but inside his head it was all chaos and confusion. He couldn't make sense of the bits and pieces. Once he tried to explain it to me in writing: I smile like an idiot. I feel that I constantly walk around with an idiotic smile on my face. It's because I don't understand anything.

– Normally Carl wasn't in the habit of smiling much, Niels Buus said. – What do you think he thought about the two of us?

– I don't know, Margrethe said. Actually I felt very comfortable in his company the last few years although it was a difficult time. We both made an effort to get closer to each other, but I didn't understand him properly. I don't think I have ever understood the more fragile people among us.

She pulled the blanket tighter around her legs and stared into space. – He wrote other things to me as well. About

279

Egon and about Lily Lund. He left some notes behind him. Most of them were written in a sort of code which I couldn't make head or tail of. But I don't think it was all delusionary.

– Lily Lund. I didn't know her at all. But once many years ago, I saw the two of you coming out from Egon's pub along with Carl.

– I think Carl was in love with Lily Lund, Margrethe said and paused for a moment. – All the way back in the old days. He was also very fond of Lars. He was the one who had a rapport with Lars. I was too heavy-handed. An Earth Climp. Where did that word come from, she thought to herself. – I organized our lives. I was always rushing around organizing. I still do that, come to think of it.

– Someone has to do it.

– But no one will thank you for it. They believe I'm the one who makes the sun rise in the morning and set in the evening.

She turned her head and looked at Niels Buus, at his cleft chin that butted out, his curvy lower lip. She could see tiny red blood vessels in the white of his eyes. He looked tired in the morning light.

– You are cold, Margrethe, he said and put his arm around her. – What about yourself. How are you managing now?

– Fine, very well. Yes, she managed just fine. She had had a few more language articles published and had established connections with some of the people in the field. And there was enough to do here in town, what with teaching and work in various groups and associations. And by the way, these days she was seeing a lot of Regitze, Lily Lund's daughter, who had a car and often came to visit her. Regitze had originally trained as a nurse, and now she was a midwife as well. Who would have thought that she could manage all that. She had four big children now, nice children that came along on the visits. – In a way they are my closest family, for all the others have died, Margrethe said. Suddenly she felt that her words sounded so inadequate and weak. What had she accomplished. Nothing. And wasn't life just something to be done with, like an exam or an exhausting day.

– And have you never thought of moving. Of coming to the big city where we are, he said and pulled her closer against his body.

She shook her head. – Once upon a time I imagined that the big city was a castle burning with excitement which sunk into the ground when I turned my back on it, she said and had to laugh at herself a little.

His hand found its way to her cheek. He brushed her hair away, gathered it in his hand and pulled it back tightly. She could feel the pull on her scalp and the touch of his fingers at the nape of her neck.

– The two of us, Niels Buus said. – We're of the same sort. We're survivors.

Outside a bird was shrieking. The morning sun was peeking through the window. Inside in the sitting room Margrethe Thiede and Niels Buus sat silently, leaning against each other.

24

Time vanished. How could that happen? When Margrethe Thiede was a child and a young girl, the days had seemed eternally long, each day a new adventure with thousands of possibilities. It was just a matter of choosing, and choosing was difficult. When you chose one thing over another, you would only limit yourself and diminish the number of possibilities.

Now the days were rushing along, gathering in a heap behind her, dissolving and melting away.

One evening, late, she was standing in her sitting room winding the grandfather clock. She didn't quite know why it was so important to her that the clock be wound every evening. Perhaps it was an old unwritten rule from grandmother Thiede's days that maintained that clocks always had to be ticking, even when the house was empty and especially if anyone in the house was ill. People die at low tide. Was that another one of grandmother Thiede's sayings? Margrethe dropped off a little, then turned the key again and thought about her childhood at the lighthouse.

Then the door bell suddenly rings. She goes to the front door, opens it and sees a young man in profile outside with one foot up on the step. In the glare from the streetlamp he appears very light, almost transparent, and at first she thinks it is Harald. But once he is inside the passageway and tries to explain himself somewhat akwardly, she can see that it is Lars who has returned.

– Come now and tell me what has happened, she says

and guides him over to the dining table. She sits down herself across from him but gets up again to bring some beer and soft drinks from the kitchen. He looks quite surprised, his shoulders are drooping as if he is very tired, but he doesn't mind having a beer with her. He has been left behind, was given permission to spend a few hours in town while the ship was refueling, or perhaps he had given himself permission. He doesn't remember asking anybody. Then he got tired of all those houses, walked out to the heath, ate blueberries and fell asleep in one of the sand dunes. And when he woke up, he took the wrong turn and didn't arrive at the harbour till it was all dark. The ship was gone, and there was nobody there who could tell him anything. Then he went looking for the seamen's hostel, but once again he lost his way and finally ended up on this road where only one single house had a light on. The ship was a cargo boat that was headed for some destination on the other side of the globe. Over there they will probably sign on someone else, for they weren't pleased with him. That's for sure. And if the kind lady would let him sleep there tonight, he would definitely pay her when he got into some money again.

Margrethe wakes up while listening. She is not afraid of this young man who comes from the sea or has been dropped from another planet. He has nice, blue eyes with a certain look of surprise. But things have to be done properly. Tomorrow a telegram will have to be sent off to the cargo boat. And anyway, he can have a bed for tonight or for a couple of nights and try to recover.

When she accompanied him upstairs to his room, she turned around on the stairs and asked: – What is your name, by the way?

– Lars, he answered.

One night or a couple of nights can easily turn into many. The boy or young man stayed with Margrethe Thiede for nearly two years. She called him alternately Harald and Lars for he was a strange mixture of the two, a dreamer and romantic who got lost on his way through life, and an energetic person with a practical grasp on things. He found work in fishing and brought money back regularly to pay for board and lodging. It felt good having someone to cook for again. Now Margrethe Thiede had more time as well with fewer hours at the school. She was soon going to retire.

Lars cleaned the gutters, nailed things in place and made himself useful in many ways. He wasn't very communicative, and she never did get his family background straight. Apparently he didn't know his parents. He had come from the sea.

She was glad to have a man in the house. Sometimes when on her evening walk, she would be followed by a couple of adolescent boys that she didn't recognize from the school. They were dressed in black leather, or clothes that looked like leather, and walked silently behind her, keeping at a distance of about ten paces. When she turned around, they would draw back. She had tried shouting to them and calling out to them, but they always drew back and refused to speak to her.

It is once again an autumn night. Lars has begun talking about moving on and getting back to the big world, and Margrethe cannot sleep. She is tossing and turning in her bed, but finally she gets up and throws her coat on top of her nightdress.

Evidently adolescent boys also sleep at night. She is all

alone and can hear her own steps on the sidewalk while passing autumnal gardens where the wind is blowing through the dark treetops. Above her head the moon is shining, the gentle moon that can make the grass look like silver puddles, its beams reaching in under the dead foliage.

She reaches the main street. The large show windows are asleep, but a lonely shop is lit up. She walks up to it and peers inside. Egon is there, sitting in his wheelchair. His hands are folded around the handle of a cane that he is holding in front of him. He is nodding his head, barely missing the handle of the cane as if he is about to fall asleep, but when he catches sight of her, he straightens up.

Around him stand wax dummies, young gentlemen in broad-striped suits and patterned ties. Their arms are stretched out, touching each other's shoulders, and their heads which are topped with wavy waxy hair are lowered as if they are about to say something very significant. In the far corner is a fellow dressed in blue jeans and a zippered black leather jacket. He is approaching the others and steps over a large pile of underwear that is placed between arrangements of socks and sweaters.

Egon is shaking his head slightly. Then he holds out the cane and motions her to come inside. She doesn't really want to, but when she steps closer to the window, the glass opens up like a cloud of steam. She takes another step and finds herself standing in the show window right in front of Egon. He reaches out for her with the cane, catches the belt on her coat with the handle and pulls her closer towards him.

– So, here you are, Margrethe, he says and looks at her with the one eye. The other one is smiling slyly, turning inward. – The two of us have gone on display, it seems.

All of a sudden she remembers that she is only wearing a nightdress, and she pulls the coat tighter around her.

– You once slapped my face. Do you remember that?

– I can do it again. You probably deserve it.

– Steady, Margrethe, Egon says. You have always been hot-tempered, and that didn't get you anywhere.

The yellow lights above the wax dummies are hot. She doesn't quite know what to answer him. He is so big. His flesh is slopping around in the wheelchair, threatening to overflow. There is much flesh but also much water in that body. She wants to slam her fists into him, but it is too hot.

– Now, why don't you wheel me out of here, Egon says and unhooks the handle of his cane from her belt. – We don't want to stay here any longer, do we?

She walks carefully around the wheelchair and nearly stumbles over the pile of sweaters. Then she turns the chair. There is a ramp, and they begin moving down the slope. She looks behind her and sees the man in the leather jacket who has taken Egon's place in the show window. With one arm, he reaches out for one of the suited gentlemen. The other arm is hanging straight down.

They wheel through long corridors that lead into retail spaces with counters and displays of all sorts of things. There are silverware and jewelry, handbags and suitcases. On large racks clothes are suspended on hangers. Dresses, shirts, coats and jackets. Egon is hunched over in the chair somewhat but is pointing at things here and there with the cane.

– You may take something if you feel so inclined, he says. – A silver spoon with an ornate handle or a letter case equipped with a lock. I own everything here. I bought all the shops on main street, don't you know? Now a department store is being built. The town is growing.

– I could certainly use a pea jacket, Margrethe says. – For Lars. Lars has come back to me.

– Now you're dreaming, Margrethe.

They have stopped in front of an aquarium where small fish swish in and out among pebbles and water plants.

– Now you're dreaming, Margrethe. Lars has been eaten by the fish. And a crying shame it is too, that nice boy. I could have made good use of him. But he didn't want to.

– Lars looks like Berre, Margrethe continues and begins pushing the chair again. – But there are parts of him that resemble Harald too. And Lily Lund.

– Lily Lund, Egon repeats. His hoarse voice sounds suddenly gentle. – She was such a little kitten.

– Not in my opinion, Margrethe says and stops so suddenly that Egon slides forward in the chair. They have stopped in front of a creaky yellow door that opens into a narrow lift.

– Yes, we're going up, Egon mumbles, and the door closes behind them.

They ride for a long time. It is very cramped. Margrethe is standing much too close to Egon. He is a maggot but also a powerful force. His whole being exudes energy.

Then the lift comes to a standstill. It hums for a long time without moving until the door begins to give and slowly slides open.

Outside the yellow door is the heath with its creeping willows, blueberry bushes and patches of reddish purple heather. The air is so clear. The moon is sailing slowly across the dark sky among the tiny flickering stars, and far out the lighthouse is flashing, lighting up the town and the sea.

Margrethe bends down and gropes with her hand under some wet greyish leaves. The willows scratch her. She pushes them up gently with the tips of her fingers, and blueberries trickle into her hand and bounce against each other, each in its own silver membrane and with a little black tuft on the bottom.

– This is where my Sea World is going to be, Egon says and points with the cane.

– There won't be a Sea World. It will be stopped.

She can feel the blueberries in her mouth, round and plump with a slight tart sweetness when she bites into them.

– Oh yes, that's true, you took up with your former boyfriend again. He was good at writing for the newspapers, but apart from that was he much of anything?

– Don't you get started on that, Margrethe says and stares out over the heath.

– I'll get my Sea World, don't you worry about that. Egon smiles roguishly. – I usually get what I want.

– Do you want some blueberries, poor Egon, Margrethe says and pours a small pile into his hand. He looks at them pensively. Then he closes his hand with its furry knuckles, and the juice runs out between his fingers.

– Why did you do that, Egon. I could have taken them home with me and given them to Lars. Why do you always have to destroy things.

– If you want to build up something, you'll have to destroy something else. You can find pleasure in doing that too.

The fog from the sea has begun to creep in and settle on the heath. A small foggy cloud rises above a couple of crooked pine trees in a hollow.

– Carl said that you were Death's messenger. That you conspired with death.

– That Carl. He could think up so many things. No, that's giving me too much credit. Those who conspire with death are up in the higher echelons, Egon says and scratches his belly with the handle of the cane. – I'm just a poor boy who has used the resources given to me so I could enjoy life. His one eye is a pool of moonlight, the other one looks cunningly at her.

The sea fog has reached Margrethe's feet and now covers the lower part of the wheels on Egon's chair. The small foggy cloud is coming closer and settles around the armrest. Suddenly Margrethe sees that it is Lily Lund in her grey dress who is sitting there halfway squatting beside Egon. He stretches out his arm and lets his hand slide under her heavy hair. His fingers move up and down her neck.

– That slender little neck, Egon says and looks at Lily Lund's bowed head. – That slender little neck.

Margrethe wants to jump up and pull Lily Lund away. But then she is gone, and the fog from the sea has crept further up covering Egon's belly.

– You are a bottom feeder, Margrethe says. You are full of rot. And now I'm leaving. Then you can sit here and look at your Sea World.

– An Earth Climp, Egon shouts after her as she is running back across the heath among the prickly willows. – An Earth Climp just like you, Margrethe.

She reaches the small houses at the outskirts of town and heads for the harbour. The streetlamps are swaying on their long stems, and the light is reflected in the black water.

A couple of larger boats are moored at the pier. The heavy ropes have been fastened to rusty iron bollards. She turns the corner by the auction hall where the dock is empty and peaceful.

But there is Egon again, sitting in his wheelchair. His

hands are clasped around the cane that is pointing straight out, resting on his swollen belly. He is slumped in his chair, looking into the beam of moonlight, but he straigthens up when he hears her steps on the pavement.

– You're taking your time, he says. – But I reckoned that we would meet again.

– How could you get down here so fast, she asks. – In the wheelchair and with those bad legs of yours.

– Bad legs, he repeats. – Yes, that sort of thing comes with old age, Margrethe dear. Surely, you haven't escaped the infirmities of old age either.

That she cannot deny. – I can't see well any longer, she answers. – There are so many things that seem impenetrable to me.

Egon is sitting there by the dock. She needs more time to figure out what Egon is all about.

– Now that we have talked about Sea World, she says, – I should perhaps ask about your son who wants to be general manager.

– My son? He only shows up once in a while when he needs money. Manager? That's not for him in any case. He would be no good at that. But it's really my Sea World that we ought to be talking about. Sit down, then we can call it a meeting.

She is standing beside him, looking somewhat hesitant. He turns his large face in her direction and smiles cunningly.

– I'm sitting here thinking of the salmon, Egon says. – Do you know, Margrethe, that when the salmon has spawned up north, it begins to decompose. It turns belly up, and the new spawn begins to eat its way through it.

– Yes, I can see that you resemble the salmon a little, Margrethe answers. His belly is so big that the jacket won't meet, and every time he takes a breath tiny quick movements make his flesh quiver under the shirt.

– That's not exactly what I meant, Egon says in a friendly way. – I was thinking of life in general. You want to do so many things, and then one day you wake up and realize that it has all come to nought.

He sighs and attempts to look miserable. Poor Egon. But his one eye is looking at her slyly.

– You haven't had an easy time of it either, Margrethe, he continues. – It was sad the way it turned out for Carl.

Margrethe sits down on a bollard diagonally opposite the wheelchair. She wraps the coat around her legs and fastens the belt. – Carl was a good person, better than most in this town, she says curtly.

– Yes, yes, Egon mumbles. – You can perhaps look at it that way too.

– He believed that you were selling information to foreign powers.

– He was a sick man, of course, but not stupid. He had his ear to the ground.

– Was there any truth in it, then? Margrethe asks and leans forward.

– So now I'm going to be interrogated too, Egon says. – He went to the police with his case. But they know me, you see. Then we teased him a little. After all, there should be room for some entertainment in life.

– Just like the way you tease me now. Keep your gorilla underlings away from me, you hear?

– Sure, sure, Egon sighs. – You have never had much of a sense of humour. That trick you played on me with Sea World was a bad joke.

Margrethe Thiede is looking towards the pier-heads where the lights are flashing their red and green beams far out to sea. The harbour is so quiet. No boats are chugging away, no men in oilskin. Further out you can see the greyish black hulls of the war ships with their bridges and observation towers.

– It was stopped. That was the most important thing, she says and turns to face Egon.

– Don't be so sure. The plans are still kept at the city hall. One day in a couple of years, time will be ripe.

– It was my impression that you had run out of steam, Egon. That you felt like the salmon that was floating belly up.

– When something is beneficial to the town, you are obliged to see it through even if some people cannot comprehend it and the red baboons are on the war path, he says piously. – But he who crosses my plans will pay for it, you know that, Margrethe, he continues in a voice that creeps along towards her and wraps itself around her arms like a rope.

– I'm not afraid of you, she yells and shakes his voice off her arms. – One day all your old dirty deals will be disclosed and scrutinized.

– Well, that's all I wanted to tell you, Egon says. – Remember it for your own sake. And now I better wheel home.

He glances at her searchingly. Then he reaches out with his cane and catches her belt with the handle. – But first you have to help me with something, Margrethe. – I have to take a piss.

He pulls her towards him. She resists, stumbles, falls down and feels a stabbing sensation in her thigh.

– Yes, you better get down on your knees, Margrethe, if you have to undo my buttons. Try digging under my belly. It's very big, for many things have been stuffed into it. At least one has had much enjoyment from that.

He pulls hard at her belt with the cane. His large white face looms above her, and the smell of old age and woollies fills her nostrils.

– Come now, Margrethe. Can't you do an old school friend a small favour here where no one but the moon can see us.

Her hand gets stuck under his bulging stomach. She can feel his stiffening member against it. Then she snatches away her hand, knocks the cane aside and crawls behind the wheelchair into the dark shadows by the auction hall.

– So, you didn't like what you found down there, Egon says. She can hear him smile. Yet plenty of others have enjoyed it.

– You're a braggart, Egon. You have always been a braggart.

He is trying to get up from the chair, pushes with his hands against the armrests, pulls himself up and stands swaying for a moment. He is so huge.

– You slapped my face once, Margrethe. We weren't so old then as we are now. But you and I, we aren't done with each other.

He has straightened himself up. His body gets bigger and bigger, blots out the world like an enormous shadow against the moon.

His shoulders begin to droop again. His legs bend, slowly. His upper body leans forward. A splash can be heard, and water sprays up around the wheelchair that is rocking against the wharf.

She is kneeling at the edge of the dock and stares at the large rings that are spreading in the water. It is as if an eye is winking at her from far below, under the moon beam.

On the wall of the auction hall hung a bleached-out lifebuoy. Margrethe noticed it when she ran back towards town. She stopped momentarily on main street and glanced at the shop window. But Egon was no longer sitting there in his wheelchair.

Lars was up and around when she came home. He was pacing back and forth in the living room with a cheese sandwich in his hand. He had been hungry and had gotten up, had noticed that her bedroom door was open and her bed empty.

– Has anything happened? he asked. His eyes were as blue and clear as the sea on a sunny day.

– I went for a walk by the harbour, she said and suddenly felt a little cold. – Then I fell down and hurt myself. And now I think I'll make us a cup of hot chocolate.

THE THIN SILENCE

One day, we know,
The thin silence will come,
The powerlessness of May,
June without a summer.

Thøger Larsen

25

Out by the lighthouse – for the lighthouse is still standing although it is more and more exposed to the elements – the sea is eating away at the sand dunes. At high tide it removes the sand. But that's the general idea, anyway. The sand has to be transferred and deposited out there where the sea is breaking. That's how they have figured it out. The sea has to be fed, and the waves forced to break further out so their beating against the beach is less violent. But the sea is not so easy to fool. It laughs at the town engineer and all his advisors, grabs a huge chunk of the feed and carries it along only to let go of it far out in the deep sea. And during the next storm it behaves just as crazily again, throws itself against the cliff and hollows it out. It doesn't help that you plant marram grass and set out spruce branches in order to keep the sand in place. Before the plantation gets a firm hold, the cliff has been devoured.

Margrethe has gone out to the lighthouse to see how bad things are. Regitze has driven her in her big car that has been a useful vehicle with all those children. Now they have of course grown up and can look after their own transportation. And Margrethe listens attentively to all Regitze's stories.

Regitze has grown heavier, almost stout. Who would have thought so. But that girl, she is no milksop. She is also good at her work, writes articles for the journal of midwifery about all the things that upset her. Now they can make pigs without eyes so the animals can just stand quietly and grow into mountains of flesh. And soon they will be able to make humans just the way people would like them, with large or small heads for different applications.

Margrethe nods. What Regitze is telling her reminds her of an old story. About the evil queen. Who is the evil queen? And was it the Carrot Fairy who told her that story. Now you have to take over, said the Carrot Fairy, and Margrethe remembers how that remark had irritated her. Now you have to take over, Regitze.

Yes, that Regitze. She is good at living. She can manage children, both her own and all those that she helps to bring into the world. And she can manage visiting Margrethe and taking care of her old father, Lily Lund's husband Berre who is just as active as always although he has sold his factory with the water treatment plant and is twice a widower.

– Now he has a new idea, Regitze tells her. – He wants to export icebergs to the desert.

– Here we need more sand to feed to the sea, and down there they have too much, Margrethe mumbles and screws up her eyes to look out the car window. The sunlight bothers her.

– He believes that one of those supertankers easily can pull an iceberg. And even if two thirds of it melts on the way, there will still be enough to make a go of it.

Margrethe closes her eyes. Behind them the iceberg sails over a green-blue ocean down to the yellow-brown desert.

– You see, down there they are eradicating cattle diseases. Consequently the cattle population is increasing. The animals crop the vegetation, and there is nothing to retain the heat from the sun. It goes straight back into the atmosphere or the biosphere or whatever it is called. Clouds are not formed, and there is no rain as a result. So now my father wants to export icebergs into the desert.

Margrethe nods, a little weary. Regitze knows so much. And what she is telling isn't without significance, especially for those who live in the desert. But it's so far away. In the past she would have written it down, found additional information and then invited an expert to give a lecture in the environmental group. We must do something about it, stop the sand that is drifting in the desert and retain the sand that is drifting around the lighthouse. Down there there is no water. Here the ground water rises year by year. And one day the Nine-wave will come, nine miles tall and nine miles wide and swallow the whole thing. Oh no, what is it that she is imagining?

She is wondering if she has enough food in the house to invite Regitze who has come for a visit unexpectedly. She would like to look after her guests but that, too, is becoming difficult.

When you grow old and have trouble seeing well, the real world doesn't really concern you so much. It's there, but it's veiled. It calls out to you from afar and makes its demands. If you begin to tackle it, you'll more often than not suffer defeat. You stumble on the stairs or pick up the wrong tin in the supermarket and come home with something that you never intended to buy. That's why it's best to keep calm, to sit quietly and let go of your needs.

Sometimes Mats Mathies comes and wants to take Margrethe out for a walk. Mats Mathies is an old man, but he is the one who takes Margrethe's arm and shepherds her.

They walk across the heath. The autumn sky is grey yet bright, the heather is done flowering. It's so big and empty, this landscape, and Mats Mathies takes her arm so she won't trip.

Then they meet an old bent-over woman whose hair looks like tangled roots. Her name is Ancient, and she points at Margrethe with her cane.

But Mats Mathies says: – It's odd, that pile of wild roses. They have hacked them off with a heather cutter and thrown them into a heap. Then they believe that they have gotten rid of them. But just watch the wild roses. They will soon be covered with frost and snow that will prevent the heat in the ground from escaping, and the roots will then be drawn into the soil. And you'll see, in the spring they will bloom again. No, they are not so easy to get rid of.

And Ancient withdraws, shakes her cane at them and disappears.

Most of the time Margrethe is sitting by the window in her sitting room. She is thinner now. Her skin is flabby here and there and slides over the bones when she rubs her arms.

Outside a branch with golden leaves is swinging up and down, in light and shade, while the children are laughing and a dog is barking in the distance. She likes to sit here and think about her life. After all, she has enjoyed a good life. She has loved two men and hated a third. The third one she killed. Maybe. She can't quite remember it. They wrote in the local paper: The town's most venerated son has died. And a little further down: Tragic accident by the harbour. But there was no mention of any details.

And Lars has returned to her even if he had to leave again. He writes often. Now he too is married. The young people are the ones that must survive. The only thing is, she cannot understand how that butterfly had the strength to rise through seventy-five fathoms of water.

In a while the neighbour will arrive with the groceries. Then they will have a cup of coffee and talk of this, that and the other thing. Of this, that and the other? When you use language casually, you don't really think of the meaning of the words. You just say what it is customary to say. The words lap back and forth like small, quiet waves. They have lost their power, but they can still bring people into friendly proximity to each other.

Then the neighbour leaves again, and Margrethe remains sitting in the thin silence.

During the night she dreams that she is dead. She is standing on top of the hill and looks out over the world that is created by language. It won't hold together any longer, is dissolving, coming apart at joints she has never noticed before. And below is the abyss, the immense darkness.

She is searching for a word that is so strong that it can fuse all the cracks. If she finds it, she will inherit the kingdom and have all her wishes come true.

She is holding Carl's fragile face between her hands. Tell me about it, Carl. His ears are so delicate, his eyes are closed. Look at me, Carl. And slowly his lids slide open. His muddy eyes stare at her, empty, without recognition. Then something stirs in them. Carl, I'm here. Don't be afraid. We're all here together.

Lily Lund is smiling from inside her loneliness, a

small, vague and secretive smile. She tosses her hair to the side and bares her neck.

And dark branches whip against her in the woods where she is running and where the black tree roots lie across the path. Egon is lurking far back in the shadows. Poor Egon. He reaches out between the branches with his butcher hands. He is Death's messenger. I'm coming now to get you.

I'm coming now to get you, I'm coming now to get you, the children chant in the school yard with their high, shrill voices. And Niels Buus catches her in his arms and holds her so tight that she cannot escape.

In the hill lives the troll. If you can guess his name, you will be his. What is his name? Where is the word that can put the world together again? The sky looks so black, mother. And behind the black sky is outer space forever expanding and moving towards death.

Margrethe Thiede Holm is standing on top of the hill while letters of her name blow away across the sea like colourful kites. Three of them collide, pink, orange, ivory. And out there three little old men are walking on the sea. They are waving and shouting. She doesn't understand what they are saying. But it doesn't matter for behind the words lies the sea, or what we call the sea, until everything merges in front of our eyes and has to be named anew.

Red and orange clouds are ablaze, and slowly the sun emerges. Sheets of light upon sheets of light. Rays trickle across the water surface. And it is still all here, the earth, the sea, the sun that rises from the bosom of the sea and shines upon this little wheel of life that will turn happily till the end of its days.

SUZANNE BRØGGER

A Fighting Pig's Too Tough to Eat
and Other Prose Texts

(translated by Marina Allemano)

*'I live in a rather invisible place where progress has passed right by,
and I am happy about that. ... In terms of train tracks, I live only
100km from Copenhagen – but in terms of time, I live thousands of
kilometres away. I live by the marshes where the marshwoman brews
her mist and I write my books – it comes to the same thing. From my
window I can see where the world ends.'*

from 'I Live as I Write and I Write as I Live'

This selection of work by Suzanne Brøgger contains her autobiographical
meditation, 'A Fighting Pig's Too Tough to Eat' – its title taken from a
folk belief in the rural district of West Sjælland in which the author lives
– as well as essays from the past twenty-five years, showing her
development from social rebel to iconoclast and visionary.

Suzanne Brøgger (b. 1944) has always been unconventional in her
lifestyle and in her writing, in a way that has often prompted comparison
with her fellow countrywoman Karen Blixen. She writes stories, poems,
plays and essays, and many of her writings transgress genre boundaries.
Her pronouncements and her activities have excited much controversy in
Denmark, and her books have been translated in more than a dozen
languages. Beginning as a polemicist, she has matured into a
philosophical writer for whom the writing process is a continuous
meditation on life, death and eros.

ISBN 1 870041 35 6
UK £10.95
(paperback, 282 pages)

ELLEN REES

On the Margins:
Nordic Women Modernists of the 1930s

This study examines the work of six women prose writers of the 1930s, placing them for the first time within the broader context of European and American literary modernism. These writers – Stina Aronson, Karen Blixen, Karo Espeseth, Hagar Olsson, Cora Sandel and Edith Øberg – have been doubly marginalized. Their work has long been viewed as anomalous within the Scandinavian literary canon, but, apart from Karen Blixen, it also remains marginalized from examinations of women writers produced outside Scandinavia. This is a 'connective study' which examines the literary strategies, preoccupations, and responses to changes in society shared across national boundaries by these writers. They all sought inspiration from foreign literature and culture, and made themselves literal or figurative exiles from their homelands.

Ellen Rees is Assistant Professor of Scandinavian Studies at the University of Oregon. She has published widely on Scandinavian prose fiction and cinema, and is currently researching a monograph on Cora Sandel.

ISBN 1 870041 59 3
UK £14.95
(paperback, 204 pages)

For further information, or to request a catalogue, contact:
Norvik Press, University of East Anglia (LLT), Norwich NR4 7TJ, England
e-mail: norvik.press@uea.ac.uk